# Underfoot

# LEANNE BANKS
## *Underfoot*

MIRA

*MIRA is a registered trademark of Harlequin Enterprises Limited,
used under licence.*

*First published in Great Britain 2007.
MIRA Books, Eton House, 18-24 Paradise Road,
Richmond, Surrey, TW9 1SR*

© Leanne Banks 2006

*ISBN: 978 0 7783 0170 7*

63-0607

*Printed and bound in Spain
by Litografia Rosés S.A., Barcelona*

Dear Reader,

Some of life's greatest pleasures are messy—hot fudge sundaes, puppies, great sex, babies. Some messes aren't always planned.

Have you ever gone through a time in your life when you thought you had everything planned? When you thought you had it all under control? You would make those really naive statements of absolute power and knowledge with words like *never* or *always*. Then something messy happens and turns your life upside down. But after a while you figure out that maybe your so-called plans weren't that great after all... Along the way, you learn that courage isn't always about physical battles. Courage is looking failure in the face, feeling afraid and busting your gut to succeed anyway. The efforts can be awkward and messy, but in this case, messy can be beautiful...

I hope you enjoy the messes—fun, sexy, heart stealing and otherwise—in *Underfoot*.

Fondly,

*Leanne*

Thank you to my readers, great friends and family who encouraged me to write and finish this book. Cindy, Rhonda, Cherry and Pam, thank you for being there for me. Special acknowledgements to other people who inspire me, my sisters Janie and Karen, my husband, Tony, and my children, Adam and Alisa. And always, the best parents in the world—mine! Thank you, Mum, for not being like Trina's mum and for teaching me common sense, and Daddy, for the gift of persistence.

This book is dedicated to all of you who have stepped up to the plate to help a child or a parent or a sibling when it was inconvenient, difficult or painful for you to do so. You make the world a better place.

# Underfoot

If you're going to walk down a primrose path,
make sure you've got a great pair of shoes.

## CHAPTER ONE

IT WAS LATE when she sank onto the barstool. Still wearing her best dressed-to-kill sexy tuxedo dress, Trina Roberts had received immediate attention from the bartender.

"Hot night?" he said. "What'll you have?"

Hot didn't cover it. Train wreck didn't cover it. Nuclear explosion didn't cover it. "Mojito, please."

"Coming up," he said.

While she waited, she took a deep breath and glanced around the bar. The crowd had thinned out. Her gaze stopped on a man seated at the other end of the bar, his head bowed over a squat glass of amber-colored liquor.

His tux tie was unfastened along with the top buttons of his shirt. She knew that profile, the hard jawline, straight nose and dark hair uncharacteristically mussed over his forehead.

Walker Gordon.

Her heart clenched for him. He looked miserable,

desolate, destroyed. She couldn't blame him. After all, he'd just been publicly dumped at the altar by Brooke Tarantino, the great-granddaughter of the founder of Bellagio Shoes. That was bad enough, but the dumping had been conducted on live television with millions of witnesses.

Trina had attended the wedding because she worked for Bellagio in PR. In fact, she'd worked with Walker, an advertising contractor that Bellagio had hired several years ago. From the beginning, she'd liked his combination of quick intelligence and sense of humor. And it didn't hurt that he had a great body and sexy eyes.

The bartender returned with her drink and she paid her tab, sipping the mojito and trying not to look at Walker. Her gaze, however, kept wandering toward him. She'd never seen him missing an ounce of confidence. He oozed solid assurance and even though she hadn't totally understood his relationship with Brooke Tarantino, he'd once revealed part of the attraction. Brooke was entirely too self-involved to ever want children. That suited him fine because he didn't want children, either. Being a father, he'd confessed, would be a surefire path to failure for him. He'd made a joke in that way that people did when they weren't completely joking, that he'd come from a long line of bad fathers and he was determined not to continue the trend.

His broad shoulders were folded forward. He leaned against the bar, his gaze vacant.

Pity mixed with anger. Why had Brooke done this? Especially this way. With a sigh, she picked up her mojito and wandered to the stool beside him.

He glanced at her and closed his eyes, but gave a nod of recognition.

"Sorry," Trina said. "Sucks to be you."

His mouth twitched slightly and he opened his eyes, taking a sip from his glass. "Can't disagree."

"I saw one reporter get you. Did anyone else—"

"I didn't move fast enough. Two more caught me before I left the church."

She winced. "Sorry."

"Can we talk about something else?"

Trina nodded, another surge of sympathy sliding through her. "Sure," she said, searching her mind for a neutral topic. She took a few sips and swallowed the last of her mojito. "So, what's your favorite game show?"

*"Jeopardy,"* he said taking a sip. "What about you?"

*"Wheel of Fortune."*

"You're a word person," he said.

"And you're a fact person," she said.

"Pretty much."

Silence fell between them. Trina felt the urge to fill it. "There was another old game show I liked. I only saw it in reruns. *Name That Tune.*"

"Oh, yeah. I think I saw it a couple of times when I stayed home from school because I was sick." He tossed back the rest of his drink and lifted two fingers toward the bartender, indicating he wanted a refill for both of them. "What kind of music do you like?"

"A little of everything. Back then I liked whatever my mother hated," she said with a smile.

His lips tilted in a half smile. "Teenage rebel?"

"Some. I just couldn't do the Stepford debutante thing. I dug in my heels and made my mother crazy. What about you?"

"My father hogged all opportunities for rebellion. He left my mother and moved to the Cayman Islands, started a financial service and married a woman down there."

Trina winced. "That doesn't sound like fun for the wife and kid he left behind. Did you ever visit him?"

"Kids, plural. I visited him once." He paused. "I come from a long line of terrible fathers. There are just some men who shouldn't reproduce. I thought marrying Brooke was a good idea because she said she didn't want any children, and she was so focused on herself that I knew…" He broke off and took a long swallow from the drink the bartender had placed in front of him.

Trina couldn't help thinking about the huge differences between Walker and Brooke. He'd probably always been studious and responsible, levelheaded to a fault. Brooke, on the other hand, was rebellious, daring and fun. She supposed it hadn't hurt that she was beautiful and her father was loaded.

What a night, she thought, feeling the mojito ease the rough edges. She took a sip of the fresh drink the bartender had placed in front of her.

"Not to dwell on the evening, but you missed some other drama. One of the reality TV hosts did a live interview with Jenny Prillaman about the degree she didn't get from design school."

Walker tore his gaze from his glass and looked at Trina. "Oh, no. You're kidding."

Trina shook her head and shuddered. "It just got worse after that. She confessed that she didn't have a degree. Alfredo Bellagio turned purple with rage and fired her on the air."

Swearing, Walker raked his hand through his hair. "Oh, what a mess. Poor kid."

"I felt sorry for her. She's nice. Very talented with or without a degree." She glanced at her watch, wondering if she should leave him to nurse his misery by himself. "I should probably go home."

"Must be nice," he said. "I'm sure as hell not going back to my condo. You can bet there will be reporters camped outside. Even if I made it inside, the phone would be ringing off the hook or friends would be pounding on the door to check on me."

She made a face. "Yeah, that wouldn't be fun." She looked at his shoulders hunched toward the bar. He usually stood so straight, everything about him confident. Not tonight. Another shot of pity stabbed at her.

"My apartment's right around the corner if you're willing to take the couch," she impulsively offered.

He glanced up at her and looked at her, really looked at her. She felt his gaze take in her face then skim over her body and back up to her eyes. "You sure?"

Something in his greenish hazel eyes made her stomach take a dip. She shook it off. It was probably just the second mojito. "Yeah."

"Okay, I'll take you up on your kind invitation," he said. "Let's just have one more for the road."

"I haven't finished my second," she said.

He took a long drink. "Swallow faster," he said and motioned again for the bartender.

Two more mojitos later, she might have been fuzzy-headed, but she had enough sense to let the bartender call a cab. She supposed they could have walked, but her coordination wasn't at peak level.

Neither was Walker's, but he helped her out of the car. "You're really nice to let me have your sofa, Trina. I always thought you were nice," he said, his voice slurring slightly.

"Thanks, Walker. I always thought you were nice and very intelligent," she said, feeling wobbly on her Bellagio heels as they walked to the elevator.

"Which floor?" he asked.

"Six," she said, aiming for the right button and missing. "Oops."

He chuckled. "Let me do it," he said, and he missed, too.

For some reason, that struck her as hilarious. They both reached for the button and finally pushed number six. The elevator, however, stopped on floors four and five due to their misses. By the time they arrived at her door, she and Walker couldn't stop laughing. She managed to find her keys in her purse. He managed to take them from her hand and eventually found the one for her door.

Trina tripped as she stepped inside, but Walker caught her against him just before he closed the door. "Whoa," he said. "No falling. You're not allowed to fall."

Grabbing his shoulders for balance, she took a deep breath and caught a draft of his aftershave. "You smell really good," she said.

"Do I?" he asked and grinned. He ducked his head into the crook of her shoulder and inhaled noisily. "You do, too."

"Thanks," she said, liking the way he felt against her. She liked the way his hair looked when it was messed up, not so smooth and perfect. And he had really sexy eyes and one dimple. "Did you know that you have a dent right here?" she asked, lifting her finger to the dimple that added charm to his hard jaw.

"Yeah, I probably got it fighting with my brother or sister," he said, his voice growing a stronger Southern drawl.

"Where are you from?"

"All over the South," he said. "Lived in too many houses and trailers to count. That's what happens when Dad doesn't pay the bills."

She shook her head in sympathy, the movement blurring her vision. "Before he died, my father spent a ton of money on a court fight for his business principles."

"Ouch," Walker said. "Fighting for your principles in court can be very expensive."

"Yeah," she said, and got distracted by his thigh pressed against hers. She studied his eyes. "Did you know that your eyes change colors?"

He shook his head. "No. I haven't looked at them much lately."

"They look very dark green right now, but they don't always look green," she said.

He leaned closer. "Yours are brown. Like cocoa. Or hot chocolate. I always liked hot chocolate."

Her heart tripped at the husky sound of his voice. "Oh." His mouth was inches away, she thought, and wondered what it would be like to kiss him. She'd wondered more than once before, but had always pushed aside her thoughts.

As she should push them aside right now. "I should get a blanket and pillow for you," she said.

"Yeah," he said and she felt his green gaze drop to her mouth. "Why do you think Brooke dumped me?"

Trina's heart squeezed tight. Her chest hurt. "I have no idea."

He met her gaze. "Really? How was I not enough? Not smart enough? Not good-looking enough? Not exciting enough?"

"I'd have to say no to all the above," she said.

"Really?" he asked and she knew the combination of liquor, his wounded ego and heart were talking. He would croak when he realized he'd discussed this with her.

"Really," she said, because she believed it and she felt sorry for him. "You're smart, entirely too good-looking, and plenty exciting."

One side of his mouth tilted upward and he

pulled her against him in an embrace. "You're really nice, Trina."

"I'm not just being nice," she told him. "I'm telling you the truth."

"You're nice. You feel really nice, too," he murmured against her hair.

She heard a change in his voice and felt her sense of gravity shift. A muted sense of warning pushed through her muddled mind. She should back away. She did, looking up at him. "I should get your blanket," she whispered again.

He nodded, but lifted his hand and slowly rubbed his finger over her lips.

Trina was surprised but mesmerized by the soft touch.

"For such a nice girl, I've always thought you had a bad-girl mouth."

Surprise bumped at her again. "Why?"

"Your lips are puffy," he said, still rubbing her mouth. "And pink. Except when you wear red lipstick. Makes a guy wonder all sorts of things about your mouth."

He was saying things he shouldn't, but his voice was low and sexy and the darkness surrounded them like a cocoon.

"Would you mind if I kiss you just once?" he asked.

It was just a kiss, her liquored-up brain told her.

One little kiss, and heaven knew she'd been curious about him. What could one little kiss hurt?

"Just one," she said and he immediately lowered his mouth to hers. He surprised her by taking his time. He rolled his lips against hers as if he wanted to feel every bit of her. Every bit of her lips, she reminded herself.

When he increased the pressure, she automatically opened her mouth and he slid his tongue just inside, just for a second. Then he flicked his tongue over her lower lip and back again.

She felt heat rise. Alcohol flush, she told herself, but everything he did made her want a little more. Make it last longer, she thought. Taste me more. Do that again.

He kept the kiss going in one form or another for minutes, until she was leaning into him, sliding her fingers into the hair at the nape of his neck. His chest felt so good and hard against her breasts and, oh, he felt better than she'd thought he would.

He took a quick breath and his mouth slid over hers again. "You feel so good," he muttered against her mouth and lowered his hands to the small of her back, pulling her lower body against his.

More than his chest was hard. His obvious arousal made her heart speed up and her mind slow down. It was so easy to let her senses take over. He smelled so good, his mouth was like a drug, and the slight gentle rhythm as he moved her against him felt too sexy for words.

Some vestige of something pushed from deep inside her brain and she pulled back. The man had been scheduled to get married tonight. His heart was hurting. His ego was hurting. "Maybe we should stop," she said.

"Yeah. Just one more," he said, kissing her again.

This one went on longer than the other and Trina felt so hot she could have been in the Caribbean on a summer afternoon. He moved one of his hands over her waist, up her rib cage to the side of her breast. He slid his thumb inside the halter tux top and just glanced her nipple.

She inhaled sharply.

He stopped and swore. "What the hell am I doing? This is crazy. I shouldn't be—" He broke off and swore. "But hell, I want you."

He lowered his hands to her hips and Trina tried to make her mind work. She felt his heart beating against her chest. She could almost taste the knot of rejection he felt in his throat, the misery, and the desire to forget it until he had more strength to deal with it. She didn't know which she felt more, turned on or sorry for him.

She lifted one of her hands to his jaw and saw the mixture of pain and arousal in his eyes.

He pressed his mouth against her palm.

"What you really want is a night of hot, mindless sex," she said.

"Yeah," he said. "With you."

*Because she was the woman who was there.* Trina sighed. He was so hot, she thought, and she really didn't want to bludgeon the poor guy's ego again tonight. In this situation, there was really only one thing a nice girl could do.

## CHAPTER TWO

*Nine months, ten days, twenty-two hours and thirty-six minutes later...*

*"WHERE ARE MY DRUGS?"* Trina screamed through the pain ripping her in half.

The nurse gently squeezed her arm. "I told you. The anesthesiologist is on his way."

"You said that hours ago," Trina accused, feeling her contracted muscles relax slightly. She wiped her sweat-dampened forehead with the back of her hand. She was in hell. The cheerful yellow chintz curtains and Yanni music playing in the background couldn't fool her. She was in pain, her mother was spouting platitudes and Nurse Beamer, aka Nurse Hatchett was her guide through labor hell.

"No, you're confused," Nurse Hatchett said. "I told you that twenty minutes ago. The anesthesiologist is with another patient right now"

"You're lying." Trina felt the beginning of another

contraction and desperation stabbed at her. Her muscles tightened around her abdomen like a vise, making it impossible to breathe. "I'm never going to have this baby, am I?"

"Of course you are," the nurse said, and placed a cool washcloth on Trina's head. "As soon as the doctor checks you, I'm sure he'll tell you to start pushing."

Trina moaned. "When is he coming? Where is he? Why isn't he here?"

"Darling, the nurse already told you," her mother said. "He's delivering another baby. He'll be here any minute."

"That's what she said about the anesthesiologist," Trina said, shaking her head.

"I really don't know why you can't just knock her out," her mother said to the nurse.

"Please knock me out," Trina pleaded. "Please."

"We don't do that anymore except for emergency C-sections," the nurse said.

"Cut me," Trina said, her contraction easing. "Please just get it over with. Where's the doctor?"

"He's coming," the nurse said.

"I don't believe it," Trina said. "He's eating donuts. Or banging someone in the closet," she added. "Men are pigs," she muttered, imagining what Walker Gordon was doing right now—drinking wine in some French bistro with a thin French woman or eating a croissant and delicious coffee for breakfast with a thin French woman. Depending on the time zone. Trina didn't even know what time zone *she* was in right now.

"Miss Roberts," a man said cheerfully as he swept into the room. "I'm Dr. Hanson. We met during one of your monthly office visits. Let me check your progress."

Trina vaguely remembered the man. After two shift changes, they were all starting to look the same. He was happy, she noticed as every muscle in her body began to tighten in another contraction. For a fleeting second before the pain gripped her, she wondered if he'd been eating donuts or getting laid. The pain took her breath again and she grasped at his arm. "I need an epidural," she begged. "Knock me out. Shoot me. Something," she said.

"Really, darling," her mother said in a chastising voice. "Where is your dignity?"

"Get her out of here," Trina told the nurse in a voice that sounded as if she was possessed. Where had that voice come from? She felt her fingers pried loose from the doctor's arm.

The doctor moved to check her. "You're ready to push," he said.

"What about my epidural?"

"It's time for you to push. You don't need an epidural."

"Says who?" Trina asked, panic cutting through her. "I want an epidural. She promised me an epidural," Trina said, pointing to the nurse.

"I promised that the doctor would be here soon," she said.

The doctor flipped through her chart. "Did this patient take prepared childbirth classes?"

"Yes, but I didn't practice the breathing because I knew I would get an epidural," she said, her abdomen tightening again.

"Lean forward and push," the nurse said, supporting Trina's shoulders.

Trina did as she was instructed. She would do anything to get out of pain. It wasn't labor. It was hell.

She continued to push for what had to be days. At some point, her mother was thrown out. Trina vaguely recalled a derogatory comment about how her hair looked.

Nurse Hatchett coached, "Just one more push."

Big fat lie. One more meant a million more.

"I can't do this much longer," Trina said, out of breath and nearly out of energy.

"Sure you can. You're almost there."

"Are you sure it's a baby?" Trina asked, wanting whatever it was to just get out of her. "Maybe the ultrasound was wrong and it's a mule. Maybe it's a beast. Or an alien. Or—"

Another contraction hit and she gave a scream as she pushed for all she was worth.

"Good girl," the nurse said.

"The baby is crowning," the doctor said.

"It's human?" Trina asked, caught between delirium and excitement.

"Sure is," the doctor said with a chuckle. "Give me another good push."

"One or two more," the nurse said. "And I really mean it this time. Watch the mirror."

Trina pushed again, and had the odd sensation that she was going to split apart. She pushed through the sensation.

"Head's out. Look at that hair," the nurse said.

Trina glanced at the mirror and felt disconnected from the image of her body and the baby's head. Still not completely birthed, the baby began to cry.

Trina watched in awe. "It's crying."

"Let me get the shoulders," the doctor said and seconds later, he held her screaming baby in his hands. "It's a girl."

Relief and elation rushed through her. She couldn't take her eyes off the baby. "It's a girl. My baby's a girl. She's okay, isn't she?"

The nurse weighed the baby, wiped her off, put a little socklike cap on her head, wrapped her in a blanket and handed her to Trina. "Eight pounds and eleven ounces."

Trina's heart overflowed at the sight of her baby, the weight of her in her arms. "You're gorgeous," she said. "You're a sweetie pie and I'm going to make your life as happy as I possibly can and I won't make you go to private girls' school if you don't want."

She glanced up at the doctor and the nurse, who, she was sure, were angels in disguise. "Thank you so much," she said, her eyes filling with tears. "Thank you."

"My pleasure," Nurse Beamer said.

"But I was a pain."

"No more than most," the nurse said with a smile. "I couldn't wait to see you with your baby in your arms."

Trina looked down at her baby and touched those tiny, tiny fingers. "I'm so glad I have you," she whispered to her daughter. "But I never want to do this again, so I'm never ever going to have sex again."

## CHAPTER THREE

ONCE UPON A TIME Trina had been in control of her life. She'd successfully distanced herself from her overbearing mother and managed her romantic life so that she enjoyed casual dates, but nothing that interfered with her plan to remain single and free of domestic responsibility. Yes, there's been a blip in keeping her love life under control by the name of Stan Roch when she'd been nineteen, but she'd taken care of that and put it behind her.

Once upon a time, although she normally kept her apartment neat and clean, she'd only been in charge of her own laundry and she only bought food she needed, which she could eat on her own schedule.

Once upon a time, she'd been on the fast track to her second promotion at the designer shoe company, Bellagio, Inc. She'd been someone management knew they could depend on to be prompt, level-headed, poised and always ready with a brilliant idea.

All that had changed as a result of her temporary

insanity fifteen months ago. As she rushed into her office late brushing food particles from her suit, she prayed no surprises would greet her.

"Good morning, Dora," she said to the PR group's assistant. "How are you? Any pressing messages?"

Dora, who Trina was convinced was determined to replace her, took a casual sip from her latte. "Yup. There's a meeting with marketing for the new season that started five minutes ago."

Trina began to sweat. She stared at Dora. "This wasn't on my schedule. Why did they start without me?"

Dora shot her a faux sympathetic glance. "Because Alfredo Bellagio called the meeting."

"Crap. Is he actually on site or just speakerphone?"

"On site." She shrugged her shoulders. "I offered to take notes for you during the meeting."

*I'll bet you did.* She felt her stomach tighten with pressure. The beginning of a panic attack. She'd never had panic attacks until fifteen months ago.

"Where are they meeting?" Trina asked.

"Umm, let me see," Dora said, slowly perusing the few papers on her desk.

Trina resisted the urge to give Dora's hair a strong yank. She was convinced that beneath Dora's silky black locks lay a pair of horns. "I guess I can call Marc Waterson's assistant. She would know."

Dora immediately lifted a piece of paper and offered it to Trina. "No need. Here's the message Ben left for you."

Executive room, she read and rushed into her office to pull her laptop from the case then checked her desk for any further messages that Dora the devil may have delayed delivering. Nothing.

Mentally reassuring herself that her tardiness was no big deal, she took the elevator up to the executive floor and gave a nod to the gatekeeper.

She turned the doorknob as quietly as possible and entered the conference room that held at first glance about a dozen Bellagio executives and key employees who all looked at her.

Trina gave a falsely confident smile and murmured, "Good morning."

She despised being late, especially for business meetings. It immediately put you behind the game, and Trina had always tried to stay on top of her game.

Bellagio was predominantly dominated by men of Italian descent with years of chauvinistic conditioning. She'd known from the beginning she would be putting herself in an uphill battle to get where she wanted to go. The chemistry of the people at the company, and the fact that they took innovative, even ballsey measures to increase their market share had been irresistible. Plus, she loved the product. Great shoes. Bellagio shoes did amazing things for a woman's legs, rear end and her self-confidence, and for her, they were free.

Taking a seat at the large table next to her PR chief, she opened her laptop and booted it up. A cute peppy blond woman resumed speaking, pointing to a Power-Point presentation with pie charts indicating public opinion polls, studies and demographic profiles.

She typed a few notes as the woman began to display proposed ads for Fall and Winter shoes. After concentrating on the ads, she suddenly noticed the ad company's logo in the corner of the screen.

Her stomach immediately drew into a tight knot of panic. Eager to get the attention away from her tardy entrance, she'd only taken a cursory glance around the room. She looked more thoroughly, her gaze taking in each person.

Leaning forward, she looked past her PR chief, past two marketing execs to VP Marc Waterson as he cocked his head to one side and there *he* was.

Trina's breath stopped in her chest. Panic roared through her. *Oh, my God, please help!* She had known that eventually she would see him again. She'd prepared for a hundred scenarios, even this one, but her brain locked up.

Walker Gordon rose to his feet beside perky girl wearing his confident, reassuring half smile. His shoulders were broad and his black suit fit his lean, muscular body well. He was obviously still working out, she observed sourly. He was so well-groomed he almost could have been a model, but Trina knew that the sexiest thing about Walker wasn't his body. It was the way his mind worked.

He was a fascinating mix of conservative and risk-taker. He came across as both solid and innovative and he didn't rely on his charm to get a deal.

"We're excited about this ad campaign, and about the prospect of working more with Bellagio," Walker said. "Thank you for letting us bid for your business again. We'd love to have your feedback."

He gave a nod of respect to Alfredo Bellagio and glanced around the room. His gaze lingered on her for a long moment and she suddenly felt self-conscious. She knew what he saw. Her hair had grown past her shoulders and was in dire need of a cut and style. Despite early mornings and nonstop days that sent her crawling to bed by 10:00 p.m., she still hadn't quite gotten rid of fifteen pounds she'd gained. Feeling his scrutiny, she wondered if he saw the dark circles she tried to hide. *Had she put on concealer this morning?* Everything had been a blur.

"What is the model wearing underneath her trench coat and how can I get her number?" a guy from marketing cracked, breaking the silence.

Trina felt light-headed. She wondered how long a person could go without breathing. She had to get out of here. Just for a moment. A week would be better. But she would take a moment.

Her oxygen-deprived brain quickly provided an option. She pressed a button on her cell phone, casually placed it on the cherry table and seconds later it vibrated.

She picked it up. "Looks like someone from the *Atlanta Constitution*," she whispered to her supervisor, Ben. "I'd better take it. Excuse me," she said, and darted out of the room.

Heading straight for the restroom, she locked the door behind her and covered her face with her trembling hands. "Oh crap, oh crap, oh crap. What am I going to do?"

When Walker had left for Paris and hadn't returned for over a year, she'd told herself the fairy tale that she would never have to talk with him again.

The memory of what had happened between them the night of his nonwedding bombarded her. Exhausted from handling the press, maximizing exposure opportunities at the same time she performed damage control, she'd slipped into a bar close to her apartment for a mojito.

And that had been the beginning of when her pity had gotten her into *mojito* trouble, Trina thought as she stared into the ladies' room mirror. She needed to pull herself out of Memoryville and get back to that meeting. Yanking a towel from the dispenser, she dampened it with cool water and pressed it against her forehead and throat.

She could do this. She could return to this meeting and pretend that she was okay-fine for a maximum of forty-five minutes. She could pretend. Pretending was what PR was all about.

Trina wasn't pretending, however, that she didn't want Bellagio to renew the advertising contract with Walker's company. She'd strongly advocated putting the contract out for bid and the board had decided to give Walker's group first shot. If they didn't pan out, then Bellagio would accept other bids.

Reentering the room, she gave a businesslike nod and returned to her seat next to her supervisor.

"I like the sophistication of this campaign," Walker said. "The models we have in mind will portray wealth and beauty. They'll be the kind of person your customer wants to be."

"Anyone mention the bar ads yet?" she whispered to her boss, Ben.

He glanced at her and shook his head. "No. Good point." He turned toward Walker. "One of the things we want to achieve with this campaign is appealing to a younger demographic. I believe we discussed via e-mail that we wanted to see an ad in a bar featuring a well-dressed woman with men surrounding her offering her drinks. And of course, she would be wearing Bellagio shoes. To target younger men, we also suggested an ad of a man watching a sports game with beautiful women on either side."

Walker shot a quick glance at perky girl.

Perky girl cleared her throat. "We'd already put together the proposal when we received that memo, but we can have something for you by the end of the week."

*Uh-oh. Busted.* Trina saw just a hint of tension in Walker's jaw, but she'd bet Miss Perky would do well to get her resume ready for some serious faxing.

"We can have it for you later this week," Walker corrected in a crisp voice. "I'll take care of it myself."

"Who's going to cover for Walker when he's in Paris?" Trina whispered to her supervisor.

Her supervisor nodded. Ben cleared his throat. "We also need to know who will be covering Bellagio. If you're handling international accounts in Paris, we need to know who our point person will be."

Expectant silence descended over the room. Trina glanced at the board members and saw that Ben had asked the question on everyone's mind. The question that would open the door for Bellagio to work with another advertising agency.

Walker's answer and subsequent absence from

her life would provide her with a peace of mind that money couldn't buy.

She turned her attention to Walker.

His jaw was set and the expression in his eyes reminded her of a gladiator going into a fight. The expression made her uneasy.

"I'll be your point man," he said. "I'm not going back to Paris."

## CHAPTER FOUR

AS SOON AS HE ANNOUNCED himself as the point man, that he wouldn't be returning to Paris, Walker felt the level of tension in the room drop at least sixty percent. The knowledge boosted his confidence and would ultimately boost earnings for his company.

Brooke Tarantino might have dumped him at the altar on live television. She might have stomped his ego into the ground and made him look like a joke. She might have succeeded in motivating him to leave Atlanta in order to get his mojo back.

But Walker was hell-bent and determined on keeping the Bellagio account. He'd nurtured this account from the beginning and it was growing bigger every year. Atlanta would burn again before he would let another agency raid his account and take the spoils.

"That's good to know," Alfredo Bellagio said. "So you'll give us some more ads on Friday and we'll think some more."

Walker nodded, feeling a shot of adrenaline. He would need to hustle to pull it together, but he could do it. He'd done it before. Everyone in the room stood, taking Alfredo's words as a signal that the meeting was adjourned.

Walker shook hands with Alfredo and one of the VPs sitting next to him. He caught sight of Trina Roberts moving toward the door and he remembered that one hot night….

Her gaze slid away from his. Curious, he thought. They'd parted on good terms. It had been a one-night stand. Damn good one from what he could remember. Unfortunately he couldn't remember much because he'd been loaded.

He sure didn't want awkwardness between them now. Not now when he needed every Bellagio insider backing him. He made a mental list of who he should contact personally. Marc Waterson would be inclined to back him. After all, his fiancée, Jenny Prillaman, had been fired as a result of the Brooke wedding debacle. Fortunately she'd been rehired. He made another mental note to contact the marketing VP.

And Trina, he thought. He may as well catch her in her office now. Turning to the assistant that had been assigned to him, he motioned toward the presentation materials. "Please go ahead and pack everything up, Stephanie. I'll be back in fifteen minutes."

He left the conference room and made his way toward Trina's office, waving at people he hadn't seen in over a year. With a nonchalance no longer feigned, he'd prepared himself for discomfort, pity, even lame jokes. A year away from Brooke Tarantino had cured him. Hell, a month away from her had cured him.

Truth was, Brooke hadn't crushed his heart. She'd just blasted his ego and temporarily disrupted some of his business plans. After a year spent developing the European market and enjoying the attention of more than one creative, attentive mademoiselle, he was as good as new.

He punched the elevator button and nodded at the receptionist. "How's it going, Thelma? I meant to ask, are your kids doing okay?"

The woman blinked. "Oh. I wouldn't have expected you to remember. It's been a long time since you've been—" She broke off and cleared her throat as if she didn't know what to say.

"And a lot has happened. All water under the bridge, now," he said cheerfully. "And your kids?"

"Good," she said, clearly relieved. "Benjamin is playing Little League this year."

He shook his head. "They grow so fast. It seems like just yesterday you were talking about his first steps."

"You're so right," she said as the elevator door slid

open. "You have a good day. It's good to see you again, Mr. Gordon."

"Walker," he corrected. "You'll be seeing me a lot more often now." He took the elevator down two floors and headed for the PR suite of offices.

A dark-haired woman sitting at the receptionist's desk gave him a thorough once-over and smiled. "How can I help you?"

Her voice oozed invitation. He smiled in return. "I just wanted to speak to Trina Roberts for a minute. Is she in her office?"

"Sure. She just returned from a meeting. You can go on in… Mr.…?"

"Gordon. Walker Gordon." He saw the moment the woman registered *who* he was.

"Oh, Brooke's—" She covered her mouth in horror.

"No problem. That's ancient history," he said, and headed for Trina's office. The door was open. She was standing in front of the window, gazing outside as if she were lost in thought. Her hair was longer than he remembered, darker blond. The style was more casual. He remembered Trina as chicly manicured from her head to her toenails. She filled out the suit she was wearing differently. She'd been model slim the last time he'd seen her.

He watched her bite her lip and wondered what else was different. "Hey. Better not let Ben see you staring out the window on company time," he joked.

She jerked around and gaped at him, her chocolate-brown eyes wide with surprise. Almost shock. "Um, hi. What are you doing here?"

"Good to see you, too," he said and laughed.

"Sorry," she said, pushing her hair behind her ear and moving toward her desk. "How was Paris?"

"Healing," he said. "But I'm ready to be back. I'd like to know you're on my side with keeping the Bellagio account. Can we get together for dinner tonight? Tomorrow night?"

She shook her head. "I'm sorry. I can't."

She refused him so quickly he blinked. "Hmm." He picked up her left hand. "I don't see signs of engagement or marriage."

"I have other commitments. Sorry." She shot him a quick glance. "Looks like things are going well for you."

"Except I'm going to need a new assistant," he said, referring to the gaffe during the presentation.

"Not a bad idea," she said with a smile and glanced at her watch. "I wish I could talk, but my schedule's packed today."

"Okay," he said, wondering at her lack of friendliness. "You're not upset about that night we—"

"No," she said before he could finish. "It was just

one of those strange things that happen. Like a meteor dropping in the desert. Or an airplane dropping frozen water on a house."

He wrinkled his brow at the comparisons she chose for the night they'd spent together. He wasn't sure he liked the second one. "I don't really remember that much about—"

"Neither do I because we were both smashed. So there's really no need to discuss it."

He nodded. "I hope it won't affect our working relationship."

"*If* we work together, I'm sure it won't be a problem. Long time ago."

"We will be working together," Walker said, determined to remove any doubt. "I'll do what it takes to keep the Bellagio account."

She didn't jump for joy at his words, making him wonder. Trina had always been friendly toward him. Not seductive, but nice. Why the change?

"You do want me for this account, don't you?"

"I want the very best for Bellagio," she said. "How can we be sure you won't head back to France?"

"Because I said I'm staying here. It's not just for business reasons," he told her. "My uncle just had heart surgery. He needs someone to live with while he recovers. I've been elected."

She looked at him in surprise. "Wow. I never saw you as the nurturing type."

"I'm not," he said. "But this is different. He showed up for my graduations, gave my sister and brother and me money every now and then. He didn't ever have any kids of his own, but he kept an eye on us after my father cut and ran."

"Gordon curse," she murmured.

"What?"

"Oh, it was something you mentioned about why you didn't want to have children. Some sort of curse, long line of fathers…"

"Yeah," he said, surprised that she recalled. "I didn't remember telling you that. I don't talk about my father much."

She shrugged. "It was a very strange night." She glanced at her watch again. "I need to run. I'm glad you're doing well."

"Same," he said. "I'll be seeing you soon and often."

"Take care," she said and slid into her chair, opening her laptop.

TRINA WATCHED the very fine backside of Walker as he left her office, and told herself to breathe. Out of the corner of her eye she caught sight of her baby daughter Maddie's picture and held it in her lap. Her fingers began to tremble.

She hadn't counted on him returning to Atlanta, let alone to Bellagio. Walker had plenty of accounts.

He didn't need Bellagio. And why put himself in a position where he had to respond to gossip and bad jokes about his failed wedding?

But she hadn't counted on his pride. Trina had convinced herself that she wouldn't meet him face-to-face again until she was on her death bed, or at least until Maddie, her daughter, graduated from high school.

She swore under her breath.

Dora burst through her doorway. "That was Walker Gordon. He's so hot. Why did Brooke dump him?"

Trina's hands continued to shake and she closed them around each other over the photo in her lap. "I couldn't say," she managed.

"But he seems like he's so *over* her." Dora twirled her finger around her hair. "You worked with him before. What do you know about him? He obviously works out. Do you know which club he belongs to? Where does he hang out?"

Trina stared at Dora in exasperation. "How would I know? He's been *hanging out* in Paris for the last year."

"Chill out. I was just asking. I'm single. He's single. I wouldn't mind a chance to help rebuild his—" She paused and smiled like a female devil. "Ego."

"I don't think his ego needs rebuilding," Trina muttered.

"Oh really?" Dora asked, her face lighting up.

"What makes you say that? Did he say anything about me? He gave me the look, you know, like he liked what he saw."

"I'm sure he did," Trina said, hoping her agreement would shoo Dora away. "You're a pretty girl."

Dora gave a coy smile. "Well, what a sweet thing to say. Thank you," she drawled. "I'm so lucky I've never had a weight problem. I can eat anything I want."

Before she'd gotten pregnant, Trina had been able to eat anything she wanted. Not so now. She gritted her teeth and smiled.

"You know, if you would lose ten pounds and cut your hair, I bet you would get out a lot more."

"I don't really want to get out a lot more right now," Trina said.

Dora appeared not to have heard her. "I'm not sure you could get Walker's attention but—"

Trina blinked at the insult. She should have seen it coming. The way Dora pulled a knife out in her sweetest tone reminded Trina of her mother. She took a deep breath. "Dora, trust me. I couldn't be less interested in getting Walker Gordon's attention."

Dora fell silent and stared at Trina for a long moment. She narrowed her eyes. "You know something. What's wrong with him?"

Gross miscalculation to reassure Dora of her lack

of interest in Walker. Her second or third miscalculation of the day.

Trina spent the rest of the day unsuccessfully dodging Dora's questions.

"Does he have a mental condition? Is he a secret sicko?" Dora asked an hour later.

"Not to my knowledge," Trina said and left for a meeting.

When she returned, Dora followed her into her office. "Is he emotionally or physically abusive?"

"No," Trina said in horror. "At least, I haven't heard that he is."

Dora sighed in obvious frustration. "Then maybe it's something super personal." She leaned closer and lowered her voice to a whisper. "Does he have a forked—" She stopped. "You know. Down there?"

"A forked wha—" She broke off as realization hit. "Absolutely not," she said, then quickly added, "Not from what I've heard."

Dora frowned. "Then why don't you want him? He's gorgeous. He's loaded. He's smart."

"It's probably hormonal," Trina manufactured. "Since I had Maddie, I'm not interested in anyone. I'm much more interested in a good night's sleep."

"Oh," Dora said with a nod of sympathy. "And that's probably why you've let yourself go."

Trina blinked. She should have seen that insult

coming. Counting to ten, she gritted her teeth. "How kind of you to notice."

Dora's eyes widened. "Oh, I didn't mean to hurt your feelings. It's just obvious you're not putting a lot of effort into your appearance. I could help you if you'd like."

"That's okay, Dora. What I'd like is for you to print the press releases for Jenny Prillaman's new designs along with the accompanying letters. I'd like to give them a quick once-over before they're sent out. Thanks," she said in a dismissive tone.

Trina took her quick lunch break at the company day-care center. Due to a bumper crop of pregnancies and babies, Bellagio had joined with another company close by to provide service for the children of their employees.

After going through three nannies, Trina had brought Maddie to the day-care center with a few reservations. She preferred one-on-one care for her daughter and also worried about infections, but she loved the proximity and the convenience of visiting Maddie when she could squeeze in a break during her workday.

She walked into the room for babies where her six-month-old daughter was being fed oatmeal by an assistant teacher. "How has she been today?"

"Sweet, but active. I think she may be an early

crawler. Good luck," the teacher said with a rueful smile.

Just then, Maddie glanced up and caught sight of Trina. She let out an earsplitting shriek and banged her fists on her high chair.

"Looks like she's happy to see you," the teacher said.

A thrill shot through Trina. Her child's adoration for her never failed to give her heart a squeeze. "How's my little carrot cake?"

Maddie gave a wide oatmeal-lined smile and Trina walked over to take over the feeding duty. She brushed a kiss over her daughter's soft head where her carrot-red topknot tilted to the right.

"And how has your day been?" Trina asked Maddie as she lifted the spoon to her daughter's rosebud mouth.

Maddie swallowed the oatmeal and made a gurgling sound and other sounds in an unintelligible language as if she were making conversation.

"Gramma Aubrey would not approve of talking with your mouth full, but we'll wait on that one. Okay?" Trina said with a nod.

Maddie nodded and opened her mouth for another bite. Trina finished feeding Maddie then cleaned her face and hands despite her baby's protests.

After changing her diaper, Trina carried Maddie

to a rocking chair in a quiet corner of the room and began to rock. After a morning that had shaken every nerve in her body, the weight of her little daughter in her arms felt so reassuring.

As Maddie relaxed, Trina felt her own heart rate and her breathing slow. The muscles in the back of her neck loosened. She would have never predicted it, but in her arms, Trina felt as if she were holding the pot of gold at the end of the rainbow.

When she'd first learned she was pregnant, she'd panicked and considered terminating the pregnancy. She wasn't in a position to be a mother. Her apartment was too small. She didn't have a husband. Plus she had a mother who would die if her daughter became an unwed mother. Aside from that, Trina had plans that didn't include children until, if, or when she should get married. And there was the fact that Trina had no mommy skills. Heck, she hadn't even done much babysitting during her teen years. What did people do with babies anyway? They seemed like little savages that cried and peed and cried and pooped and cried and ate and cried some more.

So the obvious choice had been to call the doctor to do the deed and not be pregnant anymore. She'd made a mental note to call the doctor to make an appointment tomorrow, but she'd been too busy that day. And the next tomorrow, she'd felt creepy about calling, which was hormonal, she was certain. So she told herself she would call when she didn't feel creepy about it, when she felt confident and sure and had no regrets.

That tomorrow had never arrived.

She'd hid her pregnancy reasonably well until her sixth month when her abdomen had sprouted outward. She'd avoided face-to-face contact with her mother by claiming business was taking her out of town. Lord knew, her mother could smell weight gain of anything over a pound.

People at work had reacted with surprise and curiosity. Trina had reacted as if it were perfectly normal for her to be pregnant. Pretty soon, the questions died down.

Her mother, however, had gone into a hysterical frenzy that had required heavy doses of sedatives. She'd locked herself in her bedroom for a solid week.

Trina had secretly hoped she would stay locked up longer, say a year. Or two.

Trina glanced down at Maddie, asleep on her lap. Her dark eyelashes stood out against her fair complexion. Trina had fallen in love with her daughter at first sight. What she didn't know about child rearing could fill a library, but she understood a few things about what her daughter needed. Love, food, sunshine, a bath, sleep and her mother.

Trina figured she would learn what she needed to know along the way. Lifting Maddie against her chest, she carried her to the crib marked with her name and laid her down, her heart full at the sight of her baby.

Waving to the teachers, she left to return to her office.

DESPITE TRINA'S BEST EFFORTS, Dora continued her inquisition about Walker throughout the afternoon. Every mention of his name shredded her nerves even more. Bamboo sticks under her fingernails or water torture would have been easier to bear.

Promising herself she would buy Lean Cuisine the next time she got to the grocery store, Trina picked up Maddie and grabbed a take-out sandwich through a drive-thru while Maddie sang in her car seat in the back seat.

Before she arrived at her town house, she smelled a distinctive scent that told her the first thing she would be doing when she got inside would be changing Maddie's diaper.

Grabbing Maddie's bag and her carryout sandwich, she walked inside, dumped both bags in the foyer and immediately headed for the nursery.

Just as she put on a fresh diaper, the doorbell rang three times. Trina paused. The doorbell rang again, this time five times and Trina tensed. Her mother.

"Please tell me I still have some wine in the fridge," she said to Maddie.

Maddie gave an unintelligible but sympathetic sounding response.

"Carter-Aubrey?" her mother called from the now open doorway. "Carter-Aubrey, are you there?"

Trina groaned. Her mother refused to call her by her preferred middle name. The other two just did not fit her at all. "I'm here, Mother," she called from the top of the stairs.

"Thank God you're okay," said Aubrey Carter-Elizabeth with a perfect hairstyle, dyed perfectly auburn. She wore a perfect size-four suit and sported a perfect manicure. "I looked at the mess in this foyer and was afraid your house had been looted."

"Just needed to make a quick diaper change," she said. "What brings you here?"

"Oh, look at her. She's a mess. Nanna Aubrey will get you shiny clean in no time," she said, reaching for her granddaughter. She glanced down at the fast-food bag on the floor. "Dear, you really need to eat better food. You'll never lose your baby weight if you keep eating that stuff."

"Thanks for the encouragement, Mother," Trina said with a heavy trace of sarcasm.

"I'm just looking out for your best interest. Someday you may meet the right man who will be a good father for our little Madeline and you want to be ready."

Meaning Trina clearly wasn't ready today.

Her mother studied her suit jacket. "What is that?" she asked, scraping her fingernail over the sleeve.

Trina glanced down and shrugged. "Oatmeal? Applesauce? I dunno. I don't have anything to offer you except baby food and half my sandwich. Are you interested?"

"No, thank you," her mother said, wrinkling her nose. "I just came over to see Madeline and drop off the application for the Ambrose school for girls. You probably should have signed her up the day she was born. They have a very long waiting list. It's so competitive to get in, but since you, your grandmother and I graduated from Ambrose, it shouldn't be a problem."

Trina felt her stomach twist as she led the way into her kitchen. "I haven't decided if Ambrose is the best place for Maddie. I'm looking into the Montessori school."

Aubrey gasped. "Not there. Oh, darling, there's hardly any structure, no uniforms and she'll never meet the right people."

Trina bit her tongue and lifted her fingers into a peace sign, the sign she used to tell her mother she was overstepping her bounds. Again.

Aubrey dropped her mouth. "Oh, you can't think I'm interfering by merely bringing over an application. And speaking to Owen Randall in admissions," she added.

Trina continued to hold her peace sign.

Audrey sighed. "May I give her a bath?"

"She'll love it."

Aubrey beamed at Madeline. "She's as beautiful a baby as you were. You did well." She tossed Trina a sideways glance. "Although it would have been nice if you'd at least married her father."

"Life's not perfect," Trina said. "You should know. And remember our agreement about the discussion of that subject." If Aubrey didn't bring up the subject of Maddie's father or Trina's love-life disaster when she'd been nineteen, then Trina had agreed not to bring up the subject of her father or the fact that he'd died due to an automobile accident when he'd been arguing with her mother.

Her mother sighed because her life wasn't going as planned, either. Aubrey was determined to hang on to the family home despite the fact that she didn't have nearly enough money for the upkeep. Her mother had married her father for his nouveau riche money. Her father had married her mother for her name, which provided him, an outsider, a way into Atlanta's upper class. Unfortunately her father had lost most of the money in court, suing over principle. After years spent in court, he'd lost his fight and died a month later, leaving her mother with bills.

Trina had long encouraged her mother to sell the estate to someone who could afford to refurbish it, but her mother, who had apparently watched *Gone with the Wind* way too many times, had cast herself in the role of Scarlett, determined to hang on to the family land.

Too much melodrama for Trina. She was happy with her condo, Jacuzzi bathtub, and loved the fact that her community association fees covered all the lawn work.

"You want to feed her, too?" Trina asked gently.

Her mother nodded.

"Fine. I'll get an apron for you."

# CHAPTER FIVE

AFTER FIRING STEPHANIE and temporarily comman-
deering his partner's longtime admin assistant,
putting together a skeleton ad and calling in favors
to get a cameraman, producer and some actors,
Walker dragged himself into his condo.

He heard a ball game blaring from the television
and smelled the combined scents of a Dominican
cigar and burger and fries.

Everything his uncle Harry wasn't supposed to be
consuming with the exception of alcohol.

Walker felt a headache pound through his skull.
He knew why he'd been chosen to provide a place for
Uncle Harry after his uncle had spent a couple weeks
in a rehab facility following bypass surgery. Uncle
Harry trusted Walker. Plus Walker was financially independent and the Gordon family had a sketchy
history with finances, banks, taxes and creditors.

He shrugged out of his jacket as he walked through
the wooden foyer toward the den. His balding, hard-

of-hearing uncle sat in Walker's favorite chair, holding a cigar in one hand and a beer in the other. A telltale bag advertising a fast-food burger joint lay crumpled on the TV tray beside Harry.

With a sigh, Walker crept behind his uncle and plucked the cigar and beer out of his hands.

"Hey! What are you—" Harry jerked around with an expression of indignation that quickly changed to a cagey grin. "Walker, my boy, I was wondering when you would get here."

"Obviously should have been sooner," Walker muttered. "You know you're not supposed to be smoking and drinking. And why bother with the bypass surgery if you're going to clog up your veins the second you get out of the hospital?"

"I haven't had a burger in months," Harry complained, pressing the remote to lower the TV volume. "I was due."

"How'd you get this stuff? I can't believe that home health aide allowed this."

"Oh, I sent her home early," Harry said with a dismissive wave. "And you know I'm supposed to take short walks. I chatted with one of the security guards. Real nice guy. I told him I thought I could get him a good deal on a double-wide for his thirty-year-old stepson that refuses to leave his house. He brought me dinner after he got off his shift."

"Did he bring the beer and cigar?" Walker asked, feeling like a mother and not liking it.

Uncle Harry lifted his mouth in a craggy grin. "I keep a stash handy. Hey, it's not like they're Cuban. Cubans are overrated anyway."

"And the beer?"

"Was under your bed," Harry said and wagged his head from side to side. "Pretty lame, boy. I would have expected better from you."

Walker rested his hands on his hips and bit his tongue to keep from laughing. His uncle Harry had shown up for graduations and contributed money at times when he, his mother, sister and brother had been broke.

Of course, nowadays his mother, brother and sister still had times when they provided the giant sucking sound in Walker's bank account. Or Harry's. Depending on which one picked up their cell phone first.

"Gimme back my beer and tell me what you did at work today, boy," Harry said.

"No," Walker said and took the beer and cigar to the kitchen. He dumped the beer down the drain, stubbed out the cigar and grabbed two bottles of water from the fridge. Returning to the den, he twisted the top off one and gave it to his uncle.

Harry made a face, but took a long draw.

"I almost lost a big account today."

Harry nodded, his gaze turning serious. "Almost means you can still keep it."

"Yeah," Walker said. "Bellagio Shoes."

Harry's eyes widened. "Bellagio. That Tarantino girl who dumped you at that altar in front of God and everybody. Wasn't she related to those Bellagios?"

"Yeah," Walker said and took a drink of water, wishing it was bourbon, not because he'd lost Brooke, but because he didn't want to lose the Bellagio account.

"That's why I never got married," Harry said.

"Because you were afraid of being dumped at the altar?"

"No. Because of the Gordon curse," Harry said. "We stink in the marriage and fatherhood department."

"I thought it was more of a fatherhood issue. Brooke and I had agreed not to have children."

Harry snorted. "Talk to your mom if you think it's just fatherhood. How you gonna keep the account?"

"They like me and trust me. They know I deliver. But they probably think I should have been able to keep my woman under control." Walker took another draw from his bottle of water. "I need to produce a bang-up commercial fast. If I can pull a few key Bellagio people onto my side, I think I can keep the account. Especially since I'm staying in Atlanta."

Walker thought of Trina and frowned. He wondered

why she had been so reticent with him. He'd enjoyed their friendship before he'd left for France. Trina had been fun to be around. He'd felt as if he could let down his guard with her and everything would be okay. Plus she had assured him that their one-night stand hadn't meant anything to her. Now, he didn't know what to think.

"By the way, your phone rang a couple of times, but I didn't pick up," Harry said. "Caller ID looked like it may have been your brother."

"BJ usually calls the house first," Walker said, wondering if his brother's latest troubles were financial or personal. "I'll call him. Enjoy the game, but don't sneak any more cigars or beer tonight."

Harry made a face. "Okay," he conceded. "I won't tonight."

Walker walked upstairs to his home office and sank into the leather chair behind his desk. He picked up the phone and dialed the latest number his brother had given him at the same time he opened a desk drawer and pulled out his checkbook. Conversations with BJ almost always involved his checkbook. He didn't resent it. He was just glad he had the ability. Someone had to make up for his father.

One half of a ring later, he heart his brother's voice. "Walker?"

"BJ, what's up?" Walker asked, rubbing his face. "Everything okay?"

"Could be better," BJ said. "I got a woman pregnant."

Walker's stomach clenched.

"Are you sure the baby is yours? You use protection, don't you?"

"Well, yeah, but this girl, she seems pretty sure."

"Girl," Walker echoed. "Tell me she's over eighteen," he said, praying his brother hadn't knocked up an underage teenager.

"She's twenty-two," BJ said and paused. "I think she wants me to marry her."

Walker closed his eyes and could barely stifle a groan. His younger brother had tried to pull off a lot of crazy ventures over the years—trying to use chicken manure for fuel, pet time-share sales, propelling a chain letter he was certain would yield him a fortune, real estate agent for a Caribbean island that didn't exist.

Walker had bailed him out with repeated warnings. He and his brother parted ways on many things, but one area on which they'd always agreed had been the subject of fathering. Don't just say *no*. Say *never*.

"Walker, I know we always said we wouldn't have any children, but I gotta tell you I want to be a good father for this baby. I want to be a husband for

Danielle. I never thought I would say it, but I want to be a family man."

*For how long?* Walker wondered. In all the time Walker had known his brother, BJ had exhibited the staying power of a fly. "BJ, this isn't another business investment you can dump and move on to another one. This is a human being. A person. Do you really want to take on that responsibility? And this girl? Do you love her enough to stick with her and try to get a real job and earn a real living?"

"I know the baby's a human being, and yeah, I do love Danielle. I have for a while now. I just didn't want to tell you. I can tell you don't believe in me. Can't say I blame you."

"I didn't say I don't believe in you," Walker replied. "I've always said you had great potential."

"And you've always gotten me out of trouble. You know I can be a hard worker, though," BJ said.

"Yeah," Walker admitted. Hard, just not all that focused.

"So, Danielle and I think it would be better for us to move to Atlanta. I'd like to go to work for you, big brother. It's always been my dream."

Alarm shot through him. Despite the Bellagio principle of having all those relatives work for the same organization, he'd always firmly believed that family working for family was *not* a good idea. In fact, it was a horrible idea.

"I can do it," BJ continued. "I'll do anything you ask. I'll run errands. I'll answer the phone. I'll help you sell advertising. Just give me a chance."

Walker cleared his throat. "I'm not sure you would be happy in the advertising field, BJ. You have a lot of entrepreneurial spirit. That's great, but sometimes it makes it hard to take orders from someone else."

"Walker, I need to make a fresh start if I'm going to make this work. I need your help like I've never needed it before. I gotta grow up and be somebody else's daddy."

THE NEXT MORNING, Trina's supervisor, Ben Ferguson, invited her into his office and closed the door behind him. First clue that something unusual was up.

He sat across from Trina and looked at her for a moment. She returned his glance calmly, although her stomach twisted.

"There are some changes in the works. I need to know if you want my job."

She blinked. "Excuse me?"

"If I were to move up, are you sure you want my job?"

"Of course I do," she said. "I've always wanted your job."

He laughed. "That's what I like about you, Trina. You want my job, but you don't stab me in the back to get it. You help me get promoted instead."

She smiled. "What I like about you is that you realize I'm trying to help you."

"You've made me look good. Good enough that I'm filling in for Anthony Tarantino's VP spot this summer. He's talking about retiring."

"That's great," she said. "You've got to be pleased."

"I am," he said. "But I'm going to be in a limbo phase where I'm filling in for Anthony at the same time I'm still acting PR supervisor. If you're really sure you want my position, then I need you to step up now."

"I always have."

"I hesitate to mention this, but you've had a baby and you're a single parent. Is that going to be a problem?"

"Absolutely not," Trina said, although she felt the slightest twist of uncertainty. "Women have been successfully multitasking for ages. Have you noticed a dip in my performance?"

"No. You've been late a few times and had to skip out early for a few doctor appointments, but you've always come through when Bellagio needed you."

"Thank you for noticing," she said.

Ben gave her another considering glance. "Okay. First order of business is Walker Gordon."

Trina's heart leapt. "You want me to fire him?"

Ben laughed. "Hell, no. The board is still partial to him even after the Brooke fiasco. There's a point person assigned to him from marketing and we need a point person from PR. That would be you."

She swallowed a gasp. "I thought he still needed to present a commercial before the board approved him."

Ben shrugged. "Yeah. It better be a decent commercial. But when has Walker done anything that wasn't stellar? As long as Bellagio has his personal attention and he's got his game going, we're going to go with him this time. Marc Waterson himself told me."

She swallowed seven swear words. How was she supposed to work with Walker? If he was going to stay in Atlanta, she was going to have to tell him about Maddie.

Her expression must have revealed her lack of enthusiasm. "You don't look happy about it. I always got the impression that you and Walker got along well."

"We did," she said without much conviction.

Ben wrinkled his brow. "Has something happened that I need to know—"

"Oh, no," she said quickly, her heart racing at the lie. She prayed the color of her cheeks didn't betray her. "I, uh—" She cleared her throat and gave a tight smile as she manufactured a reason for her response. "I just thought Bellagio would benefit from a fresh point of view. In terms of advertising."

Ben relaxed. "I see your point, but you gotta admit Walker has always done a good job for us. So we'll see how he handles the next campaign. And of course since you're the point person, it will be your job to make sure it's a success," Ben half joked, pausing when she remained silent.

"If you think it's going to be too much, we could turn it over to Dora."

"Oh, no," Trina said, feeling protective of her job, her future, her baby's future. "I'm up for it."

"Just because I'll be upstairs doesn't mean you can't call me for anything," he assured her.

"Thanks and congratulations," she said, rising to her feet.

"Yeah." He stood, too. "Don't spread it around. Nothing's official yet."

"Okay, I'll talk to you later," Trina said and left his office, her mind whirling. This was the promotion she had been working for since she'd started at Bellagio. She'd called in favors from old schoolmates to get exposure for Bellagio. She'd worked late and sacrificed. Finally, it was within sight. The promotion was more important than ever to her now that she was in charge of Maddie's welfare. Trina knew she could do the job. She also knew she would need support. Someone who could do her grocery shopping, occasionally prepare meals and take care of Maddie when Trina needed to work late. Her stomach twisted at that last possibility, but she didn't dwell on it.

Walking into her office, she opened a file on her computer and made notes about requirements for the position she needed. She sucked down a cup of coffee and called *Bride Magazine* to confirm a mention of Bellagio shoes in the June issue. It took some extra delving, but she learned the shoe size for the fashion editor at a top women's magazine and arranged to send her pair of Bellagio sandals.

Grabbing a Diet Coke, she started to dial marketing when her phone rang. "Trina Roberts, hello."

One beat of silence followed. "Trina, it's Walker."

Her throat tightened and she took a breath to help her relax. "Walker, hello."

"I just talked to Ben and he told me you're going to be one of my go-to people."

"That's what I hear," she said with forced cheerfulness. "What can I do for you?"

"I thought it would be good to touch base with you about the commercial and my ideas. Is a drink after work okay?"

"Let me check my schedule and I'll get right back to you. It might be easier for me if we meet at the office earlier in the afternoon."

"I'm stuck all day shooting this commercial."

"Okay, then let me call you back." She hung up,

hating the fact that her hands shook. She was going to have to get hold of herself. Reviewing her options, she called Jenny Prillaman.

"Hey, girl," Jenny said with a smile in her voice. "How's your gorgeous baby?"

"Gorgeous and growing," Trina said. "You offered to keep her every now and then. Any chance you could keep her for a little while this evening?"

"Oooh, hot date?" Jenny asked.

"Business."

"Oh," Jenny said in a disappointed tone. "I wish I could, but the wedding machine is in high gear and Marc and I have a meeting with the minister tonight."

"That's okay. No problem," Trina said.

"But you have to promise that you'll ask me again," Jenny said.

"I promise," Trina said, thinking Jenny had to be one of the sweetest people in the world. "But since you're getting married soon, you may be starting on your own babies."

"One thing at a time. Call me soon."

"Sure thing," Trina said and dialed the number of another friend who already had plans.

She winced as she regretfully dialed her last choice. "Mom, it's Trina."

"Hello, dear. I'm playing bridge."

"Okay, I'll keep it quick. Any chance you could pick up Maddie tonight and keep her for a little while?"

"Yes. Do you have a date?"

"No, business."

"Oh," her mother said, her voice full of disappointment. "I wish you would start—"

"Thanks so much, Mom. I shouldn't be long. Just pick her up at the company day care. Kill 'em at bridge," she said and hung up.

After work, Trina stopped by a salon close to the office and got a shampoo and blow-dry. With every sweep of the round brush, she rehearsed how to tell Walker about Maddie.

*I had a baby six months ago. You're the father.*

*I don't expect anything from you.*

*I don't want anything from you.*

*I don't know why the contraception didn't work. Perhaps because we were both plowed.*

*Why didn't you tell me before?* he would ask.

*I just kinda never got around to it.*

Trina rolled her eyes at herself. Lame, lame, lame. She glanced at her fingernails and wished she had time for a manicure. With Maddie-girl, she was always washing her hands after changing a diaper or before feeding or after cleaning carrots off Maddie's face.

She was glad she'd worn black today. It made her

feel less vulnerable. Exactly how was a woman supposed to dress when she told a man that she'd had his baby?

She swallowed over the bubble of panic in the back of her throat.

What could he do to her? she asked herself, trying to approach the situation rationally. He couldn't accuse her of trying to trap him into marriage. He couldn't accuse her of trapping him into being a real father to Maddie because she had resolved a long time ago to ask and expect nothing of him.

What if he didn't believe her?

She clenched her jaw. That bothered her. That really bothered her.

It probably wouldn't happen, she assured herself as she left the salon and ducked into a drugstore to pick up a compact, lipstick and mascara. She applied the cosmetics in her car, feeling as if she were putting on an extra layer of armor.

She possessed the edge here, she told herself as she walked into the bar. She had the knowledge and she had Maddie. That last thought warmed her like sunshine.

She glanced around the bar and didn't see Walker. A cowardly sliver of relief ran through her. *Oh, good, he was a no-show.*

"You beat me by seconds," a familiar male voice said from behind her.

She whispered a swear word, but managed to turn around with a smile. "I wondered if we might need to reschedule."

He shook his head. "No. I've been looking forward to this all day." He gestured toward a table across the room and waved at the bartender for service.

She felt his hand hover at her back and automatically quickened her pace.

He pulled out her chair for her. "Busy day?"

"The usual," she said, taking her seat and thinking she didn't remember him being so tall.

He sat across from her. She didn't remember his shoulders being quite so wide. She did remember the intensity in his eyes, his mouth, and the way he had kissed her that night. Frustration had mixed with some kind of carnal wanting. She'd felt the same way, frustrated from the insane almost-wedding day and curious to find out how he would handle a woman. How he would handle her. He must have felt some curiosity, too. The first time had been fast, but there had been a second. And a third.

Trina felt a rush of heat. The sensation reminded her of how two glasses of wine affected her, the warmth that spread from her chest to her face and the way her heartbeat accelerated. It was the memory of wild sex, she told herself. It wasn't specifically Walker.

A waiter approached their table. "I'll take a beer.

Whatever you have on tap," Walker said and turned to
her. "What do you like? Martini?" he asked and looked
at her for a long moment. "No, it was something else,"
he said, shaking his head with a wry grin. "Mojito."

The fact that he'd remembered her drink gave her
a thrill. A very stupid thrill, she told herself. "It's different now. I've turned into a lightweight. Pinot
Grigio," she said to the waiter.

"Lightweight," Walker echoed curiously. "When
did that happen?"

"A while ago," she said with a shrug and wished she
had a glass so she could do something with her hands.
Should she tell him before the waiter returned or after?

He nodded. "Okay. So what have you been doing
for the last year and a half?"

*Having a baby.* Not quite right, she thought,
looking away from his expectant gaze. "Working,
moving. How was Paris?" she asked, turning the conversation away from her.

"Good."

The waiter returned with their drinks and she
fiddled with the stem of her wineglass. "Hard to
come back?"

"Yes and no. It was time and I didn't want to
lose Bellagio."

She lifted her glass to her lips. "It's just another

account, isn't it? With the bonus of public humiliation and a few bad memories."

He paused a half beat and studied her carefully. "I could almost think you didn't want me around," he said in a silky but cold voice.

"Of course not," she said, forcing the words from her throat. "Everyone knows you're great at what you do. I just thought you might prefer to avoid the discomfort."

"I did that," he said and took a long draw from his beer. "The marriage to Brooke didn't work out and that was for the best, but I'm not losing Bellagio over a failed engagement."

Trina's stomach sank at the steel in his tone. She couldn't imagine how he would respond to her announcement that he was the father of her baby.

"Speaking of Bellagio, I wanted to show you some of the models I'm using for the commercial." He reached into his pocket for his PalmPilot and turned it on. He pushed some buttons and handed it to her. "What do you think?"

She looked at the headshot of a toothy blonde. "Pretty," she said. "But we're not going for perfect," she added. "We're going for Ms. And Mr. Everyday who can clean up nicely."

He nodded. "Don't want to be intimidating."

"Right," she said and took a sip of her wine,

mentally girding herself. "There have been some changes. I need to talk about them with you."

He leaned closer. "At Bellagio," he said.

She moved her head in a circle. "More with me, and it's something you should know. I, uh. We, uh—"

"Walker Gordon, when did you get back in town?" a woman's flirty Southern drawl oozed from a few steps away.

Trina glanced at her perfectly groomed and coiffed former classmate, Blair Smythe Manning Davis, twice divorced.

"Blair—" he said, obviously searching for her last name as he stood.

She beamed, her porcelain veneers gleaming as white as chalk. "You remembered me. The last time we met we were both committed, but you're single now and so am I." She shot a quick dismissing glance in Trina's direction. "It's been so long since you and I have seen each other, Walker. Would you mind if I join you? Or am I interrupting something important?" she asked as an afterthought.

Walker looked at Trina. "We're discussing business."

Blair made a clucking sound and tapped her diamond-encrusted watch. "It's way past five o'clock. Quitting time," she said and pulled a chair from another table.

Walker helped Blair with the chair. She smiled at him as she sat down then glanced again at Trina. "Hello, I'm Blair—"

"Davis," Trina finished because she couldn't resist.

Blair blinked and she studied Trina.

"Trina Roberts," she said, rescuing the woman. "You and I went to the same girls' school."

"Oh," Blair said and gave a hesitant smile. "I'll have to look you up in my yearbook."

"I've let my hair grow and I was a couple years behind you," Trina couldn't resist adding, noticing that Blair looked razor thin and had a man-eater look in her eyes. Her hair was highlighted platinum and her skin faux-tanned just this side of oompha-loompha. Two husbands down, ready for number three. She wondered if blood dripped from Blair's incisors at night.

"Really?" Blair said in disbelief and gave a forced laugh. "I'll definitely have to dig out my yearbook. But enough about me. Walker, make my dream come true and tell me you're back in town for good?"

He shot a look of discomfort toward Trina and cleared his throat. "I'm back for good."

"That's great. The Walthams are hosting a party this weekend. You absolutely must come with me."

"I'm still settling in," he said.

She gave an exaggerated pout. "You can do that anytime. I just want to borrow you on Saturday night.

For starters, anyway," she added with a seductive glint in her eye.

And so it went for twenty more minutes while Trina nursed her little glass of wine and contributed eleven nods and eight uh-huhs. The ball of apprehension in her chest turned to irritation in her stomach.

Tonight was clearly not the night that she would tell Walker about Maddie. She glanced at her watch and was forced to interrupt Blair's latest combination of gossip and flirting. "Excuse me. I hate to say this, but I have some other plans this evening, so I need to leave."

She stood and Walker rose to his feet. "Let me walk you to your car."

"Not necessary. I can find it on my own."

"I need to cover a couple more things with you," he said, frustration edging into his tone.

"Let's try meeting at my office. Give me a call in the morning."

"I'll still walk you out."

"What a gentleman," Blair said. "Let him walk you out and he can come back and chat with me."

Trina gave a tight smile. "Okay. It was great seeing you Blair. You look more amazing than ever."

"Thank you. What a sweetie you are."

Trina headed out of the bar, feeling Walker catch up to her in just a few strides.

"Were you really going to leave me with her?" he asked.

"Hey, she's a great contact. She knows everyone and talks about them, too."

He adjusted his tie. "I didn't know you went to school with her crowd."

"I may have gone to school with her, but that doesn't mean we were friends," she said, approaching her car and wondering if Walker would notice the infant safety seat in her car. At least she'd remembered to put the top up on her convertible.

She knew, however, that Walker could be very observant. Her edginess ratcheted up another notch. Not wanting to tell him he was a father in the parking lot of a bar, she quickly stepped in front of him. "Sorry I could only give you a brief reprieve from Blair. She's beautiful and well connected, though."

"And pushy as hell," he said and swore. "This didn't turn out the way I planned."

She smiled. "It happens that way sometimes."

"I'll call you in the morning," he said and she felt his gaze fall over her in some kind of combination that included masculine scrutiny.

She resisted the urge to suck in her abdomen. "Fine," she said, backing toward her car.

"We'll get together tomorrow."

"No problem," she said, fighting the jumpiness in her belly at the determined expression on his face.

He nodded. "It's good to see you again, Trina. I've missed talking to you. I always felt like I could level with you."

"Mmm," she said with a nod and lifted her hand. "Talk to you tomorrow."

Walking the rest of the way to her car, she got inside and tossed her purse on the passenger seat. She started the engine and drove out of the parking lot. In her rearview window, she saw Walker still watching her.

# CHAPTER SIX

ENTERING THE FOYER of her home, Trina kicked off her heels and plopped her purse and keys on the antique Italian credenza she'd bought at an auction.

The sound of her mother singing a wobbly, warbly rendition of a lullabye broke the silence. Trina rolled her eyes at the sound, but smiled at the same time. Trina and her mother hadn't gotten along well for about twenty-eight of Trina's twenty-nine years and they were nowhere near compatible now, but Maddie had managed to bring them to speaking terms.

Maddie had softened the edges of Aubrey's harsh, often sharp personality, and Trina found it difficult to hold a grudge when she saw her mother willing to make a fool of herself for her only grandchild.

After her lousy meeting with Walker, Trina just wanted to see her baby. She had a terrible feeling that things would change once Walker learned the truth. Now it was just Maddie and her. And while it had been hard in the beginning and Trina never would have predicted it, Maddie provided her with a haven from the insanity of the rest of the world. She tiptoed up the stairs to the nursery and peeked inside.

Her mother eyes were closed as she continued to warble. Maddie made conversational nonsense noises and waved her little hand toward Aubrey's face.

The poor child was probably trying to find a way to stop the noise her mother was making. Trina scolded herself for the wicked thought.

Aubrey's eyes opened and she immediately met Trina's gaze. Her mother's instincts about her had always amazed her. Aubrey stopped singing mid-phrase and glanced down at Maddie. She sighed. "You're wide-awake. Time for your Momma."

"Thank you for taking care of her." Maddie walked to the rocking chair and took her daughter into her arms. The soft warm weight of her filled a hollow space inside her. She looked down at her carrot-topped baby. "You smell good enough to eat," she said to Maddie. "Did your Nanna give you a bath?"

Maddie's mouth stretched into a wide smile and she chortled.

"She's just like you. Loves her bath," Aubrey said.

"Thank you, again," Maddie said, settling into the rocking chair.

"You're welcome," Aubrey said. "It was a bit short notice, but since I didn't have anything scheduled, I could help you. I don't understand why she won't go to sleep to the lullabye. It always worked for you."

"She's definitely an individual."

Aubrey sniffed. "She got that from you, too. I'll wait downstairs for you."

Trina began to stroke Maddie's forehead and talked in a soft voice. She'd found it didn't matter what she said. The stroking and the tone did the trick. "I had a totally terrible time tonight," she said softly. "I would have enjoyed being with you much more." An image of Walker raced through her mind and she paused.

Maddie squirmed as if to signal she wanted Trina to continue. Trina smiled and began to stroke Maddie's forehead again. "But let's not talk about that. Let's talk about me meeting you for lunch tomorrow. Do you think you would like sweet potatoes and green beans? Does that sound good? And if it's pretty outside, I'll take you for a stroll…"

Maddie's little body relaxed and her breathing settled into a steady rhythm. "Works like magic," Trina said and laid Maddie in the crib.

She walked downstairs and found her mother sitting in the den. Aubrey glanced up and studied her from behind her half-glasses. "You're wearing make-up," her mother observed. "And you've done something to your hair." She lifted her eyebrows. "Who did you meet tonight?"

Trina waved her hand and went to the refrigerator for a bottle of water. "Just someone from the advertising agency Bellagio has hired. No big deal." Except he was hot, and the father of her child.

"Male?" her mother asked.

"Yes, but I think he's gay," she lied. That always ended her mother's inquisitions.

"Oh," her mother said, then frowned in confusion. "Then why did you dress up?"

"Maybe I listened to my mother and decided it was time to make some effort," Trina said, swallowing a long drink of water.

"Well, I think that's wonderful. Are you going to join a weight-loss plan? I'll be happy to take care of Maddie while—"

"One thing at a time," Trina said, feeling a sharp jab of irritation. "Why do people find it necessary to comment on my weight? It's not as if I'm as big as a barn. I'm carrying ten or fifteen extra pounds. In a different century, I would still have been considered too thin for Rubenesque."

"Oh, other people are commenting," her mother said sympathetically. "I'm sorry to hear that. It's because you're just so close and it would take so little effort—lose a few pounds, get a haircut and color, put on some makeup and buy a new outfit. Then maybe you could get a date."

As if she couldn't get one now. Trina didn't really know if she could get a date. It had been so long since her last date, since the last time she'd had sex. Walker. Last sex…but it hadn't been a real date. And if skinny Blair had her way, Walker would be taking her out, maybe marrying her.

The thought irritated her. It shouldn't, she told herself, because marrying Blair would provide its own punishment for Walker. Unless he actually preferred that kind of woman.

Which was none of her business anyway.

"I told you, Mother, that I'm really not dying to date right now. And with my job changes, I'm going to have even less time than before."

"Job changes?" her mother echoed. "What job changes?"

Trina bit her tongue and wished she'd kept her mouth shut. "Nothing major, but I've been asked to take on more responsibility."

"What about Maddie?"

"I'm thinking of hiring someone to help me out. Grocery shopping, meal preparation, taking care of Maddie when I need to stay a little late."

"Well, I could shop for you and take care of Maddie, and I'm sure Hilda would be happy to cook."

Trina shook her head. Hilda had been her mother's nanny during her growing-up years. She was the only hired help still living with her mother and that was primarily because Hilda was eighty-one and had nowhere else to go. "No. Hilda has enough to do and you have a full schedule with bridge and charity."

Her mother turned silent and her lower lip began to quiver. "You don't trust me to take care of Madeline."

Trina immediately felt split in opposing directions. While Aubrey treated Maddie with grandmotherly indulgence, Trina wasn't sure when that might change to critical intrusion, and she was determined to protect Maddie and herself from the attitude she'd endured during her childhood and adolescence... hell, make that most of her entire life. "That's not true," Trina said, trying to be diplomatic. "I asked you to keep her tonight for me, didn't I? But everyday care is different."

Her mother opened her mouth to protest and Trina shook her head. "I've had a long day at work and I don't want to talk about it anymore. Thank you for taking care of Maddie tonight."

"But you should listen to me—"

"Mother, we've been over this. You may be my mother, but *I* am Maddie's mother, so what I say goes."

Her mother pressed her lips together in disapproval. "You never listen to me. I may as well go home. Good night," she said and stiffly walked out of the room.

Trina heard the slam of the front door and winced. Her stomach twisted in a knot and she closed her eyes to take a deep breath. It was all about control, her counselor had told her years ago, and her mother couldn't stand not having control.

She grabbed the mail her mother had brought in from the kitchen counter and went to the den to collapse onto the couch. Bills, advertisements. She fanned through the envelopes and paused at one that was handwritten. A letter, and the return address wasn't family. She opened it, and the salutation nearly gave her a heart attack.

*Dear Kat, How about a blast from your past? I'll never forget the time we had together in Myrtle Beach. I'm getting out of prison soon. We should get together. Write back. Affectionately, Stan*

Trina stuffed the letter back into the envelope and rushed to the kitchen to throw it in the trash can. She stared at the trash can for a moment then washed her hands with antibacterial cleanser and rinsed them thoroughly.

She never wanted to see the man again in her life. Mistake didn't cover what she'd done with Stan Roch. Nineteen, stupid and rebellious, she'd married the man.

She'd obtained a divorce six weeks later, but only after he'd been hauled off to jail for armed robbery.

Standing in the complete quiet of her home, she wondered which was worse, having her ex-husband, who happened to be an ex-convict, show up wanting to resume the relationship. Or having to tell a man that he was the father of her six-month-old daughter.

SINCE WALKER HADN'T STOPPED since five that morning, he could only squeeze in a cell call to Trina's voice mail with the message that he would drop by to talk with her after a lunch meeting.

Finding the PR receptionist reading a celebrity gossip magazine at her desk, he cleared his throat. No response. "Is Trina Roberts around?"

Dora glanced up at him blankly, then pulled an earpiece out of her ear and smiled. "Sorry. The local radio is running a contest for a cruise and I thought I'd give it a try. Sounds sweet, doesn't it?" she asked and gave him a wanna-come-with-me look.

"Yeah, sweet. I was looking for Trina."

The assistant's face fell. "Oh, she took a late lunch. I think she said something about visiting her baby."

Walker blinked. "Baby?" he echoed, surprised. No, shock was a more accurate description.

The assistant nodded. "Yeah. You didn't know? I'm surprised because you know she's still carrying a little baby weight and she's got terrible circles under her eyes. Hello? A little concealer goes a long way." She sighed and shrugged. "But I guess she's overwhelmed being a single mom. Lord knows I'd never do that."

*Baby? Single mother?* Walker tried to digest the information. He just didn't see Trina as the motherly type. He remembered her as a mix of warm but sophisticated, sharp and together. "When did, uh—"

"Oh, Maddie's six months old. And she is cute as a button. For a baby. But, you know, she's still a baby and they cry and poop and are really demanding." The assistant turned around in her chair and glanced out the window. "Oh, look, Trina's taking her for a stroll. I guess you could catch up to her if you really want. Or I could get you a cappuccino and keep you company."

"Thanks for the offer," he said. "But I'm running short on time. I'll head outside."

The assistant pouted. "Okay, but make time for a little break next time you come around."

"Have a good day," he said and walked toward the elevator. The assistant was clearly making an offer. If she weren't working for Bellagio, then he might take her up on it. Walker was unopposed to hot, uncomplicated sex, but after his relationship with Brooke had muddied the waters with Bellagio, he figured he'd better stay away from the Bellagio honeys at least until he was on firmer ground.

He took the elevator down to ground level and walked to the side of the building where he saw Trina pushing a stroller. With the sun shining brightly, the temperature in the midseventies and a slight breeze rustling through the trees, he supposed it was a good day to take a baby for a stroll. Not that he would ever have to do that kind of thing.

"Hey, Trina," he called as he caught up to her. "Trina," he said again when she didn't respond.

She came to a dead stop and turned to look at him. Her face drained of color. "Walker?"

He stared at her. "Hey, I didn't mean to startle you. The assistant told me you were out here."

Her eyes wide with fear, she gave a little nod. "Dora."

He shrugged. "Yeah, Dora. She told me you had a baby. How come you didn't tell me?" he asked, looking curiously at the stroller. His gaze landed on an infant with a blue barrette holding a wisp of carrot-colored hair in a topknot that stood straight up. She made singsong noises and moved her head from side to side. He smiled. "She's cute."

"Um, thanks," Trina said and bit her lip.

She was giving off a very weird vibe, he thought and frowned. "Are you okay?"

She took a deep breath and seemed to be trying to collect herself. "I had hoped to do this differently," she said. Meeting his gaze, she gave a choky kind of laugh. "Actually, I had hoped to never have to tell you."

"Tell me what? That you had a baby? I'm surprised, but other people do it all the time."

She took another breath, looked away and then met his gaze again. "Maddie is yours," she said.

Walker stared at Trina. The distant sounds of car horns blowing and engines humming along with the baby's babbles through the periphery of his brain. He couldn't have heard Trina correctly. "Excuse me?"

"I said Maddie is yours. You are her father." She looked at him silently. "Do the math. She was born nine months after that night you and I…"

He swore. "You think I got you pregnant that one night we had sex?"

"I know you did. I have the evidence."

Walker shook his head, wondering why she was trying to pin the pregnancy on him. Did she need money or something? "I'm sorry if you think it's me. But it can't be," he told her.

"Yes, it can and it is," Trina said, exasperation creeping into her tone. "But don't worry. I don't expect anything from you. That's why I didn't tell you when you were in Paris."

His circuits scrambled like eggs, he shook his head. "Listen, I'm sorry, Trina, but it can't be me. I'll tell you why. I had a vasectomy."

## CHAPTER SEVEN

*I HAD A VASECTOMY.*

Trina had a mental car crash. "Vasectomy," she repeated. "When? How?"

He nodded. "A couple of months before the wedding. Brooke and I had agreed that we didn't want children. How?" He gave a wry grin. "The usual way. Snip. Snip."

He jammed his hands into his pockets while she tried to digest the news.

"So you see it couldn't be me," he said.

Exactly, she agreed. Except it couldn't be anyone else unless she'd gotten pregnant by immaculate conception, and Trina had heard of only one woman who'd done that.

The problem was that she hadn't had sex with anyone in months because she'd been working double time on the reality show project for Bellagio.

"I don't know who else you were involved with at the time," he ventured.

No one. She glanced at Walker and felt an odd surge of feelings. Loss. She felt a sense of loss. Crazy. Even though she'd known he wouldn't want a child, she'd hoped that just seeing Maddie would make him at least give it a second's consideration.

She saw the flat-out determination on his face that Maddie wasn't his. Trina had envisioned a variety of responses from Walker, but never this.

"I—uh—I don't know what to say," Walker said.

Trina closed her eyes to clear her mind and at that moment she realized she'd been given a gift. She had tried to tell Walker. She'd done her ethical duty. He didn't believe her, so she didn't have to worry about it anymore. He had just released her.

"It's okay," she said, feeling a strange sense of freedom and opening her eyes. "Mistaken identity."

"You thought I was the father all this time? I wish you'd told me and I could have cleared it up sooner."

"Good point," she said, and couldn't help smiling. "I should get her back to the company nursery. Sorry if I gave you a scare."

"No, no," he said. "I'm fine. Are you okay?"

"Couldn't be better," she said and pushed the stroller to the nursery. When she pulled Maddie from the stroller, she held her against her chest for an extra moment of gratitude. She laughed to herself. The irony that Walker was dead certain that Maddie wasn't his was too sweet for words.

WALKER HAD NEVER BEEN ACCUSED of fathering a child. Even though he knew it wasn't possible, it knocked him off-kilter for the next several days.

He took care of business, of course. After delivering a new presentation to Bellagio, the account was in the bag again, where it belonged. He asked his partner's assistant to screen prospects for the assistant he'd fired on Monday and began interviewing on Friday afternoon. Two good possibilities on that front already.

His schedule was clear on Friday night. He should have been ready to celebrate, or at least relax while watching a ball game with his uncle Harry, but his comfortable leather recliner didn't feel so comfortable. His worn jeans and T-shirt didn't feel good, either. Hell, he would swear his own skin didn't feel right.

"Damnation, boy," Harry said when Walker got up for the third time in fifteen minutes. "You've been more fidgety than a female cat ready to drop a dozen kittens."

Walker twitched at his uncle's choice of analogies.

"You've been like this all week. What's your problem? Did you lose the shoe account?"

"No. I got it. Wrapped it up today."

"Good," Harry said and studied him. "Anything else bothering you?"

"Not really," Walker said, reaching for his second beer.

"Something's got you distracted. You haven't fussed at me for drinking tonight."

Walker caught sight of a beer can beside his uncle's chair. "You're not supposed to be drinking."

"The doctor said I can have one beer a day."

"This is March. If your beers represented a calendar, what month would we be in?"

"May," Harry reluctantly admitted. "Or June. But who's counting?"

"Your doctor."

Harry shrugged. "Don't try to turn this on me. What's wrong with you? Woman problems again?"

The image of Trina and her baby slid into his mind. Not his baby, he reminded himself. It couldn't be. "Not really," he said.

Harry gave a heavy put-out sounding sigh and turned off the television. "You're gonna ruin this game. Just spill it."

Walker raked his hand through his hair. "Has a woman ever tried to tell you that you were the father of her baby?"

Harry rolled his eyes. "Too many times to count. Especially if they found out I had a little money."

A little money was a huge understatement. Harry

was loaded and had been for several years. "What did you do?"

"I had one scare with a girl when I was a young buck. Turned out it was a false alarm. That's when I got snipped." He lifted his fingers in a *V*. "The big *V*."

"I got a vasectomy, too," Walker said.

"Then you're clear. She can't nail you."

She hadn't really tried to nail him, Walker thought. He frowned. "She didn't seem like the type to try to—" He resisted the word, but it was in his head like a huge billboard. "Trap me."

"Desperation," he said. "Desperation makes women and men do crazy things. Plus, she probably knows you've got a nice chunk of change in your bank account."

"She didn't ask for money, though," Walker said, unable to remain still. He took a few steps alongside the bar separating the kitchen from the den.

"That's unusual. Unless she wanted you to marry her," Harry said.

Walker shook his head. "No. She acted like she didn't really want to tell me."

"Hmm," Harry mused. "Well, if you got snipped, then you couldn't have been the one." He shrugged. "Did you get a look at the kid?"

Walker nodded. "Girl. Six months old. Cute for a baby. She had orange hair."

Harry turned quiet. "Did you say orange hair?"

"Yeah, why?"

"Hell." Harry groaned. "You don't remember what color hair you and your sister had when you were babies, do you?"

Walker felt a sinking sensation at the expression on Harry's face. He searched his memory. "I don't remember what color hair I had, but Cissy's was—" He broke off, calling back pictures of his sister as an infant. He'd only been four years old when she was born. He closed his eyes and an image appeared. Rivers of drool on her double chins, she'd screamed like a banshee. With orange hair.

He met his uncle's gaze. "You don't think—"

"Maybe you're not shooting blanks," Harry said.

"I got tested."

"How many times?" Harry asked.

"Once," he conceded, even though the doctor had encouraged a follow-up test. "I never got around to checking."

Harry shook his head. "You might have some French rolls in the oven, too."

"No, I used condoms."

Harry made a *tsking* sound of concern and shook his head again. "You sure her hair was orange?"

Walker nodded, still not believing it was possible.

Harry sighed. "You probably need to do a paternity test. If you're the father, you're just gonna have to try not to be a total loser and at least support the kid financially."

That night Walker didn't sleep. He didn't even try. How could this have happened? he asked himself as he sat in his office. He remembered the day he'd decided not to have children. He'd been fifteen years old.

He'd never lived in the same place for longer than six months because creditors had always come banging on the door. His father had often gone away for months at a time supposedly working in other locations. His father would return, but never with enough funds to bail the family out of the mountain of debt. He remembered being awakened in the middle of the night by his mother to move to a different mobile home in a different city, sometimes different state.

He remembered his brother, BJ, crying for days because they'd left behind his favorite stuffed toy. He remembered a favorite teacher and how much he'd wished he could go back to her class. She'd praised him and helped him not to feel so odd.

He'd always hoped they could stay. He remembered when the hope had died. He recalled hearing his mother cry herself to sleep at night because she didn't know where her husband was and couldn't find him. He remembered the gut-wrenching sound of his brother and sister crying out of fear.

One night he'd overheard the conversation between his uncle and his mother. "I'm sorry you got involved with him, Kathy."

His mother had made a sobbing sound. "I can

almost understand him abandoning me, but not his children. I can't understand that."

"It's a sad thing, but the Gordon men have no problem with fertility, but they're god-awful fathers. We just seem to lack the normal nurturing instincts necessary for successful fatherhood."

His mother sniffed. "What do you mean?"

"Paul didn't ever tell you our illustrious family history?"

"He said he didn't like talking about his parents."

"Our great-grandfather Paul Walker fathered, and I use that term loosely, ten children and left his wife to care for them while he traveled the world and sent her checks every now and then. Then Grandpa Paul Walker, Junior, went through three wives and six children while he hid in a lab for months at a time working on his inventions. He finally succeeded in inventing some sort of adhesive and died a week later. Then you know about Paul Walker number three."

"Yes, he's in Grand Cayman and couldn't be less interested in his kids," his mother said with disgust in her voice.

Walker. He shared the name. He shared the genes. He'd promised himself he would never do what his father had done to his children. He would make damn sure of it. He would never have children.

ON MONDAY, WALKER CALLED TRINA at the office because he didn't have her home or cell number. "Hi," he said, after she answered. "I'd like to get a DNA test done."

Dead silence followed.

"Trina? Are you there?"

"I thought you said there was no possibility— There was absolutely no way that you could be—" She broke off. "I need to close my office door. You picked a terrible time for this."

"I don't have your cell number, so I didn't have much choice. The word absolute is usually rash," he admitted. "I think we should do a test."

"I don't want Maddie hurt because she has to be stuck with a needle or her hair has to be pulled out by the roots," she said. "As far as I'm concerned, this test is unnecessary. I never asked for or expected any help or support from you."

"I know you didn't ask for help," he said, but suspected this was one of those things that could bite a guy on the ass if it weren't resolved in a quick, clean manner. "She won't have to be hurt. I already called the lab. They'll just do a swab from inside her cheek and mine."

Silence again followed. "I don't see why this is necessary at all. It's not as if you want to be a father. In fact, that's the last thing you want. I'm going to be blunt, Walker. She's an incredibly sweet child, the most precious thing in the world to me, and you don't deserve her. I'll do anything to protect her."

Walker felt as if she'd slapped his face. "I'm not going to hurt her. If she's mine, I want to make financial arrangements for her."

"I don't need your money."

"You may change your mind."

"Go to hell," she said and hung up on him.

Later that afternoon, however, Walker managed to get Trina's cell number from the assistant. That evening, after another heated exchange, she reluctantly agreed to bring Maddie to a clinic for testing.

On Friday he got the news. He was the father of the bouncing six-month-old baby girl with carrot-orange hair. After he left four unreturned messages on her voice mail, Trina finally returned his calls.

"I'm Maddie's father."

"I already told you that."

Her bored tone scraped over his nerve endings. "But I didn't know. Hell, after a vasectomy, I had to believe it wasn't me."

"Yes, but I knew how many men with whom I'd been sexually involved despite your assumption that I was so promiscuous that I couldn't keep track," she said, her tone so frigid Antarctica would have been warmer.

"I didn't say you were promiscuous. Trina, you were a very attractive, sexy woman. I figured some man was warming your bed."

"Were?" she echoed. "Did you say I *was* an attractive woman?"

Walker swore under his breath. He couldn't do anything right with this woman. "You're still an attractive, sexy woman. I was referring to the time that you and I—"

"Had sex so many times in one night that neither you nor I can remember how many."

A hot image floated through his brain. He'd been loaded, but he still recalled her straddling him on the couch, one time he took her on the floor, another from behind... His collar suddenly feeling too tight, he tugged at it and felt his body temperature rise.

He cleared his throat. "This conversation isn't about that. It's about Maddie. You and I need to talk about her future."

"I'm in charge of her future."

"Fine. I want to contribute financially. If you're such a good mother, you won't deny her my support."

Trina was silent, but Walker would almost swear he could hear the energy of her frustration singeing the sound waves. "I'll discuss it tonight at my town house. You can come over at nine o'clock. Don't be early." She gave him her address and disconnected.

WALKER PULLED HIS CAR in front of the address Trina had given him. The beams of the porch light and floodlight revealed daffodils and red tulips blooming on either side of the front porch of the brick townhome. As he walked on the sidewalk, he noticed that the tiny yard appeared well trimmed with green shrubs.

With a knot in his gut that hadn't left him since he'd received the lab results, he climbed the steps and lifted his hand to ring the doorbell.

The door swung open and Trina put her hand over the button. "No. Don't even think about ringing that bell," she said, her eyes wide with alarm. "I just got her to sleep."

"The baby," he said.

"Right." She nodded and stepped aside. "Come on in."

He stepped into the foyer, approving the combination of comfort and tradition. "Looks nice," he said. "Not too fussy."

She gave a wry smile and pushed aside a strand of hair that escaped her loose topknot. "Soon enough the tabletops will be fair game for Maddie, so I thought I'd go ahead and put any breakable things of value to me behind glass or way up high," she said, leading him down a short hallway. With the exception of the night he'd seen her naked, she was dressed more casually than he'd ever seen her. While her worn jeans clung to her round bottom, her loose T-shirt barely hinted at the curves beneath.

Accustomed to her chic, sophisticated look, he couldn't help staring at her in this more natural state. She wore no makeup, but her dark eyes and darker eyelashes along with her mouth that seemed to alternate between good girl and bad girl would get any guy's attention, he thought.

"Coffee, soda or wine?" she asked, stepping behind a breakfast bar, which separated the kitchen from a casual den.

He resisted the urge to ask if she had any bourbon. "Wine, thanks."

"Except you only tolerate wine," she said with a half smile. She pulled a glass from the cabinet and wine from the fridge.

"When did I tell you that?" he asked, accepting the glass.

"You didn't say it. You just never exhibited much enthusiasm for wine and tended to choose beer or bourbon. We ate a lot of meals together and I notice that kind of stuff. Alfredo Bellagio drinks Barolo whether he's eating fish or steak. My boss secretly likes fruity martinis. I order two and ask him to drink one."

He accepted the glass of wine she offered and saw the hint of kick in her eyes that he remembered from when they'd worked together two years ago. He felt a lift in his gut. Trina had often made him grin, just enough to take an extra breath. At the same time, something about her had made him feel at ease with her.

Until he'd returned from Paris.

Damn. Everything was different now. He felt a weird sense of loss and tossed back a big gulp of wine. He cleared his throat. "Uh, about the baby," he began, feeling his throat grow tighter with that last word.

"Maddie is her name. And I don't expect anything from you," she said. "I never did."

There was no censure in her gaze, just clear absolute acceptance. "This isn't just about you, though. It's about the baby."

Irritation crossed her face. "Stop calling her the baby. Maddie is her name."

He tossed back another gulp. "This is about Maddie's welfare."

"I can take care of her."

"I know you can, but I have to take some responsibility. Financially. I've spoken with my attorney and I want to set up an agreement. I'll pay for her college and give you monthly child support. I'm also giving you a lump sum for the time I didn't know she had been conceived."

She brushed her hair from her face and gave a dry laugh. "You're going to pay me for stretch marks, labor and delivery?" She shook her head. "I'm not sure how you compensate when the anesthesiologist doesn't give you your epidural because he's eating a donut."

Walker grimaced. "Sounds rough."

She shrugged. "It could have been worse. My labor was only nineteen hours and thirty-eight minutes long. Just curious, do big babies run in your family?"

"Maybe," he said, trying to remember anything his mother may have said about his birth weight. "I think I was nine pounds."

"Thanks," she said with a death glare.

"How big was she?"

"Eight pounds, eleven ounces, two hours of push-ing."

"Sorry," he said.

She gave a slow smile. "Maddie was so worth it."

"I never pictured you as the single-mother type."

"Me, either," she said. "But—" She broke off and cocked her head to one side, listening.

Fussy baby sounds trickled into the air. She shook her head. "I think she's teething. I'll be back in a minute," she said and jogged out of the room.

Walker stood, listening to the sound of the baby.

Maddie.

Trina's daughter.

His daughter.

His stomach clenched and he took another drink of wine, wishing again that it was bourbon. He heard Trina's footsteps on the stairs and instinctively braced himself as she entered the den with the baby in her arms.

"Teething just makes a girl mad enough to bite off a finger," Trina said as she allowed the baby to gnaw on her index finger.

"Doesn't that hurt?" he asked, taking in the sight of Maddie's mussed orange hair and teardrops on her chubby cheeks.

"No. She's still mostly a gum girl. I think I'll go ahead and give her some Orajel. Was there anything else you wanted to say?"

Walker received his invitation to leave and shrugged. "You haven't asked me how much I plan to give you."

"I don't care," she said.

He met her gaze and nodded. "And we're going to keep this confidential, right?"

"Oh, yes," she said. "I wouldn't want to try to explain this to Alfredo Bellagio. I'd just as soon not tell Maddie, either. Until she's maybe thirty or forty."

He felt a trickle of relief at the same time her words stuck in his craw. He tried to resist the urge to look at the baby again, to look for a family resemblance. It reminded him of when he'd been a kid riding a roller coaster that dropped three stories in seconds. His instinct had told him to close his eyes, but he'd been too curious, too driven to devour the whole experience.

Maddie paused from gnawing on Trina's finger like a chew toy and looked at him with wide brown eyes that seemed to take up half her face. Her baby eyelashes were darkened from her tears. No eyebrows in sight, a button nose, chubby pink cheeks and more drool on her chin and shirt than he would have thought a human that size could produce.

"Does she drool that much all the time?" he couldn't help asking.

"A lot of the time," Trina said.

"So much. You ever worry about dehydration—"

Trina laughed and Maddie's attention immediately turned to her mother's face. She stretched her rosebud mouth in a toothless smile and her eyes crinkled into half-moons.

Walker felt an odd lifting sensation in his chest. Okay, he thought, staring at Trina and Maddie. Maddie was cute. They both were cute. And they obviously had a good bond. Which was great, since he wasn't going to ruin the child by trying to be a real father to her, whatever the hell a real father was.

# CHAPTER EIGHT

TRINA PACKED some necessities for Maddie and met Jenny Prillaman in the park near the condo Jenny shared with her fiancé.

She'd liked Jenny from the first time she met her, when Jenny had been working as an assistant to another designer for Bellagio. Jenny had a big heart and Trina suspected that was part of the reason the woman had captured the interest, and now loving devotion, of Bellagio's hot VP, Marc Waterson.

As Trina drove her Mustang convertible through her old stomping grounds with an Aerosmith CD playing, she couldn't help remembering the incredibly rash and stupid thing she'd done to get away from this neighborhood and everything it had meant to her. Thank goodness she had been able to divorce Stan and put that mistake behind her. She was relieved she hadn't received any more letters from him.

Trina pulled into the parking area and immediately spotted Jenny, sitting on a bench with pad in hand, looking up and shielding her eyes from the bright sunlight.

Trina gave a big wave and plucked Maddie from her car seat, then walked toward Jenny.

"Look at her," Jenny said, meeting them halfway. "Look at those cheeks. They're so gorgeous I want to eat them!" She dropped her pad and extended her hands.

Trina smiled at the affectionate way Jenny cuddled her daughter and kissed her cheeks. At second glance, she noticed Jenny looked a little thin and had faint blue smudges beneath her eyes.

"You look like you could use some real carrot cake. Or something. What's up?"

Jenny groaned. "It's the wedding. It's turned into this big hairy deal. Between Marc's mother and my sister, the guest list has reproduced like rabbits."

"How did your sister get involved?"

Jenny sighed. "I don't know. One day she offered, and I thought it would be so much easier if I didn't have to plan it. This is my sister's area. She actually likes this kind of stuff. But it's gotten insane. Marc and I are both tired of it. We're cranky with each other."

"There's always Vegas," Trina said, feeling a surge of sympathy.

"Don't tempt me. I just keep telling myself it will be over soon."

"I was surprised it took you guys so long to do the deed in the first place."

"The entire first year I was afraid he would change his mind. Then when I really started to believe that he wouldn't, everyone wanted us to have a big bash."

"I thought you wanted to get married on the beach," Trina said, and picked up the pad Jenny had dropped onto the ground.

"I did," Jenny said glumly.

"You've got a month before the wedding. You could ask your friend Chad to take over as planner and change everything."

"That would be a ton of money and I would be hated for the rest of my life. But enough about that. What's happening with you?"

"Not much," Trina lied, her neck tightening at the thought of how Walker had reentered her life. "They're bumping up some of my responsibilities at work and it's a good time, since carrot cake is sleeping through the night. I'm thinking of hiring some extra help. I made the mistake of mentioning it to my mother and she offered her services." Trina shook her head.

"Oops."

"Oops is right. She's in interfering mode right now."

"Sounds like she needs a project," Jenny said. "Marc's grandfather is always happiest when he's working on a project."

"Good point. In my mother's case, she wants Maddie and me to be her project. I'll have to think of something."

"Dating yet?"

"No. I haven't been in the mood."

"For a year and a half?" Jenny asked.

Trina groaned. Why was everyone interested in her love life? "I just don't feel like it. I need to lose some weight."

"Wanna plan my wedding with the assistance of Marc's mother and my sister? That'll make you drop some pounds."

Trina shook her head. "That particular weight reduction method wouldn't work for me because I don't care what either of them thinks of me. Which is why you should get Chad to do it."

Maddie began to bounce up and down on Jenny's lap. Trina automatically reached for her. "The beginning of boredom. I don't think she has grasped the importance of girl talk yet. Do you mind if we stroll?"

"Not at all. So, have you decided to never have sex again?" Jenny asked.

"Maybe during labor—" She broke off. "Even though I wouldn't trade Maddie for anything, I just still feel lame about getting pregnant."

"Did you ever hear from the guy who—"

"The so-called father. Yes, as a matter of fact, I did. He wants to provide financial assistance."

"That's better than nothing."

"I suppose," Trina said. "I'd kinda hoped I wouldn't see him for a long time. Or ever."

"Were you in love with this guy?"

"Oh, no. It was a—" She couldn't reveal the fact that it had been a one-night stand. "We both had a little too much to drink and got a little too wild and—"

"You've decided to become a nun," Jenny finished for her. "If you don't show up with a date for my engagement party, then I'm setting you up with someone for my wedding."

"It's only a week until your engagement party," Trina protested.

"I never thought I would say this to you, Trina, but you've turned chicken. You're stuck in a rut."

"I'm not chicken. I'm not stuck in a rut, and you're starting to sound like my mother," she retorted. She sounded like a child, she realized quickly.

Looking at Jenny, she gasped. "Oh, no. First my mother. Now you. Is it a conspiracy, or—" She closed her eyes and shook her head. "Oh, no, does this mean she's actually right this time? That I need to get my hair cut, lose some weight and find a daddy for Maddie?"

Jenny blinked. "I wasn't recommending the hair-cut or weight loss. Or daddy for Maddie," she said.

"I just thought it might be time for you to enjoy the attention of a man again."

"Oh," Trina said, knowing her outburst had been totally unlike her. She was cool, calm and in control.

"But my friend Liz would put it a different way."

"How's that?" Trina asked cautiously. She'd met Liz and had gotten the impression that beneath the woman's blue eyes, Southern sweetness and pinup body beat the heart of a barracuda.

"She would say you need to get laid."

"I'm glad you're more sensitive than that."

Jenny gave a slow, noncommittal nod. "The thing about Liz is how often she turns out to be right."

TRINA ORDERED a rose silk dress with just a few little beads from Bluefly.com to wear to Jenny and Marc's cocktail party. A size larger than she used to wear, but who besides her mother, Dora the pain-in-the-ass assistant, Walker and a few other people would notice?

She put up her hair and stuck some sparkly bobby pins in it, switched out of her favorite Michele K running shoes for a pair of Bellagio sandals designed by Jenny.

After feeding Maddie, she grabbed a pashmina wrap from the top of her closet and gave Maddie a quick kiss and snuggle before she handed her to the babysitter. She kept the top up on her convertible so she wouldn't wreck her hair on the drive to the country club.

As she turned onto the long drive, she fought a jangle of nerves. Just business, she told herself. She'd attended cocktail parties since Maddie had been born. All business related. This one was, too, for the most part.

Go a little late, leave a lot early. Her primary mission was to make an appearance and to wish Jenny and Marc well.

Pulling to a stop in front of the country club, she stepped out of her car and gave her keys and a tip to the young, good-looking valet waiting at the curb. He shot her an appreciative wink that boosted her ego a notch. She was so grateful she considered throwing additional money at him, but restrained herself.

She entered the club and followed the noise and steady stream of catering staff dressed in crisp black and white. The party flowed from a room in the club to a garden area that twinkled with lights. A live band played and tables covered with white linens groaned under a feast of delicious-looking food.

Spotting Marc and Jenny at the head of a small receiving line, she waited at the end. Gradually moving forward, she took a breath of the cool night air and felt some of the tension ooze out of her.

*Chill,* she told herself. *Have some fun.* It was a

gorgeous night. She really liked the sitter taking care of Maddie. She had her cell phone in her teensy purse in case of emergency and she looked pretty good for a mom.

She smiled to herself.

"Your hands are empty. I can't remember if you like champagne or not," a familiar male voice said from behind her.

Trina's heart immediately jumped and the tension that had just melted away returned with a vengeance. She reluctantly turned to look at Walker. Dressed in a black suit with a black shirt and blue tie, he looked good. Really good. Too good.

She accepted the glass of champagne. "Thank you and yes, I love everything about champagne except how I feel the next morning after I drink too much."

He gave a half grin. "You look very pretty."

"Thank you. You look pretty good yourself," she said, determined to keep the conversation casual even though she had an odd feeling in her stomach.

"How's Maddie?" he asked.

"With a sitter who thinks she's the most important baby in the universe."

He nodded. "That's—"

"Trina!" Jenny opened her arms, wearing an expression of desperation. Her eyes were wide and her smile a little pinched.

Trina instinctively pulled Jenny against her and hugged her. "Sweetie, you look like you're wound a little tight tonight. I think you could use my glass of champagne."

"My sister told me I can't drink anything until we've greeted everyone," Jenny whispered.

"This is one of many times Big Sister doesn't know best," Trina murmured. "Here. Take mine. I insist."

"Trina it's good to see you. We really appreciate you coming," Marc Waterson said, extending his arm for a brief hug. He glanced behind her. "Hey, did you two come together?"

Jenny's inquisitive gaze felt like an impending personal X-ray.

"No," Trina said. "We just—"

"Just timing," Walker said. "My date said she wanted to touch up her lipstick. She should be here in just a minute."

Trina felt a squishy, icky sensation in her tummy. Why? she wondered. There wasn't, nor had there ever been, anything romantic between her and Walker. The hot night they'd shared hadn't been romantic. It had just been wild, crazy and amazing. At least, the part she remembered had been.

She didn't mind if Walker had a date. He'd always had a date before. His fiancée. And she hadn't been naive enough to think he'd been dateless in Paris.

She hadn't, however, had to deal with that reality on a daily basis. And the lipstick comment dug at her. Why did his date need to reapply her lipstick? Because they'd been making out in his car?

As if it were any of her business or concern. She gave herself a hard mental slap. "You look beautiful, Jenny. The party is amazing."

"Thanks," Jenny said. "I'll pass along the party compliment to my mother-in-law-to-be. So where's your date?"

Trina opened her mouth. "I, um—" She closed her mouth, frustrated with herself. She didn't stutter when cornered. It was one of the few practices her mother had taught her that had served her well.

Jenny's face fell. "You don't have one, do you?"

Marc shot her a surprised glance. "Jenny," he said in a chastising tone. "It's none of your bus—"

Jenny shook her head and downed another sip of champagne. "Trina and I had a little deal, and since she didn't keep her end of the bargain, we need to find her a date for our wedding."

Feeling her neck and face heat with embarrassment, Trina shook her head. "Not necessary at all. I can—"

"What if she doesn't want us to find her a date?" Marc asked.

"Thank you," Trina said.

"She hasn't been out on a date since she got

pregnant. I wouldn't be a good friend if I didn't help her get on the move again. I want somebody really good for her. I mean look at her, she's gorgeous, smart, funny, sexy."

Could this possibly be any more embarrassing? Trina wondered as she felt Walker's gaze on her like a laser. "Thank you, but—"

"And whoever it is needs to like kids. Have you seen a picture of her baby, Walker? She's the absolute cutest baby in the world. Those cheeks and that hair! Oh, and that adorable smile. Hey, Walker, maybe you can come up with some suggestions, too."

Trina felt as if she was going to shatter into a thousand tomato-red embarrassed pieces right there on the country club patio. This situation had just gotten beyond embarrassing and was out of control. She glanced around, glad to see Blair approaching.

Resisting the urge to pinch her well-intentioned friend, Trina gave Jenny a quick squeeze. "I'd better scoot. Looks like another guest is coming this way."

"Blair Davis," Jenny said with a true lack of enthusiasm.

"My date," Walker said in the most neutral tone Jenny had ever heard him use. "She insisted on re-introducing me to Atlanta society."

Trina met Jenny's gaze and had to bite her tongue

at the bewildered expression on her face. "Cheers," she said with a huge sincere smile, because the attention was off her love life and she could indeed go collect her one glass of champagne for the evening and drink it in peace.

THE REST OF THE EVENING, Walker couldn't stop thinking about Jenny Prillaman's dating-status report on Trina. With Blair talking to him nearly nonstop, he found his gaze wandering to Trina as she made her rounds.

He noticed that she smiled easily and seemed to focus on whoever conversed with her at that moment, whether it was Alfredo Bellagio and his wife or a waitress delivering appetizers. No looking over her shoulder to see if someone more important or more interesting was coming up from the rear.

He saw a guy approach her and studied her body language. She smiled and nodded, but wrapped her arms around her chest and pointed her feet in another direction.

No action here, she may as well have said to the guy. Hmm.

"Wal-ker," Blair said in a singsong voice. "You're not ignoring me, are you?"

He shook his head. "No, not at all," he lied.

"The band is playing my favorite song. Will you dance with me?"

"Sure," he said out of courtesy. He'd already decided he wasn't going out with Blair again. He took a turn around the dance floor to some sappy song with Blair rubbing herself against him and giving him the unmistakable green light.

He considered taking her up on it for a millisecond. He suspected she would be eager to please him. That never hurt, he thought. But sex with this kind of woman came with more strings than a twine factory. Worse than strings, he thought. More like barbed wire.

He spotted an ad man he'd once worked with across the room and nodded a hello to the guy. Walker had never liked Glen that much. Glen was a big social climber, if he recalled correctly.

Blair skimmed her lips against Walker's ear.

Walker felt a shiver, but he wasn't sure if it was from arousal or unease. The song thankfully drew to a close, and Walker stepped back.

Blair threw him a questioning glance.

"Hey, I see a colleague over there. Let me introduce you," he said and ushered Blair to the bar.

He introduced Glen to Blair and immediately noticed that Glen hadn't changed. The guy hit on Blair right in front of him. With a different woman that might have irritated him. God would probably punish him for it, but Walker encouraged Glen to dance with Blair.

Feeling a rush of relief, he ordered a beer. He took his first swallow and spotted Trina a few feet away. She was standing behind a palm. He asked the bartender for a glass of champagne and walked toward her.

"You've never been the wallflower type, Trina. What are you doing in the corner? Here, have some champagne."

"Sorry, can't have it," she said. "I figured it out. I have to stay sober for seventeen and a half years."

He frowned. "Seventeen and a half years?"

She nodded. "When Maddie turns eighteen, I'll get loaded. By that time, I'll be seriously overdue."

He smiled and shook his head. "What should I do with this champagne?"

"Give it to your date," she said with a smile that was almost too sweet.

"Screw that," he muttered and dumped the contents of the glass into the planter holding the palm. "And don't lecture me on wasting fine wine. I'll get Marc and Jenny a really nice wedding gift."

"Where'd you get the idea I was going to lecture you?"

He shrugged, mentally hearing his mother's complaints over the lack of money. "I don't know. With my family it was always don't waste anything," he said. "It doesn't matter. Listen, I've been thinking about what Jenny said earlier."

Trina rolled her eyes. "I was afraid you might."

"You really haven't gone out with anyone since we..."

"I haven't," she confessed. "But it's not the way it sounds. When I first found out I was pregnant, I was in shock and then there was morning sickness and then I looked like a beached whale. After labor and delivery and the sleep deprivation of her infancy, I didn't want to have sex again. And now I'm just really busy and tired."

Whoa. Walker blinked at the earful she'd given him. "So you had morning sickness, too?"

She nodded with an expression of dread at the memory. "Except it wasn't morning. Lasted most of the day."

"For how long?"

"Just three months, but—"

"Damn, that must have sucked."

"Yeah, it did," she said, but smiled.

"So the reason you never went out again wasn't because you had some—" He broke off, searching for the right word. "Some feelings for me after that night."

She stared at him for a moment, then laughed. "Oh, you mean, like I fell in love with you after our night of wild, drunken sex?" She laughed again and shook her head. "No. Nothing like that." She paused and he felt her studying his face. "I didn't mean to offend you. I mean, it was good. As much as I remember, it was. I just knew it was a one-night—"

"Don't say one-night stand."

"I'm sorry. Am I making you feel cheap?" she asked with tongue-in-cheek sympathy.

The wicked glint in her dark eyes got under his skin. He sighed in exasperation. "You're not making this easy."

"Good," she said. "Maybe you won't ask any more crazy questions."

He took a swallow of beer. "I don't like being the bad guy. Contrary to your opinion, I take my responsibilities seriously."

"I know you do. You're a stand-up guy in probably every area but having kids."

Her words scratched at him like a burr sticker, but he guessed he should be thankful she understood him so well. "Exactly. I'm not going to be good father material. So maybe you should think about finding another one for Maddie."

She blinked at him. "Excuse me?"

"I mean Jenny had a good idea. You should start dating for Maddie. For you. You're pretty. Men are going to want you. The right one is going to want Maddie, too."

Her mouth tightened. "This is none of your business. You wouldn't even know about Maddie if you'd stayed in Paris like you were supposed to."

"Supposed to," he said, unable to keep a growl from his voice. "I never intended to stay there longer than a year or two, tops."

"Yeah, sure," she said, clearly not believing him.

Her response bothered him. "I'm back and I think you should try to get a father for her."

She narrowed her eyes and met his gaze. "Just as I have no right, or interest," she added with emphasis, "in your dating life, you have no right, or need you have any interest, in mine."

"You're missing the point. You're a pretty and intelligent woman. You're nice. A little softer than you used to be. In a good way," he added when her eyes narrowed. "It shouldn't be that hard for you to find someone, but you need to open up to the idea. Before I left, I remember you as a hot woman with all the right moves to get a man's attention. I've been watching you tonight and the only signals you're sending are stop and don't even think about it."

"Maybe it's just not on my to-do list right now."

"Maybe you should change your to-do list. And when you do, stop crossing your arms over your chest when a guy talks to you. Don't automatically back away," he said and took a step closer to prove his point.

Trina stood rooted to the spot, looking as if she wanted to club him.

"Look into his eyes and smile." He paused catching a hint of her scent, something sweet mixed with a spice. He looked at her mouth and got distracted for a couple of seconds. In his opinion, her mouth had always been one of the sexiest things about her. Plump, with a natural color somewhere between pink and mauve, it reminded him of a juicy fruit that made him want to take a big bite. Forbidden fruit, he reminded himself. "Everything you used to do. Damn, you have a great mouth."

Surprise widened her eyes. "I—uh." She bit her lip. "I'm trying to figure out whether to be flattered or offended." She looked past him as if she were determined to break the connection with him. "Oh, looks like your date has tracked you down. Time for me to go."

Blair strode breathlessly to his side searching Walker's and Trina's faces. Walker would swear the woman had the search capabilities of a bloodhound. "It took me forever to find you," she chided Walker. "You shouldn't have hidden in the corner with, uh—" She stared at Trina for a long moment. "I know we've seen each other recently."

"Trina Roberts," Walker supplied. "We work together on the Bellagio account."

"Oh, coworkers," Blair said, relief crossing her face. She smiled. "It's nice to meet you again, Trina."

"Thank you," Trina said. "I hope you're enjoying yourself. Lovely dress."

"Thank you," Blair said. "It's Chanel. Just love it. Yours is cute, too," she said as an afterthought, then frowned. "What is that green thing on your shoulder? Is it part of the design?"

Walker watched Trina tug at her dress to look at the shoulder. She started to laugh. "No, that's courtesy of Maddie. A strained-green-bean kiss. Thanks for the heads-up. I should go. Have a nice evening," she said and walked away.

"A strained-green-bean kiss?" Blair echoed. "Who is Maddie?"

Three answers backed up in his throat.

Her daughter.

My daughter.

Our daughter.

But he'd agreed to strict confidentiality even if it felt slimy. "Not sure. Do you want a drink?"

Sad Fact: It's not unusual for a woman's feet to grow a half to a full size during pregnancy. Often enough, her feet will remain a larger size. Best consolation: a new wardrobe of shoes in the proper size.

## CHAPTER NINE

WHILE MADDIE SLEPT PEACEFULLY, Trina paced her bedroom as she stripped. She kicked off the Bellagio sandals, folded her pashmina and caught sight of herself in the full-length mirror as she unzipped her dress.

She studied the green-bean stain on her shoulder. Damn, it was larger than she'd expected. She wondered why no one except Blair had mentioned it to her.

Maybe everyone else had been trying to be nice. Trina cringed. That prospect was far more embarrassing than the actual cause of the stain. What bothered her was that she'd walked around as if she looked reasonably attractive and pulled together with a baby-food stain on her shoulder all evening. She felt like an idiot.

She stepped out of the dress and put it on a hanger with plans to take it to the dry cleaner.

For a while now, she'd avoided looking in the mirror when she was naked or even half-naked. The sight of her post-pregnancy body still jarred her. It seemed like every time she caught a glimpse of herself with fuller breasts and hips and a more rounded abdomen she felt as if she were looking at someone else.

Trina took a deep breath and looked at her body, really looked at it. Four sessions a week of a combination of Pilates and an elliptical had kept her lean and mean until her pregnancy. She'd taken pride in her flat abs and tight butt.

When she'd lost her cookies on the elliptical during the third month of pregnancy, her exercise regimen had gone to hell in a handbasket.

She unfastened her bra and couldn't hold back a quiet laugh at her breast size. What she would have given for these in high school. She brushed her hand over her abdomen and a memory kicked through her like a hot coal.

She hadn't thought about it in a long time. Her images of the night she'd spent with Walker had been steamy due to arousal, hazy due to mojitos.

They had made love so many times that night she'd wondered if she'd dreamed some of them. The one she remembered now was when he'd pulled her in front of a full-length mirror and made her watch while he slid his hands over her belly, her breasts and between her legs. She remembered his open mouth on her shoulder, his low groans of arousal and the dirty talk he'd whispered in her ear. Talk about how hard she made him, how he wanted to slide inside her right then and there. Soon enough, talking and touching hadn't been enough. Propping her hands against the wall beside the mirror, he'd positioned them sideways toward the mirror and he'd slid inside her from behind.

Her nipples grew taut and she felt herself grow swollen between her legs. Watching Walker's hands wrapped around her hips and seeing him huge with desire as he thrust inside her had been the most wicked, erotic experience of her life. She'd felt like a bad, bad girl that had the power to make a man go a little crazy.

Her heart pounded and her skin heated. She wrapped her hands around herself in a hug. Oh, what a night that had been. Oh.

She opened her eyes and looked in the mirror, shocked at the arousal she saw on her face, felt in her body.

She'd thought her sexual drive was still buried somewhere and she didn't know where to find it. Hadn't been that interested in finding it.

She shook her head, but felt a slow smile start in her belly and bubble up to her mouth. So, maybe Jenny was right. Maybe she was ready to start dating. Maybe she was ready, and this time she would take it slow.

THE SITUATION WITH TRINA and Maddie plagued Walker like a hangover that wouldn't go away. Still horrified that his vasectomy had failed, he had hoped that the generous financial arrangement he'd made would appease some of his guilt. He couldn't, however, dodge the fact that Maddie deserved a father. A better one than he would ever be.

He surfed the Net for information on how daughters without fathers fared and he didn't like what he learned. Trina needed to listen to him about this. She might not appreciate his interference, but she needed to hear the truth.

He called her on Monday morning. "Can you meet me for lunch?"

"Is it urgent business? I planned to grab a sandwich and spend my lunch hour with Maddie today. I'll probably take her for a stroll."

He hesitated a half beat. "Okay if I join you?"

Silence followed. "Are you sure you won't get hives or something?"

"I've never had hives in my life," he told her.

"First time for everything," she said, poking fun at him.

"Twelve-thirty?"

"Fine. Don't forget to bring your own sandwich."

He had the strange feeling that he was preparing a presentation. Deciding to eat his sandwich at his desk so he wouldn't be distracted from his task of persuasion, he reviewed his research material and met Trina and Maddie outside.

Trina pushed a stroller along the sidewalk perimeter of the office building. She stopped, bending down to say something and touch the baby, who glanced up at her and wiggled her feet. The exchange was cute, if a guy was into the baby thing. Which he wasn't.

He walked toward Trina and waited for her to glance up at him. She squinted her eyes in the sun. "Where's your sandwich?"

"I decided to walk and talk instead of eat."

She nodded and straightened. "Okay. I already ate at my desk. Maddie gets a little greedy with my food sometimes. I think it's the wanting-what-you-can't-have syndrome. What did you want? Is this about the new ads?"

"No. It's about Maddie and you." Shoving his hands into his pockets, he walked beside her. "I did some research about daughters without strong father figures and statistics indicate that girls without fathers tend not to perform as well in academics as girls who have father figures. Girls with father figures also tend to get involved in athletic activities more often. Girls with father figures exhibit more self-confidence and self-esteem. They are also more likely to graduate from high school and seek higher education."

"What did you do?" Trina asked, looking at him with a skeptical expression on her face. "Google daughters of single mothers?"

"Close," he said. Daughters without fathers. "The other thing I learned that really bothered me was that teenage girls without fathers are more likely to be promiscuous and to get pregnant before marriage."

"Don't tell me you already want to get a chastity belt for her."

"No, but we shouldn't ignore these facts."

"Statistics," Trina corrected. "You're talking about statistical probability, the same thing people use to play blackjack."

"There's no reason we can't make this information work in Maddie's favor instead of against her."

Trina shot him a wary look. "What do you mean we?"

"I mean we can cooperate."

"But you don't want to be her father," she said.

Her statement pinched, but he ignored it. "I want Maddie to have the best possible father and I know that's not me. I want you to start going out again."

"Okay," she said with a shrug.

He stopped midstride, stunned. "Okay? But the

other night you said you didn't want to date and that it was none of my business."

"It's still none of your business, but I've changed my mind." Her eyes turned smoky sexy. "I'm ready to put my toe in the water. Depending on the guy I'll put in more than my toe."

Good, he told himself to say. "Good," he forced out of his mouth even though the word felt awkward as hell. "But you'll be looking for men who will be good father figures for Maddie."

"Some," she said and began to push the stroller along the sidewalk. "I mean, if it's going to be long term, the guy would have to be crazy about both Maddie and me, but I have to be attracted to him first. I'm not going to get involved with a guy just to have a good father for Maddie, because then I'll end up unhappy and that wouldn't be fair to anyone. So Mr. Right for Maddie will also have to trip my trigger in all the right ways."

She pushed her hair behind her ear and Walker was distracted by the glint of sunlight on a tiny diamond stud earring and a small silver hoop. A memory flashed through his mind of how he had buried his nose in her neck and inhaled her scent. She'd smelled like a wicked, but sweet, combination of a hot dream and fulfillment that dragged him deeper and deeper. He remembered the sequence of insatiable wanting followed by a climax so complete he'd figured he wouldn't need sex again for days. But it had taken only minutes to feel the beginning of a burn, just minutes before his heart pounded out the start of arousal. Over and over they'd had sex…hot-as-hell sex.

He swore at the images and met Trina's searching gaze.

"You do agree, don't you?" she asked.

"Agree with what?"

"Agree that I have to want this guy for me first, and Maddie second."

Not really, he thought but swallowed the response. The idea of Trina turning into the sex siren she'd been that night with him made him feel like he needed an antacid. Which was stupid as hell, he told himself.

"I guess, but Maddie will need to be a priority in the selection process."

"Later," she said with a nod.

"What do you mean later?" he asked.

"He's going to have to float my boat before he gets a chance to float Maddie's." She looked at him for a moment. "Was this really what you wanted to discuss with me?"

"Yeah," he said. "You seemed so closed to the idea. I thought you should hear the statistics." He cleared his throat. "And I want to help."

Her eyes widened. "How?"

"Since I can't be the kind of father Maddie deserves, I want to help find a man for the two of you."

"How do you plan to do that? Take out a want ad?"

"If necessary," he said. "I doubt it will be necessary. You're pretty. She's cute. It shouldn't be that hard."

Trina smiled. "As long as you know what Maddie and I want in a man."

His gut twisted and he felt his jaw twitch, but he ignored the sensations. He had something more important to do here. Time to belly up to the bar. "Okay," he said. "What do you want in a man?"

"Intelligence, sense of humor, kindness. Passion for life and of course for me," she said, and paused. "Good in bed."

Walker shoved his hands into his pockets, feeling his jaw muscle twitch again. "How am I supposed to know if someone is good in bed?"

She shrugged. "I guess I'll have to make that call. I prefer dark hair to blondes and tall is good. Ultimately he needs to want a family." She glanced away thoughtfully. "I like a man who knows what's real and important and what isn't."

"What do you mean?"

"I mean career is important to a point, but you get your real happiness from other things."

"Such as?"

"Having your baby smile at you. Seeing her discover the world. Helping her learn to walk. Being there for the person you love at the end of a terrible day and laughing about it all. Making love when the sun comes up and knowing you're the luckiest person in the world." She met his gaze. "That will do for a start." She glanced at her watch. "I gotta run. Let me know if you find anyone interesting."

"I'll do that," he muttered as he watched her push the stroller toward the nursery. Maddie gave a happy babble and he felt a strange twist in his gut. He refused to examine it.

Late that night when Walker returned to his condo, he found his uncle playing poker with a member of the condo security, drinking beer and smoking a cigar.

Harry ducked the cigar behind his back, but a waft of smoke rose beside him.

"Don't bother trying to hide it," Walker said, pulling his tie loose as he headed for the refrigerator to grab a beer. "Just open the window and turn on the fan."

"It was just one," Harry said.

"Whatever," Walker muttered as his cell phone rang. "Walker," he replied without checking the caller ID.

"Hey, bro, it's BJ. Have you thought anymore about me coming to work with you?"

Walker swallowed a groan. "I don't know, BJ. I've never thought it was a good idea for family to work together."

"You think I'll mess everything up," BJ said.

Walker carried his beer upstairs to his office. "I didn't say that. I can be a real demanding asshole of a boss. I would drive you nuts."

BJ gave an uneasy laugh. "I'll risk it. Besides, we're kinda in a time crunch here."

Walker stopped midstride. "What do you mean in a time crunch?"

"Danielle and I want to move before the baby's born."

"That's months, isn't it?"

"More like six weeks," BJ said.

"Six weeks!" He swore under his breath. "I thought all this just happened."

"Longer than that," BJ admitted. "Danielle's mother and father are making noises about moving in with us, so we need to get out of here."

Walker sighed. "So when did you want to move?"

"Yesterday," BJ muttered. "Danielle's a dream, but her parents give new meaning to the word moochers. I need to know you'll just give me a chance to work with you. All I want is a chance. If it doesn't work out, you can let me go after thirty days."

Walker swallowed a long drink of beer. How could

he possibly turn down his brother in this situation? At least his brother was going to attempt to be a father, which was more than Walker was doing. The knowledge backed up in his throat. "Okay, where are you going to live?"

"We'll work it out," BJ said. "Just be ready for me by next week."

As Walker disconnected, he heard his uncle stomp upstairs. "What's got your shorts in a twist?" Harry asked from the doorway. "Did you find another kid that you fathered?"

Walker shot his uncle a dark look. "No, but I might as well have. BJ got a girl pregnant and they're coming to Atlanta."

Harry swore. "You're kidding."

Walker shook his head. "He's going to be working for me."

"What's he gonna do?"

"I have no idea," Walker said.

OVER THE NEXT TWO DAYS, Walker searched in vain for an appropriate position for his brother at his firm. Paragon Advertising was known as a prestigious, slick, innovative and dependable agency. His brother, God bless him, was a naive redneck who chewed tobacco and drank cheap beer.

Needing a break, Walker stopped at a sports bar

on the way home, grabbed a beer and watched a ball game on the big-screen TV.

Discussing the game with a couple of guys sitting nearby, he learned one was a brother of a friend of a friend. A commercial featuring a crying baby came on the air. Walker remembered his goal to find Maddie a father and took a second considering look at his bar mates. One was dark and seemed intelligent enough to Walker. He hadn't gotten smashed and was employed.

"Hey. Walker Gordon," he said, extending his hand.

The guy shook his hand. "Rob Brown. Always glad to meet another Braves fan."

"Good. Hey, are you married or anything?"

Rob shot him a wary look. "Why are you asking?"

"I just wondered—"

"Hey, I'm flattered, but I'm totally hetero, man. Totally."

Walker laughed and shook his head. "No. It's not for me. I have this friend. A woman. She's pretty, has a kid and I thought you two might get along."

Rob cocked his head to one side. "If she's so hot, why don't you go after her?"

Walker felt a weird clench inside him. "We've been friends forever. She's almost like my sister," he said and the lie nearly stuck in his throat. "Plus, I'm not good with kids. You don't have any addictions or diseases, do you?"

Rob laughed. "Is this a scam?"

"No. I'm serious. No addictions or diseases?"

"No, but—"

"And you like kids?"

"Yeah, I've got a bunch of nephews and nieces. I take them out all the time, but—"

"She's pretty and smart. Give her a call and tell her I sent you," Walker said, giving the guy Trina's cell number and finishing his beer. There. Trina, meet bachelor number one.

## CHAPTER TEN

"*WHO* ARE ROB, MARK AND STEVE?" Trina asked as Walker strode into her office.

The look of fury on Trina's face caught him off guard and he quickly searched his memory. "Oh, those are some guys I told to call you. Remember you said you were ready to start dating."

Shaking her head, she rose from her desk and closed the door to her office. "Have you lost your mind?"

"No. I told you I would help find someone for you."

"Getting strange calls from men I've never heard of doesn't make me want to race onto the playing field," she said. "Did you think you could maybe let *me* know you were referring these guys?"

"I told them to say I sent you," he said.

"I kinda got that message after I blew off the first two and told them they had the wrong number. What are you telling these guys anyway?"

"That you're pretty, smart, on the market and you have a baby. All of them have good jobs and like kids.

No criminal records and they're unattached. No diseases or addictions."

"If you really want me to respond to these guys without hanging up, then I'd like a little more information. Leave a voice mail on my cell or send me an e-mail with how you met them and what you know about them. Otherwise, you're getting a little too close to the whole pimp thing."

He nodded, watching her push her hair behind her ear.

She met his gaze silently for a long moment. "What's wrong?"

He shook his head. "Nothing. Why?"

"Yes, there is. I can see it, feel it," she said, her irritation warring with her concern. "I can tell."

"How?" he asked, pushing back some of his own irritation. Walker had always been a believer in not letting anyone see him sweat. The possibility that Trina could bothered him.

"I don't know," she said. "I can just tell. I sense it or something. I could always tell when you and Brooke were fighting without you saying anything."

He frowned. "How did you know?"

She shrugged and looked away as she walked behind her desk. "I told you I don't know how I know. I just do. So, what's wrong?"

"It's my brother."

Concern crossed her face. "Is he ill?"

"No. He's moving to Atlanta and wants to work for me," he added, his gut tightening at the prospect.

"Is he insane or a criminal? Is he socially insulting?"

"Not quite insane, usually not a criminal. He doesn't intend to be socially insulting."

Her eyes widened. "Really? Have to say when I think of your brother, I picture someone like you."

He shook his head. "He's not. He didn't go to college. He's tried a few pyramid sales programs that didn't work. Don't get me wrong. He's a nice guy. But now he's gotten a girl pregnant and wants to marry her."

Her mouth formed a perfect O. "Wow."

"Yeah." He shoved his hands into his pockets.

"How pregnant?" she ventured.

"About eight months."

Trina nodded. "At least she won't be alone for some of the rough parts."

"Like you were," he said, and felt a weird, protective instinct appear out of nowhere.

"I did okay," she said in a small, still voice.

But he saw something else in her eyes that made his insides ache. He lifted his hand to her cheek. "I'm sorry I wasn't there for you."

"You wouldn't have wanted to be there for me. It was a messy, emotional time."

"You want to know something crazy?"

"What?"

"When it comes to having kids, I wish I were more like my brother, BJ," he said, shaking his head at the irony.

"Why?"

"Because he actually thinks he has a shot at being a decent father, and he's either crazy enough or brave enough to get married and give it all a try."

"It probably helps if the two people involved have strong feelings for each other," she said.

"Yeah," he muttered, and slid his thumb over Trina's mouth. He'd always liked her mouth, the way she curved it upward in a smile, the way she moved it to express her surprise or laughter, the way she had opened it when he'd kissed her. A hot image of Trina naked, her open mouth moving down his chest to his abdomen and lower shot through him.

"What are you doing?" she whispered.

"Thinking," he said, rubbing her bottom lip again.

"Thinking about what?"

"About what you were like," he said. "That night."

"I didn't know you remembered," she said, her eyes widening in surprise.

"I may not remember everything, but I remember enough."

Her gaze met his as she closed her hand over his

wrist, but didn't move his hand away from her face. He looked into her dark eyes and remembered the kick of her passion. She'd surprised him with her lack of inhibition. And just when he'd thought she'd turned into a sexual she-devil, he remembered, there had been tenderness in her touch.

"Sometimes, it's better not to remember," she told him and pulled his hand from her face. He immediately felt the loss. Damn odd, he thought. He was making more of this than he should.

"Maybe you're right."

"I am. We both have something to lose if the truth about Maddie gets back to Alfredo Bellagio. He's so Italian," she said. "If he ever found out you're Maddie's father…"

Walker's gut twisted. "What do you mean?"

"He would think you should be raising your own baby."

"I'm going to do better than that," Walker said. "You and I have worked out a generous financial agreement and I'm going to help you find a husband."

She met his gaze with a frozen smile. "I never really said I would get married."

"But we covered this. I told you all the research about daughters without father figures. You said you were willing to start looking."

"I'm willing to start looking for a *date*. But I don't

know about marriage. I may feel the same way about marriage that you feel about fatherhood."

"Why?"

She looked away from him. "I didn't have a great example. My parents' marriage wasn't the best. They probably shouldn't have stayed together. It sure didn't look like a love match to me. And—" She broke off and knitted her fingers together, fidgeting.

Walker stared at her in disbelief. Trina wasn't a fidgeter. "And what?"

"I think it's a lot easier to avoid picking the wrong person by not getting married than it is to pick the right person."

"That's a switch. I thought most women wanted to get married."

"It's not that different from your point of view about becoming a father. It's avoidance."

FRIDAY NIGHT, WALKER SAT in front of the tube with a cold one. His uncle Harry was smelling up his den with cigar smoke and playing poker. Walker had thought about hitting the club scene, but he wasn't in the mood. His cell phone rang, interrupting his boredom.

"Hi, this is Trina."

Something inside him brightened and he pulled out of his slump. "What's up?"

"Do you have Mark Fisher's number?"

Walker searched his memory for the name. "Mark Fisher?"

"He's one of the guys you told to call me."

"Oh. Works for the government," he recalled. "I don't have his number."

She groaned.

"Why?"

"I was going to meet him for dinner, but my baby-sitter cancelled at the last minute. I don't want to ask my mother. She'll put me through the third degree."

"You don't have his number?"

"No. We made arrangements early this week and several people have called me since then. I hate for him to think I ditched him."

Walker stood. An idea occurred to him that he im-mediately rejected. "How long did you plan to be out?"

"It depends on whether I like Mark or not," she said with a husky laugh.

His gut twisted at the sexy undertone, but he pushed the feeling aside. If he really wanted to help find a father for Maddie, then he needed to remove as many obstacles for Trina as he could.

He wasn't making a lifetime commitment, he reminded himself. Just one night. So why did he feel like he was climbing the ladder to jump off the high diving board?

He forced the words through his tight throat. "You want me to take care of her?"

Silence followed. "You don't know how."

Irritation bled through him. "I could do it for one evening. I'm reasonably intelligent. I could do it for a few hours," he repeated. "Unless you're breast-feeding or something."

"No. I only did that for a few weeks." She paused. "Would you really do it?"

"Yeah."

"Maybe I could just have a drink and an appetizer, then leave. That wouldn't take long. Maybe an hour and a half."

"Where are you supposed to meet him?"

Trina named a trendy, exclusive restaurant.

"Sounds nice."

"Yes, but I'm not sure you can—"

He felt a surge of impatience. "What do I need to do? Feed her? Take her for a stroll? Change a diaper?" Okay, he wasn't looking forward to that last one, but he could do it. "What's the worst that could happen?"

"You could hurt her," Trina said, and the fear in her voice sliced him in half.

Walker swore. "I wouldn't hurt her."

"You wouldn't mean to hurt her," she said. "You might accidentally hurt her. Like you're supposed to lay her on her tummy in the crib and always pull the side of the crib up or she could try to climb out. And you can't put her on the floor and leave her because she can roll like nobody's business."

"Noted," Walker said.

"And even if you didn't hurt her, you might scare her."

"I'm not that ugly."

"It's not about looks. It's because you're a man. She's not used to being around men very much."

"Maybe she should get used to being around men, since we represent about half of the world population."

Trina sighed.

Walker's impatience kicked at him again. "Hey, you want Mark to think you're ditching him. It's no big deal to me."

"No. I don't want that. Okay," she said, reluctance oozing from her voice. "Come over now, so I can tell you everything you need to know."

An hour later, Walker's brain was nearly exploding from Trina's lecture. *No need to feed Maddie, because she'd already fed the baby, changed her diaper and given her a bath. He could, however, give her a bottle and two animal cookies. No more.* Trina gave him Maddie's favorite books and toys and supplied him with emergency phone numbers. She made him repeat her cell number to him four times.

He was insulted, but withstood Trina's treatment

because he could tell she was nervous. "You've covered everything six times," he said. "Go knock Mark on his butt."

She sighed. "I'm not sure I have that ability anymore," she murmured, then smiled. "But I'll give it a shot. Call for any reason."

"Will do," he said, and she walked out of the house, leaving him with a strange sensation in his gut. He pushed the feeling aside and looked at Maddie. She sat on a quilt in the middle of the floor of the den, making singsong noises as she studied her fist.

Despite his repeated reassurances to Trina, he struggled with a sudden dearth of confidence. He'd always considered babies alien beings. Maddie, with her carrot-orange hair pulled into a short spiky topknot and huge brown eyes, was no different.

His secret hope was that she would fall asleep on the quilt for two hours and he could turn on the television and watch the ball game. At the moment, he held his breath, unsure how to approach the beast.

She continued staring at her fist, making unintelligible sounds for another moment, then two.

His cell phone rang and he cursed the sound, immediately answering it. "Walker," he said.

"What is she doing?" Trina asked.

"She *was* happily staring at her fist until you called," he told her.

"Oh, well, what is she doing now?"

"Looking at me."

"Has she put her thumb in her mouth?"

Walker watched Maddie lift her thumb to her mouth. "Yes."

"I knew it," Trina said. "That's what she does when she's scared. I knew you would scare her."

"She's not crying or screaming. She's fine. Go meet your date and leave me alone." He turned off his phone and moved toward the baby. Her eyes seemed to grow larger the closer he got.

She stared at him a long moment, then let out a bloodcurdling scream of terror and burst into tears.

Walker swore, feeling every muscle in his body tense. "It's okay," he tried to say in the same reassuring tone he reserved for small pets. "You're going to be okay. I won't hurt you."

Maddie continued to scream and he felt a tug of desperation. "There's no need to get upset." His cell phone rang again. He checked the caller ID. Trina. He didn't pick up.

He felt the back of his neck grow damp from perspiration. He rolled the plastic ball toward Maddie. "There, look at that. Isn't that fun?"

She continued to howl.

He swore again and pulled out a book. "Look here. Feel the bunny."

Maddie would have none of it.

Walker would die before he admitted it, but he didn't want to pick her up. Especially when she was screaming. He glanced around the room and caught sight of the box of animal cookies. He opened the box, pulled out one and waved it in front of Maddie's face.

She abruptly turned silent. Giving a cough and a hiccup, she looked at the cookie, then at him, then back at the cookie. Tears clinging to her baby eyelashes, she reached out, took the cookie and stuffed it into her mouth.

Walker felt a rush of relief. "The secret to world peace. Animal cookies." He looked inside the box. Trina had left instructions. Only two cookies allowed. "Screw that," he said to himself. He had an hour and fifty-seven minutes to go.

TRINA SKIPPED the first two courses and proceeded directly to an entrée of crab cakes with mixed seasonal vegetables on the side. Sipping one glass of wine, she barely resisted the urge to call Walker every other minute. She skipped dessert and coffee, made her excuses and sped home.

She pushed open the door to a completely quiet house. Deathly quiet, she thought, her imagination running wild. Ditching her shoes at the bottom of the steps, she ran upstairs to the nursery, where Walker sat in the rocking chair, leaning forward, watching the crib.

She glanced at the crib where Maddie lay sprawled, her cheeks flushed and her breath even as she slept. Trina looked at Walker again. He reminded her of a silent sentry, guarding the palace princess.

A stupid romantic notion, she told herself. "Why are you sitting there just watching her?"

He didn't look away. "Because I didn't pull up the side of the crib. I didn't want her to wake up."

"Oh, I'll do that."

He immediately rose. "On your clock," he said in a low voice.

She did a double take, looking into his eyes, and saw a hint of frazzled fear. The sight warmed her heart. How many times had she felt the same way? How many times had she been willing to sell her soul if Maddie would sleep for longer than fifteen minutes?

"How long did she scream?" Trina whispered.

"In dog years? Seven," he said. "Why didn't you warn me?"

"I told you that you would scare her."

"I didn't do anything."

"You didn't have to. You just weren't me, and I'm the parent of the moment. Actually I'm the parent of the year, probably the lifetime—"

"Nice of you to show a little pity by leaving the box of animal cookies."

"How many are left?"

"Between the two of us, none," he said and raked his hand through his hair. "How do you do this every day?"

She felt a wave of protectiveness for Maddie. "She doesn't scream all the time. Didn't she stop screaming tonight?"

He gave a noncommittal nod. "Yeah, but she likes constant motion. If she's not rolling, she likes to be moving in some way—held while walking, strolling. What are you going to do when she's really mobile?"

"I don't know. I'm about to get a part-time nanny."

"I can see why. I don't know how you've done it so far."

"She's worth it," Trina said. "My little sunshine." She pulled up the side of the crib and Maddie didn't move a muscle. "Yep, she's out. Thanks for coming."

She led the way out of the room into the hallway and pulled the door partway closed.

"How was the date?" Walker asked.

"It was fine. I was a little edgy about leaving Maddie, so I ate fast. I couldn't give a complete review of the food."

"What about the guy?"

"Mark," she said, feeling suddenly aware of how

close Walker stood to her. She took a step back. "He was nice. Asked me out again."

"Are you going?"

"I don't know. I have to check my schedule and my babysitter's schedule."

"Did he work for you?"

"He was good-looking, could carry a conversation. I didn't kiss him. I guess I'll find out more about chemistry if we go out again."

She felt his gaze skim over her and tried not to feel self-conscious.

"You look pretty," he said.

"Thanks," she said and smiled. "He said something along those lines, too."

Walker rested his hands on his hips and looked at her curiously. "What? What'd he say?"

"None of your business," she said, reluctant to disclose a lot of details about the date to Walker. It felt strange.

"C'mon. I set this up. What did he say?"

"He said I was a lot hotter than he'd expected," she said and led the way downstairs. She turned when she reached the door. "Happy?"

"Yeah. You think he was trying to get in your pants on the first date?"

"It's possible. Isn't that what most guys do?" she asked. "He may have just been giving me a genuine compliment, but I guess you consider that too much of a stretch."

"No. I didn't say that," Walker said. "You are hot. You and I have just always been friends. Except for that one night."

The memory of that one hot night hung between them. Trina met his gaze, and she felt an unwelcome zinging sensation. "Yep," she said, willing the breathlessness from her voice. "One night that will not be repeated."

"Right," he said, nodding his head. "G'night, Trina. Call me if you need something. I'm around."

With her heart beating faster than it should, she watched him walk toward his car. Visceral images of the night they'd shared flew through her brain like laser lights. The truth was she couldn't remember having a sexual experience like the night she'd had with Walker.

That was a memory issue, she tried to tell herself. She'd been told by more than one mother that part of a woman's memory went out the door with her placenta.

Trina groaned. Okay, so sex in general was a hazy, fuzzy memory. That meant she definitely needed to make some new memories.

## CHAPTER ELEVEN

ON SUNDAY NIGHT, Jenny Prillaman paid a visit for a girls' night at Trina's house. After Jenny wore out Maddie, Trina put her baby to bed and fixed a martini for Jenny and herself.

Settling herself in front of the television for a rerun of *Desperate Housewives,* Jenny pulled out a pad of paper for herself, a coloring book for Trina and her box of Crayola crayons for a coloring session.

Trina shook her head. "This is serious regression, Jenny. Is the wedding situation that bad?"

"It's a healthy stress relief," Jenny said, and took a sip of her martini before she began to draw. "You're great at making martinis. No matter how hard I try, mine taste like cough medicine. How's the dating scene? I have a guy in mind for you and I'm not taking no for an answer."

"I've ventured out and my answer is yes," Trina said. "Even though you're talking about my dating life in order to throw the discussion off your upcoming nuptials."

Jenny looked at her in surprise. "You went on a date and didn't tell me?"

"I wanted to wait and see how it went. If it was a disaster, I didn't want to rehash it."

Jenny lit up. "So it wasn't a disaster? Will you go out with him again?"

"Probably. It wasn't love or lust at first sight, but he was nice."

Jenny met her gaze and took another sip of her martini. "Didn't exactly cause a forest fire."

"No, but—"

"Well, I have a guy for you. He's hot, very hot."

"But is he nice?"

"Nice, but not too nice. Funny, employed."

"Does he like kids?"

Jenny paused. "I think so. I'll have to check on that. He's an engineer."

"That sounds interesting," she said, picturing a supergeek as she colored a Loony Tunes character.

Jenny tossed her a chastising glance. "Stop that. He's a construction engineer. He builds these super resorts all over the world."

"So why would he come to Atlanta?"

"Aside from attending my huge, train wreck of a

wedding, his company is based here. So can I tell him to call you?"

Trina shrugged. "May as well. Just make sure I know his full name and let me know if you really do talk to him. Walker has been throwing me fresh meat, too," she muttered.

Jenny raised her eyebrows. "Walker? I always wondered if the two of you would hook up if he and Brooke weren't together."

Trina felt her cheeks heat and frowned at the sensation, lifting her martini glass to take a sip. "No chance. I'm not his type. He's not mine."

"Why not? You're pretty and intelligent."

"I'm not a high-profile heiress," Trina said.

"You really think that's what he wants after his experience with Brooke?" Jenny asked doubtfully.

Trina shrugged. "I don't know. He's not my type, either. Doesn't want kids."

Jenny blinked. "That surprises me. He seems like the all-American guy who will eventually settle down and have a family."

"I think maybe he didn't have the best experience with his own father."

"Hmm." Jenny gave a sad smile. "I always had a wonderful relationship with my father. It was devastating when he died."

Jenny and Trina had bonded even more when

they'd learned they both lost their fathers during their growing-up years. "Something tells me your dad will be with you on your wedding day."

Jenny's eyes turned shiny with tears and she waved her hand in front of her face. "Not at that circus," she said.

Trina sneaked a glance at Jenny's doodling pad and winced. "Is that a chicken running around a wedding cake with your sister's head on top? A little too Picasso for a joyous wedding, don't you think?"

Jenny made a face. "I wish I had the nerve to suggest Vegas. And it seems like all Marc and I do is fight. His mother. My sister."

Trina felt an ugly sense of foreboding. "Oh, no, you're not going to pull a Brooke, are you?"

Jenny shook her head. "No, but in a crazy way, she's becoming my hero. I mean, she had the nerve to walk out on the wedding of the century with cameras rolling for live TV."

"Except the live TV didn't catch her sneaking out the back door. They just caught Walker left standing at the altar," Trina said. "And you being fired."

"True and true," Jenny said.

"Are you sure you still want to get married?"

"I want to *be* married to Marc. I know that without a doubt. I just seriously dread this whole wedding thing."

Trina felt sorry for her friend. "If you change your mind about any of it, you can call me and I'll do whatever you ask. Except kill a member of the Bellagio family," she added. "I have to make a living."

Jenny gave a rough laugh and clinked her martini glass against Trina's. "Thanks for the offer. I may give you a call. In the meantime, I'm sending David Owen your way."

"Who's David Owen?"

"The hot guy who is going to rock your world."

Trina would settle for a minor explosion that lasted one evening.

AFTER TRINA MANAGED to successfully dodge her mother for two and a half weeks, Aubrey ambushed her when she arrived home on Tuesday night. Trina suspected her mother had been circling her house like a buzzard, since Aubrey showed up just ten minutes after she'd walked through the door.

"Hello Carter-Aubrey. I was in the neighborhood, so I thought I would stop by. Have you hired anyone to help with Madeline yet?" Aubrey asked and stretched her hands to reach for the baby. "How is my little princess?"

"No, I haven't gotten around to hiring anyone, but it's on my list. As you can see, Maddie's thriving," she said as she handed her daughter to her mother.

"So she is," her mother said with more than a note of surprise in her voice. "I just wish you had done this the right way, Carter-Aubrey. Gotten married, had Maddie and then quit your job so you could stay home with her."

"I probably wouldn't quit my job even if I were married. I have the perfect situation with Maddie's nursery in the same building."

"Yes, well, mark my words, child rearing doesn't get easier. You wait until Maddie hits her teens and you'll be wishing for all the help you can find."

"I think I will wait," Trina said lightly. "I have twelve and a half years before I need to deal with that."

"Then, just when you think you've successfully managed to get your daughter through high school and ready for college, she takes off with a motorcycle gang member."

"Old news," Trina interjected, not wanting to review the huge mistake. "Over and done with. Ancient history. Did I tell you that I'm dating again?" she asked, because she knew that change in subject would stop her mother's harping.

Her mother turned silent for a moment, staring at Trina. "That's wonderful," she said. "I hear Gregory Benson is single again. His mother is in my Thursday morning bridge club. I'll see what I can do."

"No need," Trina said. "My friends already have several guys lined up for me."

"What kind of guys? What friends?" her mother asked.

"Jenny Prillaman," Trina said. "Marc Waterson's fiancée."

Her mother gave a cautious nod of approval. "Who else?"

*Not that it's really any of your business.* "One of the officers at the advertising company that Bellagio uses. We've known each other a few years and he has introduced me to some men."

"How nice. I don't believe I caught his name," her mother said.

"I don't think you know him," Trina said, and poured a glass of water for her mother. "But I'm going out with one of his friends tomorrow night."

"I can babysit," her mother offered. "That way, I can meet him."

"Actually, I'm meeting him at a restaurant," Trina said.

Her mother frowned, jiggling Maddie in her arms. "If he's a gentleman, he would pick you up."

"Even though she may not know the difference, I don't want to bring a man into Maddie's life until I've gotten to know him a little bit. If I drive, I control when I leave."

Her mother nodded. "That's admirable, dear. But you must let me take care of Maddie and save your sitter for another time."

Trina reluctantly agreed and met Steve at a noisy sports bar, his choice. A game played on the large-screen televisions and she could barely make out her conversation with Steve from all the yelling. After four beers, Steve began to slide his hand through her hair and touch her. He murmured something in her ear that she couldn't understand, but since she had the feeling she didn't really want to know, she decided it was time to go.

She glanced at her watch and shook her head. "I'm sorry. I have an early meeting tomorrow morning. Thanks for dinner, though."

Steve looked disappointed. "Maybe Friday? That way we can make a long evening of it."

"I'm sorry. Family gathering that night. Thanks again," she said and quickly rose to leave. She walked outside to her car and got inside.

Starting the engine, she pulled out of the parking lot with a sigh of relief, distantly noticing that her steering wheel seemed to be pulling to one side and the car wobbled unevenly. She drove a little farther, but the thumpity-thump sensation worsened. Flat tire? She groaned. What a night. Yucky date and an inquisition awaited her from her mother at home.

Pulling to the side of the road, she got out and walked around the car, inspecting the tire. There it was. Passenger's side tire flat as a pancake. She immediately called her road service company on her cell phone and was assured someone would be there to help her soon.

If she weren't dressed in a skirt, she would change it herself, she thought, after several drivers had stopped to offer assistance.

Another two moments passed and a familiar luxury car slowed. A balding man with a comb-over poked his head out the window. "You need some help?"

Something about the man was vaguely familiar, but she couldn't quite put her finger on what it was. "No, I'm waiting for—"

Walker leaned across the older man. "Trina, it's me, Walker. What happened?"

"Just a flat tire," she said, still wondering who the other man was. "The auto service should be here to change it any minute. I would have changed it, but I'm not dressed for it."

"Trina?" the older man said. "Is this the lady you got preg—"

"Yes, Harry," Walker said, overriding the other man. "Hang on a minute. I can change it," he said and pulled to the side of the road in front of her.

Both men got out of the car and approached her.

Walker was dressed casually in jeans and a black T-shirt. She hadn't seen him dressed in anything except a suit. Except the time she'd seen him naked. She pushed that thought from her head. "You really don't need to do this. The car service should be here any second."

"A pretty girl like you shouldn't be standing out in the road when it's dark like this," the older man said.

"Trina Roberts, this is my uncle Harry," Walker said and gave her a look of apology. "He knows about Maddie."

"Oh," she said, surprised.

Harry extended his hand. "Walker's been letting me stay with him since he got back from France. I had a little surgery and wanted to keep it on the down-low," he added in a low voice.

Clueless, but wanting to be polite, Trina nodded. "I hope you're recovering well."

"As well as can be expected considering he's smoking cigars and drinking beer after bypass surgery," Walker muttered in a dark tone. "Pop your trunk and I'll get your spare tire."

"You don't really need to do this," she began, but stalled at the take-no-prisoners expression on Walker's face. "Okay," she murmured and used her remote to open her trunk. Walker got out the jack and the spare and began to remove the flat tire.

"You look mighty nice," Harry said and craned to look in the car. "No baby tonight."

"My mother's keeping her. I had a date."

"With who?" Walker asked as he put on the spare.

"Steve Fortune. It was a second date." Last date, she thought.

"He didn't walk you to your car?" Walker asked, tightening the bolts.

"I think he may have had a few too many beers," she said. "I decided not to hang around."

Walker glanced over his shoulder at her. "Did he get pushy?"

"Not really. I left before then."

"And he didn't walk you to your car?" Walker repeated in disgust and stood. "I'm gonna have to do a better job screening these guys."

"That's why I drive myself and meet them until I get to know them better."

He popped the trunk on his car and tossed her tire inside. "I'll take this in for you to get it patched."

"I really can do it. I've been taking care of my tires for a long time," she told him.

He held up his hand in a gesture to stop.

"You know, Trina, you're a lot prettier than I thought you would be," Harry said.

Trina blinked at Harry's double-edged compliment. She looked at Walker. "That's nice of you to say. Do you mind me asking why you thought I might have been unattractive?" she asked, giving Walker a hard look. "Ugly?" she couldn't resist adding.

"Well, no, I didn't say ugly," Harry backtracked, looking as if he sensed he'd stepped into a mess. "I just thought whoever Walker had knocked up from a one-night stand might not be easy on the eyes, if you know what I mean?"

Trina looked at Walker.

He rubbed his face and muttered, "Thanks, Uncle Harry. Just for the record, Trina, the only thing I've told Harry about your appearance is that you're pretty. He has drawn his own conclusions."

"Well, what was I supposed to think? When you found out you might be a father, you acted like you were going to a funeral. And you sure as hell didn't act like you wanted to marry her."

"You have no room to talk, old man. You said you gave yourself the gift of a vasectomy when you turned twenty-one, and half the reason you're staying at my place is because you're hiding from a woman who wants to marry you."

"She just wants my money," Harry said.

Recognition hit Trina. "You're Harry the Happy Mobile Home Seller."

Harry beamed and puffed out his chest. "You must recognize me from my television commercials."

"Only viewed on late-night television," Walker said.

"Walker here got me a deal. You wouldn't think a commercial that aired after midnight would do a damn bit of good, but my business has gone up twenty-three percent since I started doing those commercials."

"I used to see them when Maddie wasn't sleeping through the night," Trina said, smiling at the memory of the over-the-top commercials that had featured Harry and the mobile homes. "They really break up the monotony of middle-of-the-night programming."

"Maddie," Harry echoed. "I hear she has red hair. I'd like to see her sometime."

"We could arrange that," Trina said, sensing that Harry had a good heart.

Harry turned to Walker. "You know, you could do a lot worse than her."

A moment of silence hung between the three of them. Walker looked at her with a strange expression on his face that made something inside her hurt.

"I didn't want to marry him, either."

Harry looked at her in disbelief. "Why not? He's a good guy. Makes good money. Drives a nice car. He's educated and doesn't get drunk too often. As far as I can see, he oughta get drunk more often."

"Considering that's how Trina got pregnant," Walker interjected.

"Walker also doesn't want children," Trina said. "Plus he was engaged to Brooke Tarantino, a beautiful heiress. Who wants to follow that act? Plus he can be a real workaholic."

"Whoa," Walker said. "I'm not a workaholic."

"Yes, you are," Trina said. "And that's okay with me because I'm not counting on you to be my husband or Maddie's father."

"Body blow," Harry said to Walker. "That's a new one. She didn't want to marry you."

Walker ground his teeth. "And that's good, Uncle Harry, because Gordon men are rotten husbands and even worse fathers."

Harry paused then nodded. "Yep. Can't disagree on that one."

"We'll follow you home," Walker said, opening her car door for her.

"Why?"

"Because you only have one spare tire and I don't want anything happening to you."

She smiled. "Terrified you might have to do the father thing if I should croak?"

Walker froze. "You've got a contingency plan, don't you?"

"If you mean, do I have a will and trust already set up for Maddie? Yes. I did that before she was born."

"So who is supposed to take over for you?" he asked.

"I've got it covered. You don't need to worry about it," she said and started her engine.

She could tell he didn't like her answer and she suspected he would ask her again. Maybe she would tell him. Maybe she wouldn't. Walker did terrible things to her ego and at the moment she was peeved enough to cause him some frustration, no matter how small. Okay, so it wasn't mature, but even Trina needed a little break from taking the high road all the time.

Driving home, she spotted Walker's car in her rearview mirror throughout the drive. As she pulled onto her driveway, she flashed her lights in a good-bye. She drove into her garage and mentally prepared herself for her mother's grilling. She stepped out of her car and opened the door that led to her kitchen, expecting to hear her mother's voice.

She heard the doorbell ring instead. Seconds later, she heard her mother's voice. "Hello? Who's there?"

Trina joined her mother in the foyer.

"There are two men out there," her mother whispered.

Trina glanced through the peephole and swallowed a groan. Walker and his uncle Harry. "Uh, that's someone I work with. I got a flat tire on the way home and he changed it for me."

"You got a flat tire? That's dangerous," her mother said.

"That's why I have an auto service."

"What happened on your date?"

The doorbell rang. "I think we need to answer the door."

Trina opened the door and started talking before they could say a word. "Walker, Harry, this is my mother, Aubrey Roberts. She's taking care of Maddie tonight."

"It's nice to meet you, Mrs. Roberts," Walker said, extending his hand.

"And you," her mother said.

"I'm happy to meet you," Harry interjected. "I was hoping I could see the baby if she's not asleep."

"Actually I've already put her to bed," Aubrey said, her mouth thinning in disapproval.

Trina threw Walker a questioning look.

Walker rolled his eyes. "You know, he just had surgery. He said he wanted to see my—uh—"

Her heart stopped. Her mother didn't know who was Maddie's father. Her alarm must've shown on her face.

"Uh, a baby. He said it would have a healing effect on him."

"A healing effect," Trina echoed.

"I can understand that. Babies have a magical effect on people," Aubrey said.

Trina looked at her mother as if she'd grown a

third head. Or a fourth. She gave her head a tiny shake to clear it. "Maddie's in bed, right?" she asked her mother.

Aubrey nodded. "I fed her, bathed her, read six books to her and put her to bed."

"Okay. Would you like to look at her in her crib? She's asleep"

"Sure," Harry said, tugging at his comb-over.

"Okay," Trina said. "The nursery's upstairs. Just remember to be quiet, please."

"I can do that," Harry said.

She kicked off her shoes and led the way upstairs. Opening the door, she stepped inside and moved to Maddie's crib, where her baby girl lay sprawled on her back, relaxed in sleep with her lips pursed like a rosebud. The moonlight from the window illuminated her little body, reflecting off her carrot-red hair.

"She's got the Gordon hair," Harry said in a low voice.

"What do you mean?" Trina whispered.

"The Gordon kids have red hair when they're little. Turns blond or brown when they grow up. Walker's sister's hair looked just like that."

Trina felt an odd awareness of family and heredity. She looked at Maddie and it hit her hard that her baby was more than hers. Even though Walker didn't want her, Maddie was his, too.

"Bet she's a pistol," Harry said.

Trina smiled and nodded. "She is, but she's a sweetie, too."

"If it wouldn't be too much trouble, I'd like to see her when she's awake sometime."

She looked at Harry and the longing in his eyes got to her. "I think that could be arranged."

He gave her a slow smile. "You're a great girl. Keeper material," he said with a wink.

She laughed at his obvious flirting. "Gotta catch me first. We should go," she said and turned around to find Walker in the doorway watching them. Her heart jumped in her chest, but she reined in her reaction and walked toward the door.

"Careful with Harry," Walker muttered. "He'll have you hook, line and sinker if you're not careful."

"I like him," she said. "He's nice."

"And it doesn't hurt that he already has a crush on you."

She smiled. "In his own way, he's affirming. You're just jealous because you can't wrap women around your finger the way he does."

"Are you saying I need to take lessons?" Walker asked.

# CHAPTER TWELVE

*I DON'T UNDERSTAND why you don't just go ahead and marry her. She's a pretty girl and nice. Plus she had your baby. What else do you need?*

*Are you of all people conveniently forgetting the Gordon curse?*

*Oh,* was all Uncle Harry had said on their drive back from Trina's house.

"Yeah, oh," Walker was still muttering to himself as he stared at the ceiling. Images of Trina and Maddie streamed through his mind like nonstop video. It didn't matter if he closed his eyes or kept them open. The images continued.

Sighing, he closed his eyes and tried to think about the Braves. That lasted four seconds before an image of Trina smiling floated along. Walker began to count sheep, backwards. Down by a thousand, he finally drifted off...

The woman had come-get-me eyes and a mouth that made his blood pool in his crotch. She opened her puffy lips before he rubbed his mouth over hers and tasted her with his tongue.

A little noise of invitation vibrated from her, kicking up his body temperature. He slid his hand down her bare back. She was naked, thank goodness, and he lingered over the slightly rounded curve of her ass and squeezed.

She wiggled against him and he realized he was naked, too. And hard. Her small breasts brushed his chest, and he felt the urge to get inside her rise to another level.

Something hazy in his mind told him he'd just had her and he wanted to take his time. Try telling his lower body that. He lifted one of his hands to her breast and rubbed his thumb over her nipple, liking the quick, stiff response.

Feeling as if he were eating her mouth, he lowered his hand between her legs and found her wet and swollen. She made another sexy little sound that affected him like the pure grade moonshine one of his cousins had given him one time.

Breaking away from her wicked, addicting lips, he slid down to flick his tongue over first one nipple then the other. Then he dove lower with open-mouth kisses on her belly. And lower still, he tugged on her sweet spot while she bloomed in his mouth. Her moans moved over him like an intimate touch and he grew harder and harder. Her erotic response made him sweat.

When her knees buckled and she let out a sexy sound of release, he caught her against him and backed onto the sofa. Her legs trembling, he spread her thighs and lowered her onto him, inch by inch, evoking a groan with every movement that sent him deeper into her.

He was so hot he didn't know who was groaning—her or him. He drew her mouth back to his. "You're amazing," he muttered as he kissed her. "Can't get enough of you…"

She began to move, sliding up and down his shaft. Vaguely, he knew he'd gone over the edge before. He should have been done, but she felt so good, pumping him. Soft, tight, wet and so sexy. So sweet. He wanted to take care of her again, but he felt himself climb higher again. Every intimate squeeze and stroke stole his sanity and breath. The sight of her breasts inches from his mouth drove him nuts.

Scooping his hands around her bottom, he guided her over him as he drew one of her nipples into his mouth. The dual sensations nearly pushed him into pure sexual delirium. But it was her voice, her soft, breathy, husky moans that kicked him into the stratosphere.

His climax rushed through him, echoing into her.

Walker woke up in a sweat. It took less than a second to realize he was so hard he would have a tough time walking. One second later, he remembered something about Trina Roberts.

She was a moaner.

WALKER'S DREAM about Trina haunted him. The images called up memories that had been lost due to alcohol and time. As more memories returned, he recalled the sound of her breath as she'd climaxed, the intimate sensation of skin against skin as he lay nude with her. He remembered how soft and sweet she'd felt in his arms. All the remembering made him feel weird as hell.

Battling the memories three days in a row, he arrived home to a sight guaranteed to blast any sexual thoughts from his brain. Uncle Harry, BJ and Danielle, the last looking as if she were going to pop triplets any minute.

"Hey, Walker," BJ said with too much enthusiasm. "Uncle Harry said you wouldn't mind if Danielle and I stayed here for a couple days until we find a place to live."

Walker shot Harry a questioning look and Harry shrugged his shoulders.

BJ continued, "I don't want Danielle to get worn out from too many moves. Danielle, *this* is my brother, Walker, the smartest man alive."

Danielle extended her hand and smiled. "It's wonderful to meet you. BJ never stops talking about you."

"Thank you," Walker said, shaking her hand. "BJ has told me about you, too. Do you need to sit down? You look further along than I thought you would be."

She laughed, her eyes crinkling as she smiled. "It's part illusion. I'm short, so the watermelon looks even bigger. I've got about five more weeks."

"And you're sure you're only having one baby?" he couldn't help but ask.

"Only one," she said, laughing again. "I can show you the ultrasound picture if you want proof. It's so nice of you to give BJ a chance. We really want to make a fresh start for us and the baby. And we won't stay here long," she added. "I promise."

"It's nice to meet you," Walker said. She seemed nice, he thought. Just so young with long brown hair that reminded him of a high school kid and so vulnerable with that *watermelon*. He raked his hand through his hair.

"And I plan to work, too," she added. "I'm just not sure who will hire me looking like this, but if you know of anyone, please tell me."

BJ gave his Budweiser cap a tug. "I'm ready to start work tomorrow."

"Good." Walker forced the word from his mouth. The whole situation made him feel as if someone had thrown acid on his nerve endings. He had to get out of here. "Good. Hey, uh, Harry, how about you order some pizza. I just stopped by to change shirts before I head out to meet a, uh—colleague." He pulled fifty dollars from his pocket. "Pizza's on me."

Walker went upstairs to change his shirt, his mind going a million miles a minute. Soon enough, Danielle was going to pop out a little Gordon, and Walker knew BJ wasn't ready for a full-time job let alone being a husband or a father. The prospect of disaster loomed, making his stomach knot. How in the world could he fix this situation? He couldn't even fix his own with Trina. At least he and Trina weren't broke, though. BJ's naiveté and financial need were bad enough, but add in the terrible Gordon fathering genes and… Walker began to sweat. He had to get out of the house. He felt as if he were suffocating.

Returning downstairs, he waved to BJ and Danielle as he headed for the foyer. Uncle Harry stopped him at the door. "You're leaving them with me?" he asked.

"You let them in," Walker whispered. "You invited them to stay here."

"And you would have been able to turn a woman who looked like that out on the street?" Harry demanded.

"No," Walker admitted. "But I got to get my head

on straight about this. BJ doesn't have a clue what
he's gotten himself into, and I'm not sure Danielle
does, either. I didn't ask for this, but I feel responsible as hell for some reason, so I need to make a plan
and I can't do it here."

"You're going to Charley's, aren't you?" Harry
asked, naming a local sports bar. "Let me go with you."

"No," Walker said. "You have to be the host. I'll
be back later."

Walker did go to Charley's, drank a beer and
stared at the game for forty-five minutes. He mentally
went through half a dozen scenarios for BJ and
Danielle and none of them were good.

Too restless to continue sitting at the bar, but
nowhere near ready to return home, he drove around
for a while. He wasn't sure he made a conscious
decision, but his car ended up at Trina's town house.
He sat in front with the engine running for several
moments, debating whether to stop or leave.

He finally put the car in Park, cut the engine and
walked to her front door. Glancing at his watch, he hesitated before he rang the doorbell. Was Maddie asleep?

He tapped gently on the door and a moment later,
Trina appeared with Maddie wrapped in a bath towel,
her carrot hair sticking straight out and her baby skin
glowing. He caught a whiff of baby powder and took
another sniff.

"I know," Trina said. "She smells good enough to eat. What's up?"

He stared at her for a long moment and shrugged.

"If you can't find the words, it must be a doozy." She opened the door wider. "Come on in. Walk with me while I get her ready for bed."

He followed her upstairs where she put a diaper on Maddie while Maddie craned to look at him.

"Curious little booger, aren't you? You remember Walker," Trina said. "He's the one who gave you half a box of animal cookies." She pulled a gown over Maddie's head and tugged her little arms through the sleeves. Maddie popped her thumb into her mouth

"Uh-oh," Trina said. "She's still afraid of you."

"I have to bribe her with animal cookies," Walker said. "She obviously senses the rotten father gene."

"She senses your discomfort," Trina said, scooping up Maddie. "Don't you, carrot cake?" She rubbed her finger under Maddie's chin and Maddie pulled her thumb out of her mouth and giggled. Trina laughed and tickled the baby again. "Who needs animal cookies when I can eat you?" she said and buried her mouth in Maddie's neck.

The sound of Maddie's peals of laughter tugged at him. He couldn't help smiling. Hell, he'd have to be dead not to smile. At the same time, though, it made him feel lower than a worm.

Trina laughed, then looked at him and her smile faded. "If you don't tell me what's bothering you, I can't help."

"I'm not sure you can help anyway."

"Then why did you come here?" she asked, her question a direct hit.

"My car came here," he said, shooting her an ironic grin.

She lifted her eyebrows. "All on its own? You didn't touch the steering wheel?"

"I'm sure I helped," he said and shrugged. "I wanted to be with you."

She nodded. "Okay, then spill it. Did you get someone else pregnant? Are you getting married?"

"No and no. My brother showed up at my house."

"The one that's pregnant," she ventured.

"The one who got a woman pregnant."

"And he wants to work for you."

"And my uncle invited him and his pregnant girl-friend to stay at my house until they found a place of their own."

She cringed. "Oh, wow."

"Oh, yeah."

"I bet having both of them in your house makes you feel like you got bit on your insides by a million mosquitoes."

"Hadn't thought of that exact analogy, but it

works. Worst part is I still don't know what job I can give my brother."

"He could probably answer the phone," she said, gently swaying to keep Maddie happy. Maddie rested her face against Trina's arm.

"I don't know," Walker said, afraid of how his brother might greet potential clients. What if he tried to sell them a time-share?

She sighed. "Well, everyone has skills. Everyone," she repeated and glanced at Maddie. "Somebody's getting sleepy. Go downstairs," she said. "There's a pad of paper and a pen on the kitchen counter. Make a list of your brother's skills, talents and potential abilities. I'll be down in five minutes. Shoo," she said when he didn't move.

Walker left the room and paused outside the door while Trina pushed it partway closed. She turned out the light and soon after he heard the slight squeak of the rocking chair. She spoke in a hushed, soothing tone. He couldn't hear the words, but the tone was pure magic. He could imagine Maddie's eyelids drooping and her breaths growing even.

He felt his own heart rate settle down. Odd, he thought, and went downstairs to make the list.

Moments later, she joined him on the sofa and looked at the one item on his list.

"Can draw?" she said. "Your brother can draw?"

"Yeah. We moved a lot," he said, still leaning forward, drumming his pen against the notepad. "He would draw pictures when we were in the car."

"Okay," she said and took the pad of paper from him. She tucked her feet beneath her. "Can he drive?"

"Yeah," Walker said, leaning against the back of the couch. "He may even have a clean record."

"That's good," she said. "Speaks English. Any other languages?"

"Not to my knowledge and he definitely doesn't speak the Queen's English."

"Neither do you or I," she said. "He can read?"

Walker nodded.

"And write? Do basic math?"

"Yes to both."

"Computer skills?"

"Not sure. I know he can use the Internet," he said, remembering the scam BJ had gotten involved in years ago.

"It sounds like he's probably very teachable," Trina said. "So I think you should have your office manager do a skills inventory with him, instruct him on company policy, dress code, and hire him as an assistant. You can tell your office manager what salary he'll get. Or you can ask your office manager to suggest an appropriate salary. And tell your office manager that your brother is to do whatever she tells BJ to do."

Walker leaned back and narrowed his eyes. "You're basically saying I should pawn him off on my office manager."

"Is he ready to work with you?"

Walker paused, then shook his head. "No, but that's what he wants."

"Most of us have to work for what we want. Most of us don't get it the second we want it."

"No instant gratification," he said, and he couldn't stop his mind from wandering to the wicked dream he'd had about her. That night he'd spent with her had given gratification new meaning.

"Right," she said. "BJ may catch on more quickly than you expect."

Walker rubbed his face, trying not to doubt the possibility.

"It's often harder to try to train a member of your own family. You can't detach yourself from the little things that go wrong. But someone else can put it in perspective. Look at it this way. BJ has got to be better than the worst temp your office manager has had."

"I hadn't thought of it that way." He stretched his arm along the top of the sofa toward her. "How'd you get so smart?"

She smiled. "Care to guess how many Bellagios have spent some time in the PR department? Alfredo can be a tough bird. He gives members of his family a shot, but if they can't cut it, then they get to stay assistant forever or they get tired of the lack of prestige and leave."

"I have my own opinion, but why do you think you've been successful at Bellagio?"

"Inside the company, I serve as a diffuser. I'm not volatile. Outside the company, I have a few connections that of course lead to other connections. I put the product in front of influential people." She pushed her hair behind her ear. "You've made me curious. What are your thoughts?"

"You're right about the diffusion angle, but I think you underestimate how smart they know you are. You're excellent at exploiting opportunities for exposure."

"I prefer the term maximize," she corrected, but her tone was playful...sexy.

Her long bangs fell from behind her ear and he reached up to push it back.

"Gotta admit, I'm curious," Walker said.

Trina bit her tongue, refusing to ask him for more information. It would only lead to trouble. Pleasurable trouble, but still trouble.

"I wonder what it would be like to kiss you when I'm not smashed," he said, leaning closer.

"Terrible," she said, wondering where all the oxygen in the room had gone. She took a deep breath and caught some of his aftershave. The scent made her want to bury her head in his throat.

He gave a half grin. "Terrible?" he echoed.

She nodded. "Yes. Very terrible."

"Maybe we should find out so we don't wonder."

"This part of *we* isn't wondering," she lied.

"Are you afraid to kiss me?"

Oh, no. A dare. Trina closed her eyes. She fought back the urge to push him back on the sofa and lay one on him that would make his head spin into next week. She opened her eyes and forced a smile. "I'm not afraid. I'm just cautious and sensible. And not curious."

"Then I'll let you be cautious and sensible while I'm curious, okay?" he said and lowered his head.

She could have pushed him away, slapped him, kicked him, but she wanted to smell his aftershave for just another second. Or two.

He rubbed his mouth against hers, dragging his lips from side to side, pressing with gentle curiosity. His mouth felt good.

Trina sighed. Okay, so maybe she was a little curious. She relaxed a smidge and he continued to test her lips, tugging at her lower lip with both of his.

He slid his tongue over the seam, just dipping inside before he rubbed his mouth over hers again.

She instinctively tilted her head to feel more of his

mouth. He slid his tongue past her lips again and she felt the sensation of the kiss zing through her bloodstream. The heat of it traveled down her throat to her chest, to her breasts. Her nipples began to tingle and she fought the urge to rub against him, but she couldn't hold back the involuntary sound that bubbled from the back of her throat.

Walker slipped his hand behind her head to cradle her neck and deepened the kiss. Another little sound vibrated from inside her.

Walker pulled back just enough to catch a breath. "So, I didn't dream it after all," he muttered.

She didn't want him to stop massaging the back of her head, unless he moved his hand somewhere else on her body…anywhere else on her body.

"Oh, yeah," he murmured and took her mouth again.

Trina felt her body temperature spike as they tangled in a kiss that seemed to hum *sex, sex, sex....*

"I can't believe it took me this long to remember," he said.

"Remember what?" she asked, opening her mouth against his.

"Oh, God, the noises you make. The moans," he said.

"What moans?"

He laughed and the sexy sound gave her goose bumps. "Those sounds you make when I kiss you."

She felt a sliver of self-consciousness. "I didn't know you could hear them," she said, pulling back.

He laughed, still massaging the back of her head. "Honey, you could provide the audio for an award-winning porn movie."

He was making fun of her, she realized and felt the burn of humiliation. "That's not very nice," she said and tried to stand. His hand tangled in her hair, causing a stinging pain that brought tears to her eyes. "Ouch!"

"For Pete's sake, let me get my hand out of your hair." He untangled his fingers and frowned. "What's your problem?"

"I don't like being compared to a porn actress."

"You're taking it the wrong way. It was a compliment. It's every guy's fantasy to have a woman that moans or screams. Or both."

"It's also every guy's fantasy to have sex with twin cheerleaders," she retorted.

"That's different," he said. "You have to believe me. You make these noises when we're kissing like I taste better than ice cream." He raked his hand through his hair and blew a stream of air from his lips as if he were a little overheated, too.

Trina took a second look at him. He did look a little worked up. His eyes had a hungry look. She lowered her gaze to his pelvis and her suspicion was confirmed. Aroused.

Her embarrassment easing a half degree, she folded her arms over her chest. "It might be easier to take that as a compliment if we hadn't had a one-night stand."

"Damn shame I was so drunk. I wish I could remember more."

"You mean remember that it all started with Brooke leaving you at the altar?"

He leaned back, his legs still spread open, appearing as if he didn't mind her seeing the obvious ridge of his arousal. "And the next thing you want to remind me is that it was pity sex," he said.

"There's that," she said and knew she was about to deliver the verbal equivalent of icy water. "And the fact that that wild drunken evening produced your baby daughter."

He shot her a dark look and stood. "Nice shot, Trina. But I won't forget that you're a moaner, and if you're honest, you won't forget that I'm the one who can make you moan." He snagged her hand, taking her by surprise, then lifted her hand to brush a kiss over her wrist. "Thanks for solving my problem with my brother. Thanks for the moans. G'night."

Trina frowned as she watched him swagger out of the den, down the hallway and out her front door. *What was that all about? Why was he acting like this? As if he wanted some kind of relationship, sexual relationship, with her?*

Trina bit her lip. She wasn't his type, not even before she'd had Maddie, and she sure as heck wasn't now. Sure she'd been cool, confident and in control before she'd had Maddie, but she'd never possessed a tenth of Brooke Tarantino's flash and glamour. She never would.

And she didn't care about that, especially now with Maddie. She might have been good enough for pity sex for Walker, but not for more than a night.

And that was fine with her. She narrowed her eyes. He'd deliberately egged her on, daring her. She felt a twist in her stomach. He made her wish she could push back with the same ease he'd tried to seduce her. Some small, very bad part of her wanted to bother him as much as he'd bothered her. Just once, she'd like to have the power to wreck his equilibrium and his sleep. She'd like to get him so worked up he could barely think, let alone speak.

Trina forced herself to take a mind-clearing breath. Not likely.

## CHAPTER THIRTEEN

THREE DAYS LATER, Trina completed plans for a party hosted by Bellagio at the national shoe convention. She kept eyeing the clock because Walker had said he wanted to meet with her, about business, he'd emphasized, at the end of the day.

Walker strode through the door just after four-thirty. "Sorry this is so late. I spent the afternoon upstairs with marketing. They're getting nervous about the product, since Sal has decided not to return full-time. Jenny's in demand."

"I know," Trina said. "You wouldn't believe how many requests for her appearance we get. And what she really wants to do is lock herself in a room and draw."

"Let's do some brainstorming," he said.

"I'd like to be in on this," Dora said, giving Walker a covetous look.

"It will be work," Trina warned.

"I know," Dora said with a huffy sound in her voice.

Trina said. "Okay, I need to grab Maddie. I'll just bring her back here."

"During our meeting?" Dora asked in horror.

"It's called multitasking. I'll load her up on Cheerios. Back in a few," she said, wondering if Dora would have Walker's clothes off by the time she returned.

Not her worry, she told herself as she walked toward the nursery. "Go for it, Dora," she muttered under her breath. Maybe if someone else took care of Walker's sexual needs, Trina wouldn't feel so aware of him as a man, a very hot man.

Scowling at herself, she pushed the thought from her mind and picked up Maddie, who didn't need an immediate diaper change and appeared to be in a good mood.

Returning to the office, she found Walker talking on his cell phone and Dora looking at him in disgust.

Walker gave Trina a quick nod. "I'll check back with you tomorrow. Thanks," he said. "New account," he explained and glanced at Maddie for several seconds.

Seeming to tear his gaze away, he looked at Trina. "Any ideas?"

"They need to hire more designers," Trina said, sitting down and digging a bag of Cheerios out of one of her desk drawers. She spread a blanket on the

floor beside her, set Maddie down and put some
Cheerios on a napkin. "But that's not going to take
care of things immediately. Jenny has been great for
us, but she's got her hands full and marketing wants
to make a big move into women's active shoes.
Totally new market for us."

"We should get some celebrities to wear our
shoes," Dora said.

"Good point," Trina said, smiling at Maddie as
she picked up one Cheerio at a time and ate it. "I
have a list of celebrities and their shoe sizes. We can
send out samples. Donate to charity. The challenge
is making these shoes seem more glamorous to
wear. Tennis shoes can be cute and fun, but not that
glamorous."

"We're working on that with the ad campaign,"
Walker said.

"We're targeting the working woman at the end of
the day. It's more about comfort than spiked heels."

"Yeah, hausfrau types and mothers like you,"
Dora added, looking at Walker for approval.

He shot her a quick quizzical glance. "I don't
think PR or anyone else should be using the term
hausfrau," he said.

"We'll pitch articles with women's magazines.
Tied in with a sweepstakes," Trina said. "We could

pair the shoes with something relaxing like a trip to a spa."

"Good," Walker said, nodding his head and holding her gaze.

Trina felt a zinging sensation at the look in his eyes.

Dora cleared her throat and Trina blinked, pulling her gaze away from Walker. "Okay, let's add—"

Her phone rang and she checked her watch. "After five. Unusual. Just a second," she said and picked it up. "Trina Roberts."

"Miss Roberts, we have someone here by the name of BJ Gordon. He said he wants to see Walker Gordon."

Surprise shot through her. "Oh, BJ Gordon," she echoed and caught Walker's expression of bewilderment. "Sure, send him on up." She hung up the phone.

"BJ?" he said. "What does he want? He left for an appointment with Danielle."

"Who's BJ? Who's Danielle?" Dora asked.

"My brother and his, uh, fiancée," Walker said, rising. "I'll—"

"Walker, my man!" said a young man wearing slightly rumpled khaki slacks and a pullover. Trina immediately glimpsed his resemblance to Walker along with the differences. BJ was heavier, his hair lighter with more curl and his eyes glinted with good humor. He didn't appear to have Walker's edge. Beside him stood a very pregnant, very young woman with long brown hair. "We have some good news and we were in the area, so I thought I'd stop by to see you."

Maddie began to nod her head. She picked up a Cheerio and tried to stick it up her nose. "Oops," Trina murmured, scooping up the cereal. "I guess that game is over." She picked up Maddie and stood, recognizing the first sign of dangerous boredom.

"Oops," BJ said. "Did I interrupt something? I thought you would be finished."

Walker's face clouded with exasperation.

"We were just wrapping up," Trina said, saving Walker from responding.

"BJ and Danielle, this is Trina Roberts, senior Public Relations rep for Bellagio. Her assistant, Dora Forentino."

"Technically not Trina's assistant," Dora corrected. "I'm the departmental assistant."

Walker exchanged a commiserating glance with Trina, and she couldn't help smiling.

"Sorry to interrupt," BJ said. "But we're really excited. The doctor said Danielle's cervix is thinning out and she's dilated a centimeter."

"TMI," Dora said, covering her ears. "I like to pretend that the stork delivers the baby."

"That's great news," Trina interjected. "You're doing some of the work before labor, so maybe that will make your labor easier."

"That's what I'm hoping," Danielle said and glanced at Maddie. "Is she yours? She's adorable."

"Thanks. Yes, her name is Maddie."

"Gotta love that carrot hair," BJ said. "Runs in our family, too."

Trina froze, looking at Walker, who also seemed to freeze. He recovered quickly. "Yeah, so congratulations on your good doctor visit."

"That's not all," Danielle said. "We've found a place to live."

Walker dropped his jaw, his face revealing sheer relief. "That's terrific. Where is it?"

"It's a little house in an older neighborhood. The only downside is we can't move in for two more weeks."

Walker's face froze again. "Two weeks," Walker echoed.

"Yeah, so you don't mind if we stay just two more weeks, do you?" BJ asked.

Trina looked at Walker with his rock-hard jaw. She'd seen him slice a competitor to ribbons in a fair fight. She knew he could be ruthless, but refusing his brother would be the equivalent to stomping on a puppy. A puppy with the potential of making a big mess, she thought, glancing at Danielle.

"Two weeks longer won't be a problem," Walker said in a reassuring voice.

"Thanks. I'll make it up to you," BJ said. "You wait and see."

Walker nodded. "Just take care of your family and that will be good enough for me."

BJ turned solemn. "Yeah, I'll do that."

"I can't believe that's Walker's brother," Dora whispered. "They're like night and day."

"Not unusual for siblings," Trina murmured.

"Yeah, but Walker is so—"

"I guess we should go. Danielle said she's hungry. Eating for two, you know," BJ said.

"Hot," Dora whispered. "And his brother is goofy."

Trina's irritation shot over the edge. "Shut up, Dora. Haven't you heard that it's classy to be kind instead of snarky?"

The room turned abruptly silent. BJ and Danielle shot her wary glances and Walker and Dora looked at her in surprise.

Trina cleared her throat and pushed her lips into a smile. "It's time for me to scoot, too. I'm sure Maddie needs a diaper change by now. It was so nice meeting you, BJ and Danielle. Good luck with your delivery."

The younger couple smiled. "Thank you," Danielle said. "I won't be able to get a job until after the baby is born, so if you need a babysitter, please give me a call. I have a lot of experience. Lots of young cousins," she said.

"Great idea," BJ said. "You can call Walker."

Trina felt Walker's gaze on her, but didn't look at him. Instead she nodded and gathered her purse and stuffed the blanket into Maddie's bag. "I may do that. Thank you for the offer."

"Please do," Danielle said. "Pleasure to meet you, Dora."

"Oh, and you, too," Dora managed.

"G'night," BJ said. "See you later, Walker."

Walker nodded. "I should walk you to your car," he said to Trina.

"What about me?" Dora asked.

Trina stared at the PR assistant in surprise. Dora looked miffed. "You can walk Dora to her car," she said, swallowing a chuckle. "I can find the way to my car with no problem."

"I needed to discuss one other item of business with you," he said. "But I can walk you to your car first if you like, Dora," he said in a lethally cool voice. "Are you ready to go now?"

Dora looked uncertain, then nodded. "Sure. I can grab my purse on the way out."

While Trina watched the two of them leave, she suspected Walker would make it clear to Dora that he wasn't interested and she might as well give it up, all the while exhibiting the most gentlemanly manners on earth. She couldn't muster any pity for

Dora. The woman's lack of tact and kindness set Trina's teeth on edge.

"Dora needs a personality makeover," Trina whispered to Maddie.

Maddie responded by grabbing a handful of her momma's hair as Trina left the office and headed for her car. Part of her wouldn't mind if Walker changed his mind and gave Dora what she was asking for. Who knew? Maybe Dora would be nicer if she got laid. She wouldn't think about how that theory could very well apply to herself. Fastening Maddie into her infant seat, she tossed her purse and Maddie's bag in the back seat and rounded the car to the driver's side.

"Helluva afternoon," Walker muttered from behind her. "I don't suppose you have any bourbon at your house,"

"Sorry. Fresh out. All I've got is white wine and animal crackers."

He shook his head and stuffed his hands into his pockets.

"You really don't want to go home, do you?" she asked.

"You think they would notice if I stayed at a hotel for the next two weeks?" he ventured.

"You're a nicer guy than I thought."

He sighed. "I hate to disappoint him. He reminds me of—"

"A puppy," she interjected.

"Yeah.

She wanted to hug him, which was just plain stupid. Even though he was over six feet tall with muscles in all the right places and could take care of himself in an alley or the boardroom, she liked that he had a soft spot for his brother. She liked it a lot.

Reining in the feelings, she stepped back. "You're tough. You can handle it. Those two weeks will fly by."

"Kinda like labor," he said with dark humor.

She laughed. "Everybody has to take their turn."

THE BEAUTIFUL METHODIST CHURCH was packed for the nuptials of Marc Waterson and Jenny Prillaman. Trina's mother had insisted on keeping carrot cake overnight. Although Trina was a little nervous about her first night away from Maddie, she decided to make the best of it.

She'd ordered another dress from Bluefly.com since she had so little time for shopping these days. Wearing the requisite Bellagio shoes and bag, with her hair freshly blown out, she allowed a groomsman dressed in a tux with tails to escort her to a seat on the bride's side of the church.

The sanctuary bloomed with flowers, each pew adorned with a pink-and-white arrangement with ribbons. A harpist played classical music. The church was decorated so beautifully it could have been a movie set.

She wondered how much medication Jenny needed at this point.

"Mind if I sit here?" Walker asked.

Trina glanced up and felt her stomach jump. Oh, he looked so good. "Not at all," she said and scooted over. "Anything to get out of the house?" she couldn't resist asking.

He shot her a sideways glance. "Anything," he agreed. "The calendar may say my brother has only been living with me for six days, but I'm sure it's six years."

"Yes," she said. "Sounds a lot like labor."

"You look beautiful," he said.

"Thank you. See any strained green beans?" she asked, glancing at her shoulder.

"No, but I didn't notice them last time either."

"Good." She deliberately looked away from his flirting gaze. It made her feel odd. She forced herself to do some people watching, wondering if the guy Jenny had mentioned was here yet.

Hearing a rush of murmurs and whispers, she glanced toward the back of the sanctuary and what she saw whacked her like a two by four. Her brain just stopped as Brooke Tarantino, long and lean with legs up to her shoulders, walked down the aisle with a groomsman.

Her hair currently blond, Walker's ex wore a body-hugging dress that Trina suspected she hadn't bought online and heels designed by Jenny. A pair of dark sunglasses perched on her nose.

Trina bit her lip, but didn't look at Walker, although she suspected she was in the minority. Gawk at Brooke, then gawk at Walker.

"You okay?" she asked in a low voice without turning her head.

"Fine. I'm just glad I won't be the one waiting at the altar this time," he said in a dry tone.

She couldn't help smiling and she gave in to the urge to look at him. Then she gave in to the urge to surreptitiously scoot her hand closer to his and wrap her fingers around his.

He leaned closer and whispered in her ear, "Does this mean I get another night of pity sex?"

She dug her nails into his palm, then pulled back her hand. "Sure. You want another baby?"

He winced. "Low blow, Trina."

The organist saved her from responding. A little girl and boy were pulled down the aisle in a white cart pulled by one of the poor groomsmen. The little boy and girl threw rose petals onto the white aisle runner. Soon after, a very pregnant bridesmaid dressed in purple organza walked down the aisle while escorted by another groomsman.

"Good grief," Walker muttered. "Is it in the water?"

"I think that's Anna. She used to live next door to Jenny. She married one of Marc's cousins."

Then a blond bombshell of a woman strutted next to a gorgeous tall, dark and handsome man dressed in black except for his purple tie.

"Chad and Liz," Trina said. "Jenny told me he wanted to be a bridesmaid and this seemed the easiest way." She glanced at the front of the church. "But I wonder why Marc and the minister aren't up front. Odd, isn't it?"

"Damn smart as far as I'm concerned."

She shook her head then watched as Chad and Liz continued walking past the rest of the wedding party, up the steps to the elevated platform.

Liz smiled. "Welcome to all of you who know and love Marc and Jenny. Marc and Jenny would especially like to thank his mother Jean and Jenny's sister Victoria for planning this amazing event. Their talents and tastes are unsurpassed."

An uneasy suspicion grew in Trina's stomach. "You don't think she called it off, do you?"

"At least she didn't leave him at the altar on live TV."

"Marc and Jenny send their sincere regrets that they cannot be here today," Liz said.

A wave of murmurs passed through the crowd. "Oh, no," Trina said.

"And the reason they can't be here," Chad said, "is because Marc Waterson kidnapped his bride this morning and married her on the beach."

"We have a video of the short ceremony and would like to share it with you," Liz said, and Trina watched in amazement as the groomsmen set up a large screen on the elevated platform and the lights in the church were dimmed.

The screen lit with the images of Marc Waterson heartbreakingly handsome in a tux, Jenny Prillaman in a wedding gown, wisps of her hair escaping the updo. The ocean water reflected the sun, looking as if diamonds sparkled on top of the sea. A man in a suit held a Bible and a man and woman Trina didn't recognize stood on either side of Marc and Jenny.

"We're gathered here this gorgeous day to celebrate the marriage of Marc Waterson and Jenny Prillaman…"

Trina watched in awe as the couple exchanged vows, surprising herself by tearing up at the emotion and love she saw on their faces. Sniffing, she felt Walker's gaze on her, but she didn't look at him.

"I now pronounce you man and wife," the man said. "You may kiss your bride."

Marc picked Jenny up and swung her around, giving a glimpse of her bare feet as he lifted her. Carrying her in his arms, he gave her a long kiss. When he finally pulled back slightly, Jenny and Marc, beaming, waved at the camera. "Have fun at the party!" they said at the same time. Marc set her down and they walked away, hand in hand.

"They almost make it look possible, don't they?" Walker murmured.

She glanced at him and saw a flash of something different in his gaze as he looked at her. She couldn't quite name it, but it made her heart turn over and seemed to squeeze the oxygen from her lungs.

"Yeah, almost," she said.

The lights in the sanctuary brightened. "We have our instructions," Liz said.

"Party!" Chad said, and the organist broke out the Wagner.

"Are you going to the reception?" Walker asked as Trina stood.

"Might as well," she said. "My mother's taking care of Maddie."

"Sure you don't want a ride?"

"I have my own car," she said.

"See you there," he said, and she saw that dark, searching kind of look in his eyes again. Trina scooted into the crowd.

THE WEDDING PARTY, along with Jenny's family and Marc's mother, greeted guests as they arrived at the country club. With the band playing a combination of rock and rhythm and blues, the dance floor filled up in no time.

Trina waved at Liz. "Great performance with Chad," she said.

"The most challenging part was selling the idea to Marc's mother and Jenny's sister. They were both so hysterical I had to throw water on them."

"You're kidding," Trina said, unable to swallow a chuckle.

"No," Liz said. "Wrecked their hair and shocked them into listening to me. This probably worked out for the best. Those two wanted the attention more than Jenny and Marc did. I'm too practical to be romantic, but I think they may have the real deal."

Liz looked at Trina again and frowned. "I just remembered something Jenny asked me to do. She wanted me to introduce you to some guy." She snapped her fingers as if she were trying to remember the name. "David Somebody... David Owen," Liz said. "Do you know what he looks like?"

"No idea," Trina said. "It's no big deal. I don't need to meet him tonight."

Liz shook her head. "Nuh-uh. Jenny made me promise and she also said you might try to wiggle out

of it. No problem. I can find him. Don't go any-
where," she said and whirled away.

Trina immediately got nervous. Liz struck her as
one of the most testicularly enhanced women she'd
ever met. After all, she'd subdued Marc's mother and
Jenny's sister with a glass of water. Maybe this was
a good time for a trip to the powder room.

"Ladies and gentleman," Liz announced, using
one of the band microphones, "sorry to interrupt.
This won't take a second. David Owen, please see me
at the cake table ASAP." Liz kissed one of the band
members on the cheek and strutted away.

Trina felt another shot of panic. This was definitely time for the powder room. She glanced
toward the doorway and her gaze skidded to an
abrupt halt.

Brooke Tarantino stood next to Walker. With her
hand on his arm, she leaned into him, speaking
intently. He seemed to be listening just as intently.

"They look cozy, don't they?" said a man standing
next to her.

Something inside her turned upside down and she
felt a sudden stab of queasiness.

"You'd almost think she was begging his forgive-
ness. I wonder if he'll fall for it," the man added.

Trina tore her gaze from the sight of Brooke and

Walker to look at the man beside her. Chad Garcia, in tux and purple tie, in all his splendor.

"Chad, I'm Trina. I'm not sure you remember—"

"Of course I remember you. I saw you on QVC talking up our Jenny." He glanced toward the dance floor. "I'm ready to take a break from playing the gorgeous, wonderful host. You wanna dance?"

She blinked.

"I'm great on the dance floor. Come on," he said and took her hand.

"But—"

"C'mon. I know you came alone. I'll make you look great. After I get done with you every hetero guy in the place will be lined up to dance with you."

"I'm not sure—"

"I'll take care of that. The only problem is none of those straight guys can dance like me. Tough trade-off, but there it is," he said and pulled her into dance position.

The band began to play a song by Santana and it was all Trina could do to keep up with Chad. He made it fun, laughing when she misstepped, but covering for her. He pulled her close and shocked her by putting his lips on her neck.

"What are you doing?"

He laughed again. "Relax. It's part of the dance, and don't look now, but Walker's watching."

Trina gaped at him. "You're way too perceptive," she said, wondering how much he knew.

"Jenny says the same thing. My ability to read faces is a gift and curse. You looked like someone had kicked you." He smiled, revealing his gleaming white teeth. "You don't look that way anymore."

He spun her a few more times and the song finally ended.

"Trina," Liz called from several feet away. "Chad, are you causing trouble again? Jenny specifically told me to introduce her to David."

"So introduce her," he said.

Liz grabbed her hand and dragged Trina off the dance floor. "He's such a show-off."

"Nice show-off," Trina said.

"Yeah, too bad he's gay. Come with me. You're gonna like what Mama Liz has for you. David," Liz said, and a tall guy with blond hair and a curious, amused gaze glanced toward them.

He casually lifted his hand. "Right here."

"This is Trina Roberts. Jenny told me that you had to meet her."

His eyes crinkled in amusement. "I can see why I'd like to meet her, but why would she want to meet me?" he joked and extended his hand. "David Owen. Nice to meet you. Nice of Jenny to do me this favor."

His flattery oozed over some part of her ego that

she hadn't known had been wounded and she smiled in return. "It's nice to meet you, too."

"How about a drink after that dance? I sure wouldn't want to try to follow that's guy's dance ability."

She laughed. "A drink would be great. I had a tough time keeping up with him."

He lifted a glass of champagne from a waiter's tray and offered it to her. "You looked like you did pretty good to me."

"That's the thing. He knows how to make his partner look good, regardless of any rusty ability she may have," she said, ready to turn the attention away from herself. "How do you know Marc and Jenny?"

"I went to school with Marc. We were in the same fraternity."

"I bet you've got some wild stories."

"He's a married man now. My lips are sealed. Jenny told me about you, too."

"Oh, really.

He nodded. "She said she'd like us to meet, but I had to pass her test."

"And did you?"

"I guess."

"I'm a single mother," she blurted out.

"I know," he said. "I travel a lot, so I don't get much of an opportunity to meet a quality woman. Let's trade e-mail addresses and phone numbers. Okay?"

## CHAPTER FOURTEEN

"WALKER, I KNOW IT'S A LOT to ask," Brooke said. "But I'm really in a bad spot. My father is still angry with me and…"

Walker caught sight of Trina, alone for the first time, at the reception. He'd watched her dance with Chad and chat with some guy who looked interested in engaging her in more than conversation.

The prospect made his stomach burn. It didn't help that Brooke kept appearing at his side asking for his help. He saw Trina look his way and she met his gaze for a long moment that made something inside him feel like a cool stream was easing all his rough places. Then she looked to his left and away.

Brooke's voice continued in his left ear. "If you could just help me this one time—"

"I'll talk to you later," Walker said, cutting her off and heading for Trina.

Dora stepped directly in his path and smiled with

scary determination. "I'd love to steal you onto the dance floor."

"Not now, thanks," Walker said and continued around her. Waving a few times at people who called his name, he wove through the crowd and finally arrived in front of Trina.

"Hi," he said.

"Hi yourself," she said and smiled.

"You've been busy," he said.

She lifted her eyebrows. "So have you."

"Take me away," he dared her.

She paused, her expression torn. "I've already done that before."

"So let me take you away."

She met his gaze and he saw a shot of vulnerability deepen her dark eyes. "I don't want to do anything to make me feel like somebody's little mistake again."

Although she'd often joked about their night of pity sex, in that moment he could see that she carried some shame from it. Her shame stabbed at him.

"Okay. I can still take you away. It doesn't have to be for a wild night of—"

Trina's eyes grew round. "Brooke! It's great to see you. You look lovely."

Brooke looked at Trina for a long moment. "I know I've met you. You work for Bellagio and you did the QVC thing. Great job, by the way. I'm sorry I don't remember your name."

"Trina Roberts," Walker said. "She works in PR for Bellagio."

"Oh, nice to meet you again, Trina," Brooke said.

"Brooke has been talking to me this evening about wanting to work for Bellagio in some capacity," Walker said to Trina.

Trina blinked. "Really?"

Brooke gave an uneasy smile. "Yes, Daddy is still unhappy about what happened—" She glanced at Walker. "You know what I mean. And uh, I'm—" she lowered her voice "—having some cash-flow issues."

"You need a job," Trina said, disbelief in her voice.

"Yeah, I guess I do."

Trina was silent for a moment, then looked at Walker. "What about the new activewear line?"

"What about it?" he asked.

"Maybe Brooke could promote it," Trina said.

"You mean model?" Brooke said, lighting up.

"Not exactly," Trina said. "The position calls for more of a spokesperson or representative. We'll be promoting the new line in department stores, at women's trade shows. Maybe you could do that."

"I guess it's possible," Walker said, impressed that Trina had come up with the idea so quickly.

"What kind of shoes are they?" Brooke asked. "Are they Jenny's shoes?"

Trina shook her head. "Activewear."

Brooke stared at her for a long moment. "Tennis shoes? You want me to represent tennis shoes?"

"You'd need approval for marketing, but it might work," Walker said.

"But tennis shoes," Brooke repeated with a complete lack of enthusiasm.

"Do you want to think it over and get back to me next week?" Trina asked.

Brooke opened her mouth, then closed it, sighing. "Uh, yes, I'll get back to you." She glanced at Walker. "Good to see you doing so well."

"Thanks. Take care," he said and turned back to Trina as Brooke walked away. "You want to go somewhere else?"

"I'm not having sex with you," she said.

"Okay, I repeat. You ready to leave? We can go someplace else."

"What did you have in mind?"

"I'll figure it out," he said and grinned. "We both know it won't be my house."

She finally smiled. "Okay. I need to take my car home. I guess you can follow me."

FORTY-FIVE MINUTES LATER, Walker picked up a pint of the ice cream of Trina's choice, chocolate mocha, and drove her Mustang to a scenic little place he'd discovered a few years ago. He drove her car down a dirt road to an oversize pond partly surrounded by trees, bushes and honeysuckle.

"I still don't understand why you wanted to bring my car," she said, as he lowered the top to her Mustang convertible and she got a better look at the scenery. It was a clear night and the moonlight served as a spotlight on the pond.

"Okay, now I understand. This is nice. Whose property are we trespassing on?"

"Mine," he said and opened the carton of ice cream.

"Really?"

"You sound surprised," he said, giving her one of the plastic spoons. "First bite is yours."

She took the spoon in her hand, but was too busy still looking around to take a bite. "You just seem like the condo-with-every-imaginable-service kind of man."

"I am," he said. "And I have one of those. But I was born a redneck," he confessed.

She met his gaze, a slow smile forming on her lips. "And this fulfills your latent redneck needs?"

He chuckled. "I guess. I don't get out here very often and I haven't done anything about putting a house on it."

"Or a mobile home," Trina added.

"Harry has offered."

"So what do you do with it?"

"I come out here and sit. It's quiet. It's nice. It's mine."

She took one bite and a second, then made a little moaning sound as she licked the spoon.

His gut tightened at the image of her tongue wrapped around… He took the carton from her. "If you're going to moan, I'm not going to let you have any more ice cream," he threatened.

"You shouldn't have gotten my favorite ice cream if I wasn't supposed to eat it and make noise."

He took a bite to cool off the unwelcome heat rising inside him. She'd told him she wouldn't have sex with him. So why did he have this overwhelming urge to talk her out of her pretty blue silk dress and into the back seat?

"Why did you bring me here?" she asked, tilting the carton in his hand and dipping her spoon into it.

"Because I wanted to," he said.

"Upset about Brooke?"

"No," he answered, surprised she'd asked. "That's history for me."

"How was it seeing her again? She did look beautiful," Trina mused.

"I guess," he said. "The first thing I thought when I saw her was I was glad she wasn't my problem."

"Really?"

He nodded. "And damn if she didn't try to drag me

into her cash-flow situation at the reception." He met Trina's gaze. "Nice of you to offer her a solution."

Trina smiled. "I'm not sure she was thrilled with it."

"There's always fast food," he offered dryly.

She laughed then turned thoughtful. "I thought you would want to be with someone who would appease your ego," she ventured.

"My ego is no longer crushed, but if you're offering to appease…"

"I'm not. You still haven't answered my question. Why me?"

Her question made him feel restless. "I like being with you." He sighed. "When Brooke and I were together, she took up all of my nonbusiness time and she wanted some of that, too. I think I knew I couldn't please her, but for a redneck guy, she was the ultimate fantasy."

"Trophy, sign of ultimate success," she said.

"It was like being with her screwed up my vision and my hearing. I neglected my family and a lot of friends. It just messed me up, and I had this feeling the whole time we were engaged that it was going to end bad."

"And it did," Trina said quietly.

"Not really. There was no way I was going to be able to maintain her. She went over the edge when I went on business trips. It sounds corny, but I didn't like who I was with her."

"And I'm comfortable," she said. "Like an old hot water bottle."

Hearing a slight edge in her voice, he studied her face, but she appeared calm. "More like hot chocolate," he said. "Your eyes remind me of hot chocolate."

She frowned. "I can't tell if you think I'm a slut or a pacifier."

Walker felt like she'd slapped him, and swore. "Neither. I think we got drunk and I got lucky on one of the worst nights of my life." He leaned closer. "I just wish I hadn't been so drunk so I could remember it better. And if I can't have that, then I'd like to repeat the experience minus the alcohol. And as far as you being a pacifier, I haven't needed or wanted one of those for a long time. I just feel good with you. Is that a crime?" he asked and swore again.

Frustrated, he got out of the car and walked toward the pond. He took a deep breath and raked his hand though his hair. God, what a mess his life had become.

He heard a twig snap just before Trina slid her arm through his. "Sorry," she said.

"Yeah. The thing that sucks about all this is I was so damn wrapped up in winning the trophy that I couldn't see anyone else. I couldn't see you. I wonder if things between you and me could have been different if—"

"Don't go there," she said.

"Why?" he asking, looking down at her.

"Because things *are* different," she whispered.

The night was beautiful and she was, too. Her blue dress flowed over her the same way he imagined water would. Her hair was windblown and her eyes were so dark and sexy he felt he could dive inside her. He wanted to shut her up in the best and worst possible way. He slid his fingers through her hair and tilted her head upward.

"I told you I'm not going to have sex with you."

"That doesn't mean I can't kiss you," he muttered and took her mouth. She tasted like chocolate mocha ice cream and the sensation of her plump lips against his was as good as it was going to get. At least for this moment.

He felt the second she gave in to the kiss. Her body leaned into his and she lifted her arms around his neck. That little bit of encouragement lit his wick and he slid one of his hands to her lower back and rubbed his other over her waist up to her rib cage.

"You taste so good," he murmured against her mouth.

"You like the ice cream."

"No, it's your mouth." He sucked on her lower lip. "I want to eat it."

He caught her little intake of breath and tasted her again. The silk of her dress provided a terrible tease for his fingers as he skimmed his hand over her rib cage. Just enough to keep him from feeling her naked skin.

Her soft, almost unheard, moan vibrated through his mouth and cranked him up another notch. He wanted to touch her breasts. He wanted to touch her everywhere.

Sliding around her back, he found her zipper and pulled it down, at the same time that he deepened the kiss and pushed his leg between hers.

Squeezing her bottom, he pushed down the little strap from her dress and cupped her bare breast.

She opened her mouth, to protest or gasp, and he touched her already stiff nipple. Whatever she'd been going to say turned to a sexy moan.

The sound drove him nuts. He picked her up and carried her to the car, setting her on the hood.

"What are you—"

Stepping between her legs, he kissed her again. Her legs straddling his hips made him want to thrust inside her where he knew she was warm and wet. He fingered her nipples and lowered his head to take one of them into his mouth.

He heard an annoying beeping sound, but ignored it. The sensation of her stiff nipple on his tongue drowned everything out. The annoying beep sounded again.

"Oh, God, stop," she said, pushing his head back. Her eyes dark with arousal, she bit her lip and pulled up her dress. "Your cell."

The reality finally permeated his brain and he followed the beeping noise to the back seat of the car where he'd flung his jacket and cell phone. He picked it up just as it stopped ringing, frowning at the number on the caller ID.

"BJ?" he muttered, wondering what in hell— The phone rang again and he picked up. "What's up?"

"It's Danielle," BJ said. "She thinks she might be in labor and my truck won't start. And Harry's gone and left his cell phone here."

"Problem?" Trina asked, pulling her dress back together.

"Danielle may be in labor. BJ's truck won't start."

Trina's eyes widened. "Oh, no. How far apart are the contractions?"

"How far apart are the contractions?"

"I think about ten minutes," BJ said.

"Ten," he repeated to Trina.

"We should have time to get there. In the meantime, she should call her doctor."

"Okay, BJ, I'll be there as soon as I can. Trina says to call the doctor."

He turned off the phone and met Trina's gaze. "You okay?"

"Yeah," she said. "Amazing how a reminder of pregnancy can cool things off, isn't it?"

He couldn't help chuckling, moving around the car to open the door for her. "Yeah. Works like ice water."

WITH THE TOP DOWN on her Mustang convertible, Walker took the freeway toward his condo. The wind wrecked her hair, but it sure cleared her head.

What was wrong with her? Why did she keep putting herself through this insanity with Walker? What in the world did she hope to achieve?

She wondered if some stupid part of her secretly believed that they should be together because of Maddie. "Dumb," she muttered.

"Did you say something?" Walker asked.

"No." Nothing she wanted him to hear. She knew she found him extremely attractive, and before Maddie she'd been drawn to him. She'd sensed some kind of gut-level connection between them and had always wondered if he would have noticed her if he hadn't been engaged to the gorgeous, filthy rich Brooke Tarantino.

She'd always known, however, that she wouldn't

want to follow Brooke Tarantino. How could she not feel like second choice?

"You're too quiet," he said. "You're thinking. Hate it when you do that."

"Despite evidence to the contrary, you picked the wrong girl to take to the pond if you wanted one that doesn't do any thinking. I told you that at the wedding reception."

Taking the exit to his condo, he immediately pulled the car to the side of the road.

"What are you doing?"

He turned to her. "Tell me something. Do you think I'm a scumbag?"

She shook her head.

"Do you like me? For the most part," he added.

She nodded. "I guess."

"Do you want to be with me?"

Trina's breath stopped in her throat.

"Tell me the truth, Trina. Do you want to be with me?"

*Yes, but*— She bit her lip. "I have a hard time believing you want to be with me when you could be with someone like Brooke."

"And what do you think it would take to make you believe I'd rather be with you?"

*Date me publicly.* Except that could be a nightmare if people found out he'd fathered Maddie.

*Tell me you can't live without me.* She gave herself a mental eye roll. Ridiculous.

*Love Maddie.* The truth of that wish cut like a knife. She needed to get a one-way ticket out of la-la land.

"I don't know. We had a pretty tough start."

He nodded and held her gaze for a moment, then put the car in gear. "Okay."

Trina had the ugly feeling that she'd just slashed any chance she had with him. Not that there'd really ever been a chance anyway.

They rode the rest of the way in silence. When Walker pulled into the parking lot for his condominium, BJ and Danielle trudged toward them.

"Hey, nice wheels," he said, admiring Trina's Mustang.

"Thanks," she said and looked at Danielle. "How are you?"

Danielle gave a sheepish smile. "I think it may have been false labor. The doctor told me to walk for a while to see if it passed and it seems like the contractions are slowing down."

"Probably my fault," BJ said and slid his arm around Danielle. "Since Harry and you were gone, we, uh—got a little romantic."

Silence followed and Trina stole a glance at Walker. She watched his jaw work for a few seconds, then he cleared his throat. "Uh, Trina would you mind walking Danielle back to my condo?"

"No," Trina said. "I don't mind except I don't know where your condo is."

"I can show you," Danielle offered. "Maybe you can help me not feel so stupid for thinking I'm in labor when I'm not."

"You're not stupid," Trina said and joined the young woman as she lumbered across the parking lot. "You're pregnant. You're allowed some practice runs."

"But how do you know when it's the real thing?" Danielle asked.

"The contractions get more and more intense and they don't stop until you have a baby," Trina said. "You may just breeze through labor. It may be quick and easy. But just in case," Trina said as she followed Danielle, "make sure there's an anesthesiologist ready to give you your epidural. And it would help if you have someone with you who will help you with the doctor."

"Oh, well, BJ will stand up for me. He has promised," Danielle said as they reached a front door.

"Good," Trina said. "That will help."

"BJ!" Walker's voice carried across the parking lot. "The next time you get in a romantic mood before your baby comes into this world, I am going to knock you into next week. Take a cold shower, dammit!"

Danielle stared across the parking lot. "Oh, no, I don't want them fighting on my behalf."

Trina detected a note of melodrama, which she knew could be attributed to water retention. That was what she'd always blamed it on, anyway. "Oh, no, Walker just wants you and the baby to be okay. They're both looking after you. Let's go get you some water."

An hour later, Walker drove her back to her condo. After putting the top up on her Mustang, he walked her to her front door. He looked so exasperated and tired she had to resist another urge to hug him and tell him he was a good guy to help his brother and uncle.

She crossed her arms over her chest. "Interesting evening," she said.

"Yep. A laugh a minute." He raked his hand through his hair and sighed. He looked into her eyes. "Would you do me a favor?"

"What?" she asked, immediately on guard.

"No, it's not sex, although I wouldn't turn you down if you invited me inside."

Trina bit her tongue to ensure her own silence.

"Okay," he said. "Would you pretend for just two minutes that none of the bad stuff that has happened between us ever happened? And just let me kiss you good night?"

His request was unexpected and almost sweet. She took a deep breath.

"That hard?"

"Well there's a lot of water under this bridge," she said.

"Okay," he said and started to turn away.

She reached out to snag his arm. "Wait a minute."

He slowly turned around to face her. "You can do it?"

"For one minute," she said, and he lowered his mouth to hers. Gentle as a butterfly, he took her mouth. She let him, focusing on the moment, focusing on his mouth and a hushed expectancy. A bit of hope mixed with electricity and desire.

He pulled back and his eyes were filled with something that made her think that he was thinking about her and no one else.

"Thanks, Trina. Sweet dreams," he said, lifting his finger to her mouth.

"You, too," she said and watched him walk away, thinking she could have gone for longer than sixty seconds.

# CHAPTER FIFTEEN

"MY TALENTS ARE BEING WASTED here," Dora announced. "I'm leaving Bellagio."

Trina looked up from an advance press plan for an appearance by Sal in New York. "Are you sure that's what you want? If you're not happy in PR, then maybe—"

"You can find another paper-pusher position for me? No, thanks," she said in a huff. "I got a job with a cruise line. I'm in charge of group-party planning and I start day after tomorrow, so I can't give you any notice."

"It would have been nice if—"

"Yeah, well, lots of things would be nice. Like if Walker Gordon could have gone out with me. Instead of feeling obligated to be with you."

Even though Trina knew she shouldn't let Dora bother her, the woman's words stung. "Walker has never been obligated to me for anything," Trina retorted. "Not for Maddie or my position or anything else." She cut herself off. "But this is an unnecessary discussion. I appreciate all of your hard work here, Dora, and I hope you'll be happy and successful in your next position."

"I will be," she said. "I'm taking a long lunch and I'll be leaving early." She paused. "Why would Walker feel obligated for Maddie?"

Trina felt caught. She swallowed a lump of panic. "Because he's a nice guy. You've seen him with his brother."

As soon as Dora left, Trina reined in her feelings and called personnel to inform them of Dora's departure. She also requested a temp. With her supervisor tied up in his new position, Trina would need to arrange for a replacement before she got stuck with another distant relative or friend of someone's wife. She began to make notes for the qualifications and skills necessary for the position.

Late that afternoon, Walker stopped by to confirm plans for the advertising tie-in with Sal's trip. Midway through their conversation, his cell phone rang and he excused himself to take the call.

"How hard can it be to get pink roses and yellow daisies by Saturday?" he asked.

Trina stared at him.

He returned her questioning glance with a shrug. "Okay, just forget it. I'll find someone else," he said and disconnected the call. "For Pete's sake, you'd think I was asking for the Hope Diamond."

"Must ask. Why do you need flowers?"

"Since Danielle had her scare the other night, she wants to get married and she wants a real wedding. I told BJ I would pay for it, within reason."

"And you're planning it?" she asked.

"It can't be that big a deal. Roses, a cake and a minister. What else do you need?"

"Men are so naive," she said. "My mother is the queen of pulling a special event together in no time. She has contacts with florists, caterers, everyone."

"You think she would do it?"

"Probably, but I have to warn you, she can be—" She searched for the right word. "Difficult."

"I can stand anyone for a week. It's not like I have to live with her," he said. "Remember my current living situation."

"She's very controlling," Trina warned.

"I know the type," he said. "Detail oriented. Almost obsessive."

"You can remove the almost part and you'll have it right."

"Then let's give her something to do."

With a lot of trepidation, Trina talked to her mother that evening. "You need to remember that this won't be a traditional wedding. It's about making Danielle happy."

"How pregnant does she look?" her mother asked. "Some women look good their entire pregnancy."

"She's pretty, but she looks like she's going to pop," Trina said. "If you can't stand doing this because it doesn't fit the traditional mold—"

"No, no. This may be my only opportunity. I would have been happy to plan your wedding in the delivery room if you'd married your child's father."

"Mother," Trina said in her best warning voice.

"Never mind. I need to get moving if we're going to make this happen by Saturday. I need to speak with Danielle right away."

The entire week, she waited for a tearful, hysterical call from Danielle that her mother had done something to hurt her feelings or offend her.

Saturday dawned and the world still spun on its axis. Her favorite sitter arrived to take care of Maddie and Trina drove to her mother's home, where the wedding would take place.

Danielle had said she wanted the ceremony for her, BJ and the baby, so the attendees included Uncle Harry, Walker, Trina's mother, the minister and Trina. Her mother's house, she noticed as she walked through the front door, was decorated beautifully with flowers. Classical music played softly in the background.

Walker wandered toward her with a cup of coffee in his hand. "Hey there. Your mother has done a terrific job. Did you really grow up here?"

"I really did," she said, a mix of nostalgia and sadness hitting her at once.

"It's beautiful."

"Yes. I'm sure my mother has told you it's in the national registery of historic homes," she said and lowered her voice. "It's a money pit."

"Careful," he said with a glint in his eyes. "Your sentimental streak is showing."

"Just because it's a lovely house doesn't mean everything that happened inside here was all that lovely."

He studied her. "What wasn't so lovely?"

She shook her head. "This isn't the occasion for that discussion."

"Fine," he said. "I'll take a rain check."

Or not, she thought, but didn't say anything as she walked toward the sound of voices on the back porch. The small group of people stood clustered together. BJ wore a dark suit and Danielle was dressed in a white stretchy gown that celebrated her pregnancy rather than concealed it. Tiny embroidered rosebuds lined the straps, scoop neck and fluttery calf-length hem. Her dark hair was pulled into a half updo with a spray of baby's breath. She looked radiant.

She walked toward Trina as she entered the room. "I don't know how to thank you for all this."

"I didn't do anything," Trina protested.

"Yes, you did. You hooked us up with your mother and she has worked miracles. And look at this amazing setting for our wedding. I can't believe I'm getting married in a historical mansion. Walker has been so generous to give us this, and your mother thought of everything." Danielle eyes grew shiny. "I just feel so lucky."

Trina's heart squeezed at the emotion on Danielle's face. "And you look beautiful. Where did you find this dress? It's perfect."

"One of the stores you recommended," Danielle said. "I wouldn't have spent that much money, but Walker said to get what I wanted."

Wearing a broad smile on his face, BJ walked to Danielle's side. "Isn't she the most beautiful woman in the world?"

"She is," Trina said, approving his adoration.

"She's beautiful. Just remember you've already had your honeymoon," Walker said.

"Carter-Aubrey," her mother said. "There you are."

"Carter-Aubrey?" Walker echoed. "Who's that?"

"Me, unfortunately. My mother knew she wasn't

going to get pregnant again, so she had to cover all her bases with me. My full name is Carter-Aubrey Katherine. When I left home, I chose the one I liked best, my middle name, and shortened it to Trina."

She turned from Walker and said, "You've done an amazing job, Mother."

"Do you think so?" Aubrey asked as Danielle and BJ moved toward Uncle Harry. "It's certainly not traditional."

"No, but look how happy Danielle and BJ are. That's what's important."

"Very nice job, Mrs. Roberts," Walker said. "I can't thank you enough. I wish you would allow us to pay you."

"Oh, no, I couldn't do that," Aubrey said. "I'm not a professional."

"It's better than professional," Trina said. "It's personalized. And I think it would be very appropriate for you to accept Walker's offer."

"It wouldn't be right," Aubrey said. "But Harold did suggest that I open the house for special events, for a fee, of course. He's quite the shrewd businessman, isn't he?" She glanced at her watch and made a fluttering gesture. "It's time."

Trina couldn't remember seeing her mother this excited. "She loves this," Trina whispered to Walker.

"Good thing somebody does," he said in a dry tone.

Trina took her place as a witness to the simple, sweet ceremony with the minister guiding Danielle and BJ through their vows of love and commitment. Even though she knew too well the same couple who were dewy-eyed with devotion one day could be at each other's throats the next, she couldn't stop the unwelcome knot of longing that formed in her throat, or the wish that things would go well for Danielle and BJ and their baby.

Hearing her mother sniff, Trina did the same to her surprise. She felt Walker look at her, but dodged his gaze.

Vows were spoken, rings exchanged and the minister pronounced them husband and wife.

"Hear, hear," Harry said, and Trina and Walker joined his applause. Danielle and BJ hugged everyone at least twice.

Her mother clapped her hands. "Now we'll have a toast. With punch," she added firmly. "If the bride can't drink, then no one else can, either."

Harry and BJ groaned in protest. "Not even a beer?" BJ asked.

"Absolutely not," Aubrey said and looked at Harry. "Would you mind doing the honors, Harold?"

Trina did a double take at her mother's tone. Was she flirting with Harry? She glanced at Harry, with his bad comb-over and good ol' boy manner.

He winked at her mother and lifted a glass of punch. "I'm honored you would ask me, Aubrey," he said and cleared his throat. "BJ and Danielle, may your life together be blessed with love, laughter and happiness and may you both know the true joy of marriage and parenthood."

"Hear, hear," the group echoed.

Trina helped her mother's longtime employee, Hilda, serve platters of miniquiches, breakfast soufflé, fruit, Southern-style ham biscuits and entirely too much other food.

"Carter-Aubrey," her mother said while Trina returned a tray to the kitchen. "It's very nice of you to help me."

"You did so much. This is the least I can do."

"Do you really think it went well?"

Surprised at her mother's lack of confidence, she squeezed her arm. "Are you kidding? You should do this more often."

"I don't know," Aubrey said, lifting her hand to her neck. "Harold said he thought I would make a killing if I opened the house for small private parties or events. He even said he would help me. I didn't realize I would like it so much."

Even though she and her mother had argued more than they'd agreed, Trina couldn't help feeling happy for her mother. "I'm proud of you," Trina said. "You helped give BJ and Danielle a special day to remember."

Aubrey's eyes teared. "I don't think you've ever told me that you're proud of me."

"Well, I should have because I am." She pulled her mother in for a hug and heard Aubrey give a little sigh.

"Now, if only you would get married to someone right for you and Maddie, that would be a dream come true."

Trina immediately withdrew. "No need to get carried away."

"Darling, just because you had a bad experience doesn't mean you should totally give up on men."

"I haven't. I'm just taking a long pause on the whole marriage thing."

"But you have a daughter to consider now," her mother said. "And you're still young, but you're not getting any younger."

"Personally," Walker said from the doorway, "I've been a lot happier getting older."

Her mother waved her hand. "You're a man. Men are allowed to age. Women aren't. That's why I want Carter-Aubrey to open up to the idea of marriage." Aubrey gave Walker a considering glance. "You know, it wouldn't hurt you to think about giving marriage another try."

"Mother, don't even start," Trina said, torn

between embarrassment and frustration. She glanced at her watch. "I should give one more round of wishes to BJ and Danielle before I head home."

"So soon?" Aubrey protested.

The last five minutes had passed with glacierlike speed. "Yep. Gotta go. Great job, Mother," she said and gave hugs to BJ, Danielle and Harry.

"When am I going to get to see that baby again?" Harry asked.

"You name the time."

"I'm headed back to work soon, but I may be spending some time with your mother."

Trina felt a shot of alarm. "She may add to your risk for stress-related illness and diseases. That's all I'll say."

"I've usually been the one to give an ulcer, not get one," he told her with a wily grin.

"If you say so, but just remember I warned you," she said and headed for the front door. Walker joined her just as she opened the door.

"I'll walk with you outside," he said.

"The marital bliss getting to you?" she asked, smiling.

"From what I heard of your conversation, Carter-Aubrey, you didn't sound like you were a big proponent of the institution, either." He stepped outside on the front porch. "I don't think you ever told me why you're so skittish about marriage. Did you get left at the altar?"

"No," she said. Unfortunately. "My parents fought all the time. My father died in an automobile accident while he and my mother were arguing."

He cringed and shook his head. "I'm sorry. I can see why that would make you think twice or more."

She nodded. "Yeah. I had my own bad experience with a guy when I was nineteen. That made an impression, too."

"Carter-Aubrey got her heart broke?"

"*Trina* got involved with a guy because my mother couldn't stand him."

"Aubrey was right?"

"In spades," she said and felt a swell of humiliation even after all these years.

"You look upset. This guy must've taken you for a ride."

"I was a willing, if ignorant, participant. More embarrassing than anything else," she said, pushing unwelcome memories aside.

"Funny how BJ and Danielle almost make it all look possible," he mused as they walked down the steps toward her car.

"Maybe it's better not to overthink," she said. "I have an annoying tendency to get into trouble when I don't think everything through. I was kinda surprised you encouraged this wedding by paying for it since you're dead set against Gordons being fathers."

"In BJ's case, the deed is done."

"It is with you, too," she couldn't help reminding him.

"Yeah, but BJ believes he's got a shot at being a decent father. I can't ignore history and I sure as hell don't want to repeat it." He sighed. "So how's Maddie?"

"Awesome," she said, smiling. "I think she could roll her way to Canada and she's trying very hard to crawl. She looks a little orange, though. I may need to cut down on the carrots and sweet potatoes, but she acts like she could eat them till they're coming out of her ears. Oh, and she's gotten into animal sounds. There's this cute little toy that—" Trina broke off, realizing she'd given Walker a lot more information than he'd probably wanted. "She's fine. Just fine. I should go. Bye," she said, opening her car door and getting inside.

"Why is she orange?" he asked.

"The chemical in sweet potatoes and carrots can give skin an orange cast. It shows up more on her feet."

He nodded, closing her car door. "Give her an animal cookie and tell her it's from me."

His request surprised her. Any interest he showed in Maddie surprised her because he'd made it clear he would provide financial support, but he wouldn't be a real dad. He would just try to help find one for her.

She felt a flicker of hope that maybe he would see how wonderful Maddie was and grow to adore her. Trina reined it in because hope could be a dangerous thing.

After she arrived home, she played with Maddie and went through the last two days of mail. Her heart stopped when she saw a letter written in a scrawl that created a sick feeling of déjà vu. She looked at the letter and wanted to burn it. She remembered that Stan had bothered her with letters when he'd first been incarcerated, years ago, but he'd eventually stopped.

Taking a deep breath, she opened the letter.

*Dear Kat, You didn't write me back. We really need to see each other. So much unfinished between us...*

Wrong, she thought, feeling panic slice through her. She grabbed Maddie and headed for a kitchen drawer that held notepads, mailing supplies and stamps. Pulling out what she needed, she returned to the den to compose a brief note.

*Dear Stan, Please do not write or contact me again. Do not visit me. Our relationship is over.*

*Everything between us is finished. Good luck with your new life. I'm not a part of it. Sincerely, Katherine*

She reread the note, making sure her message was crystal clear. Placing his letter and hers in an envelope, she addressed the envelope and put a stamp on it. Scooping up Maddie, she walked the letter out to her mailbox and put it inside. She wanted every remnant of Stan out of her house, out of her life.

Whoever said you can't fight Mother Nature when it comes to your height never stepped into a pair of three-inch heels.

## CHAPTER SIXTEEN

TRINA ARRIVED AT HER OFFICE Monday morning to find a friendly new face at the receptionist's desk. "Hi, I'm Amelia Parker," the woman said with a deep Southern drawl that no Northern university had beaten out of her. She stood and extended her hand. "I'm Bellagio's floating temp, and I hope you'll let me know what I can do to help."

"Thank you," Trina said, shaking Amelia's hand. "I'm Trina Roberts and I'm so glad you're here."

Amelia smiled. "I've already made coffee and if you'll tell me where you'd like me to start, I'll get moving."

"I sent out prepublicity for Sal's appearance in New York City. I would like you to do some e-mail follow-up. I'm not sure what Dora had on her computer, so I'll send you the list from mine. Then there's a charitable group that Bellagio plans to donate shoes to— it's for women from abused situations who are seeking employment. Marc Waterson will make that appearance in Washington, D.C. I'm working with the charity for a combined press release. Do you think you could draft something if I send you the facts?"

"Of course," Amelia said. "I worked in marketing for a while and did that kind of thing."

Good manners. No insults. The young woman was a little chubby with unfashionable but beautiful clear white skin that would never tan. She wore a ladylike pink sweater set and skirt. Helpful, cheerful, not bitter. Trina felt her nerve endings smooth out.

"Wonderful," she said. "And thank you so much for the coffee." Trina went to her office thrilled with the absence of hostility emanating from the outer office.

After getting Amelia started, she began work on her own projects. As part of the launch for the active-wear line, Trina wanted to arrange an on-air coupon giveaway for a pair of Bellagio shoes for a studio audience. Oprah was obviously at the top of her list, but she would research others. She was on a follow-up call for media for Sal's New York City appear-ance, when Amelia appeared in the doorway.

The temp shoved a note in front of her. *Mr. Alfredo Bellagio is on line two waiting for you.*

Surprised, Trina quickly ended her call and picked up line two. "Trina Roberts, how can I help you?" she said, wondering why the president of Bellagio had called her. Mr. Bellagio never called her personally.

"Trina, this is Alfredo Bellagio," he said. Although his accent always reminded her of the movie *The Godfather,* she reminded herself that he was usually fair. When he wasn't, he made amends. "How are you?"

"I'm great, sir. And you?"

"I'm good. How's your bambino?"

"Sweet and growing fast."

"I'm glad," he said and sighed. "I want to talk with you about some things. When can you join me for dinner?"

What things? Trina felt a knot of anxiety form in her stomach. "I'm open most nights this week. I just need a little notice to get a sitter."

"Okay, how about Tuesday or Thursday?" he asked.

"Either one should be fine."

"Good. I'll let you know which I choose. You have a good day, now. Yes?"

"Yes, sir. Thank you and you have a good day, too, sir," she said and hung up, frowning. What was that all about? she wondered, bothered. Stewing over it for thirty minutes, she tried to push it aside. She wouldn't find out until dinner.

Mr. Bellagio's assistant called back to confirm dinner for Tuesday evening at 6:00 p.m. at a restaurant near the office. Trina made a call to check availability for her favorite babysitter, but the woman was busy. She decided to give Danielle a try via Walker. Trina knew her mother's presence would only jack her nerves up more.

"Hey, Trina," Walker said from his cell.

She ignored the automatic physical reaction his voice generated. "Something's come up. I need a sitter for tomorrow night. Can you ask Danielle for me?"

"Sure. What time do you need her?"

"Dinner's at 6:00 p.m. so five-thirty would be fine."

"Dinner?" he echoed.

"Yeah, why?"

"Just curious. I have dinner plans, too. Meeting the big Bellagio at that Italian restaurant near your offices."

Trina paused. "Hmm. He invited me, too. I wonder if he invited anyone else."

"Maybe he's thinking about a new product or promotion and wants our input."

"He usually wants input from his VPs," she said and shrugged. "You're probably right. I guess I'll see you and Mr. Bellagio tomorrow night. Please ask Danielle to call me to confirm."

"I'll do that. Just curious," he said. "Have you booked any other dates this week?"

She drew a temporary blank, then realization hit her. "Oh, you mean with romantic possibilities?" His pointed question irritated her, especially after their little kissing scene near his country pond. One minute he was kissing her, the next he was pushing her into another man's arms. She scowled. "I realize I'm not progressing at the speed you'd like because you'd like your guilt over Maddie immediately assuaged, but I have other things to do. I'd appreciate it if you would stop pushing me—"

"I'm not pushing," he said. "I'm not even recommending. I was just curious. I'll tell Danielle to call you. See you tomorrow night," he said and hung up.

Confused, she pulled the phone receiver from her ear and stared at it for a long moment. The annoying fast busy tone snapped her out of her daze. "Weird," she muttered and hung up the phone. "This is just weird."

One thing that hadn't been weird, however, was Amelia's work performance. She stepped into Dora's position and brought everything up to speed by late afternoon.

"Thank you. You've done an amazing job," Trina told her as she labeled new file folders. "I'm surprised Bellagio hasn't offered to make you a permanent employee."

"Oh, they have," Amelia said. "But I'm engaged and it wouldn't be fair to tell Bellagio I planned to stay in Atlanta if my fiancé gets a job somewhere else. I need to be ready to go with him."

Trina nodded, feeling a trickle of disappointment.

Amelia could make her life so much easier. "When are you getting married?"

"I don't know. William is on the fast track in sales. He says we need to be prepared for his next promotion and transfer. William is determined to be a success and I'll go wherever he goes." She paused. "William and I will be together forever. It's our destiny." She smiled. "He asked me to marry him when he was in the fifth grade and I was in fourth grade and we've been together ever since."

Trina stared at the temp in disbelief. "You've been together that long?"

Amelia's cheeks flamed. "Oh, not *together* that way," she said. "We've just always known that we wanted to spend our lives together." She sighed. "With so many marriages busted up before the first anniversary, it's hard for a lot of people to understand William and me. We just got very, very lucky with love."

Although the notion of meeting that special someone in elementary school seemed far-fetched, Amelia's sincerity tugged at something inside her. The same part of her that had fallen in love with the story of Cinderella and had fantasized about being rescued from her mother's home by a rebel on a motorcycle. The same fantasy that had gotten her in trouble at nineteen with Stan.

Still, wouldn't it be nice, she thought, if love could

have been that easy for her. She felt a little stab of envy. "That's very rare," she said. "You're right. You're very, very lucky."

"I know," Amelia said.

"If William makes a change in career plans, then you be sure to let me know."

THE FOLLOWING EVENING Trina wore one of her more forgiving black dresses with Bellagio heels. She wanted to project the image of sophistication and dependability. Maddie, however, destroyed that image in record time when, obviously full, she chuckled and blew applesauce all over the front of Trina's most forgiving black dress.

That meant Trina had to change into one of her less forgiving black dresses that required suck-you-in undergarments. No room for pasta tonight, she thought glumly as she answered the doorbell.

BJ let out a wolf whistle and Danielle nodded in approval.

"You are one hot mama," BJ said. "You're going to knock the men on their assses."

"Maybe I should change, since it's a business dinner," Trina said, biting her lip.

"No," Danielle said as she and BJ entered the foyer. "I read in a women's magazine that it's still a man's world, so a woman should use every edge she has."

Although Trina wouldn't normally depend on advice dispensed from a woman's magazine, she couldn't discount the statement. Plus she was dealing with an Italian. "Okay, I'll stick with this, but I'll take a sweater."

"Anything special we need to know for the little one?" BJ asked.

"You can put her to bed between eight and eight-thirty. She's already been fed and bathed. She sometimes gets a little tense around new people so I'm leaving you a box of animal crackers. The magic elixir."

Danielle smiled. "It was Cheerios for my little sister."

"Cheerios is a close second. If you have any questions or problems, please don't hesitate to call my cell," Trina said.

Ten minutes later, she left the house with her sweater and purse in tow, wishing she knew exactly the purpose for this dinner meeting. How could she possibly prepare when she didn't know why Alfredo had arranged it? She fussed and fumed the entire drive to the restaurant then pulled herself together as she allowed the valet to take her car.

Entering the fine Italian restaurant, she announced her reservation to the hostess and was led to a table for three where Walker already sat.

He immediately rose to his feet, looking gorgeous

and relaxed. She envied the latter quality and resented the former; she also resented the jumpy feeling he caused inside her. She didn't need any distractions when she was dealing with the president of her company.

"Wow, you look hot," he said, his gaze drifting over her in approval.

"No, I don't," she said. "I look professional and dependable, because this is my second choice dress because Maddie got applesauce and oatmeal all over the front of my first choice."

"Ooops," he said, pulling out her chair. "I guess I shouldn't add the word bedable and say the second choice looks damn good to me."

"That's right. You shouldn't. A glass of Pinot Grigio and a glass of Barolo for Mr. Bellagio," she said to the waiter and took a deep breath.

"Beer, whatever you have on draft," Walker said.

"I'd breathe so much easier if I knew why we were here."

"Since he invited us for dinner, it can't be that bad. It's a lot cheaper to fire someone during work hours. The end of the day is the best time. If you're going to get any work out of them, you've already gotten it. You tell them to go ahead and clear out their desk. They don't need to come back."

Trina's stomach clenched. She didn't want to get

fired. She didn't want to leave Bellagio. "It sounds like you have a lot of experience."

"Enough," he said and put his hand over hers on the table. "He's not going to fire you. And if he did, my company, along with a dozen others, would hire you in a heartbeat."

She took a deep breath. "I don't want to make any big changes right now," she said. "I like my condo. I love the on-site nursery. They love Maddie."

"Trust me. Alfredo is not going to fire you," he said. "You should relax. This place has great food and you're not paying for it."

"I can't eat pasta in this dress," she hissed.

The waiter returned with the beer and wine. Trina immediately took a big swallow of hers.

"Drink up," Walker said. "Here comes Alfredo."

A shot of panic burst through her, nearly causing her to spray Walker with her gulp of wine. She turned her head away, swallowing hard and praying she wouldn't choke.

"Trina, Walker!" Alfredo said in his booming voice as he walked to the table. "I'm so glad you could join me tonight."

Walker stood and Trina followed him to her feet. "Wouldn't miss it," Walker said.

"I'm honored to be invited," Trina said, extending her hand.

The barrel-chested president of Bellagio might be short in stature, but his personality and demeanor were giant-sized. Alfredo surprised the stuffing out of her by giving her a big hug. "No need to be formal. We're all family here."

He took a seat and looked at his glass of wine and lifted it to his lips for a taste. "My favorite," he said with a broad smile. "Which one of you ordered this?"

"It was Trina. She's on the ball as usual."

"Smart girl," he said, giving Walker a nudge with his elbow. "Smart and pretty girl. Now tell me what did you think of Marc and Jenny's wedding? They pulled one over on us."

"We can't be too upset after that great party afterward," Trina said, wondering when the small talk would be over, wondering when she could find out the real reason for this dinner.

"That Marc, he's a clever man. Kidnapping his nervous bride," Alfredo said, nodding as he lifted his glass.

"Probably helps if the bride wants to be kidnapped," Walker said, sliding a quick wry glance at Trina.

"True, true," Alfredo said. "But marriage is good for a man. Children, they provide meaning, heritage."

The waiter arrived at the table just then, saving Trina and Walker from responding.

Trina ordered the fish special and told herself to

follow Walker's suggestion to enjoy the meal, but found herself sitting on the edge of her seat waiting. And waiting.

Throughout the serving of the bread, salad and main course, Alfredo jumped from topic to topic. He asked Trina about Maddie and asked Walker if he was glad to be back in the States. Walker talked about a few quick trips he'd taken to Italy while living in France.

Trina resisted the urge to drum her fingers on the table and say, *Could we get on with this, please?*

When the waiter asked for dessert orders, she passed, but Alfredo insisted that she order something.

"Okay, tiramisu, but I'd like to share it," she said. "So please bring extra forks."

"That's the right idea. Sharing," Alfredo said and ordered a cup of coffee.

The conversation lulled after the waiter left and Trina glanced at Walker, sensing he felt the same expectancy she did.

Alfredo sighed and put his folded hands on the table. "You're probably wondering why I invited the two of you here tonight," he said.

Trina smiled and nodded, in contrast to her desire to wrap her hands around his neck and jerk the explanation out of him.

Walker chuckled. "Aside from enjoying our company."

Alfredo smiled at the joke, then turned serious. "This is a difficult subject to broach. My wife, she says it's none of my business. But you two, you're like family. You've been through some rough times and good times with Bellagio. You've both been loyal to Bellagio."

Can I buy a vowel? Trina thought and managed another encouraging smile.

Alfredo sighed again and nodded. "Family is the most important thing in the world, and a child, even a bambino needs the mother and the father."

And...

Alfredo narrowed his eyes and looked away then turned to Walker. "It has come to my attention that you are the father of Trina's bambino."

*Ho-ly crap.*

Trina was sure her jaw dropped to her knees...at the same moment that her throat completely closed.

She watched Walker's face. Surprise lasted a few seconds, then he nodded. "That's correct."

Alfredo pressed his lips together. "Again, this is none of my business, but I care for both of you. I know you were going to marry Brooke. I don't want you to think that you can't marry Trina because of that."

Trina wondered if her jaw had fallen the rest of the

way to the floor. Alfredo wasn't really suggesting—
She had to nip this before it got even more ridiculous.

She cleared her throat. "Walker has been very generous, even though Maddie wasn't planned. He has insisted on providing financial support."

Alfredo nodded. "As a good father should. Even though you and Walker didn't plan the bambino, she still deserves a family. If you were Italian, you would be married."

Trina coughed over the choking sensation in the back of her throat. "I've always admired the longevity of your marriage, Mr. Bellagio, but I've also seen the effects of a married couple who don't really love each other and who fight incessantly. Walker and I haven't developed the kind of relationship that I believe would be the basis for a good marriage."

Alfredo cocked his head to one side. "I should tell you that marriage is an ongoing negotiation." He waved his hand. "Even now my wife and I, we negotiate at least once a week. Sometimes about dinner, about my cigars, her shopping, my mother. *Capisca?*" He smiled. "You just try to keep the negotiations pleasant and remember you're dealing with a person who is good in the heart."

The waiter arrived with the tiramsu and coffee. Trina didn't know how she could squeeze a fraction of a bite down her throat, but she picked up one of the forks to do something with her hand. She looked at Walker and found him studying her.

"I hope you'll consider my advice. A bambino is the most important thing in the world. So spend some time together, take your daughter's mother out and give her a good time. Be nice to each other."

Silence followed. Walker glanced from Trina to Alfredo to Trina again. "I think it's excellent advice and I plan to follow it."

Trina dropped her fork.

## CHAPTER SEVENTEEN

"HAVE YOU LOST YOUR MIND?" Trina asked Walker after he walked her to her car.

"He makes a good case," Walker said.

"For what? Insanity," Trina said. "You've made it perfectly clear that you don't want to marry me and that you don't want children."

"Trina, you gotta admit our situation has been as clear as mud. I think that underneath all the chauvinistic family stuff, he had a good point. You and I have never even attempted to date."

She crossed her arms over her chest. "Maybe there's an excellent reason for that, since you're a child hater."

"I'm not a child hater. I just didn't want to have any kids because I didn't want to carry on my father's legacy."

"Which brings up the same issue that will never go away. Maddie," Trina said.

"I think we should date."

"Why? Because you're afraid you'll lose the account with Bellagio," she said, tossing out the possibility like a piece of raw meat, seeing if he would bite.

He stood silent for a full moment. Her suspicions rose exponentially. "That's what it is. You don't want to date me out of any sincere desire. It's just part of the game. Part of keeping the Bellagio account."

Disgusted, she turned away and unlocked her car door. He put his hand on the door to keep her from getting in the car.

"I can't get a break with you, Trina. Why can't we just—" He sighed. "Date? Get to know each other. Give each other a chance."

"Other than your attitude toward Maddie," she began.

"That's not really fair. You told me that you weren't going to introduce men to Maddie until you found out if those men worked for you. Why don't you find out if I work for you? Are you afraid?"

*Yes. I'm terrified.* "What if you work for me, but you still can't handle Maddie?"

"You were willing to take that chance with men you didn't even know. You should take that chance with me."

Terror slid through her like ice water. What if she found out she had feelings for Walker? Big feelings?

Feelings she'd never had before. And what if she fell for him and he never fell for her? And Maddie?

She felt his hand on her shoulder and she closed her eyes.

"The trouble is I never had a chance to get to know you. I've had sex with you, but I don't know what your favorite flower is. Your favorite ice cream is mocha chocolate, but I don't know your favorite candy. Favorite place, favorite movie, favorite music. What's guaranteed to make you laugh? I don't know any of that and I'd like to."

"Daisies, chocolate-covered peanuts, my Jacuzzi surrounded by candles, *Thelma and Louise* and *Beauty and the Beast,* depending on my mood, Aerosmith, the boys from the Blue Collar tour." She turned around and met his gaze. "Done in less than sixty seconds."

She looked into his eyes and saw things that bothered her—determination, interest, more determination.

"Let me take you out on Friday night," he said.

"Where?"

"Let me figure that out," he said.

"But how should I dress?"

"I'll tell you on Thursday. I'll pick you up Friday at six-thirty." He opened her car door and she got inside.

"Have you thought about how you're going to explain that Maddie is yours once it really gets out?" Trina asked him. "If Mr. Bellagio knows then other people must know, too. Eventually, you'll have to tell your family. Eventually, God help me, I'll have to tell my mother."

"I survived a public dumping on television. You'd be surprised what I can handle," Walker said.

She knew he was strong and tough. She'd always liked that about him. She also knew, however, that his kryptonite weighed less than twenty pounds and couldn't quite crawl, let alone walk, but she had the power to make big strong Walker sweat rivers.

TRINA SPENT THE REST of her week focused on work and Maddie. Each day Amelia greeted her with coffee and kind words and followed up with efficiency.

While reviewing the job description for the PR assistant, she found herself wanting to add "must be kind and make coffee." She stopped by personnel and chatted with the director. "I want to keep my temp," she told the director.

The woman smiled. "Everyone wants to keep Amelia, but as I'm sure she told you, she doesn't feel right committing to long-term employment with Bellagio when she needs to be ready to move."

"Aren't there some things we could do to get her to reconsider?" Trina asked.

"She's been offered everything from free shoes to a trip to Tahiti," the director said. "It's difficult to accept, but she's one of those rare people who can't be bought or bribed."

Trina groaned. "How is it that she's worked in several different departments?"

"She's incredibly adaptable. We usually put her in positions where there's been an abrupt firing, resignation or an emergency medical situation."

"So I got her because Dora walked with no notice," Trina concluded.

"Exactly. The department head she was working for before calls me daily asking to reassign her back to his department."

"Well, thank you for holding the line," Trina said, feeling a little miffed at her assistant being poached.

"I won't hold it forever," the personnel director said. "If someone else quits or gets fired, if Amelia is still here, out she goes."

Trina nodded, glum. A thought struck her. "So what are your favorite flowers?"

The personnel director just laughed. She returned to her office and met with her supervisor, Ben Ferguson. He gave her the great news that a new position, in addition to the general assistant's position, had been approved for the department. The two of them banged out the duties, both agreeing that the new rep would take over most of the traveling assignments.

Trina was so thrilled she closed the door to her office and did a little dance on the top of her desk.

Midjive, the door opened and Ben caught her. He stared at her blankly for a long moment.

Trina glanced at picture hanging next to her desk and blew the dust off the top of it. "Housekeeping is always missing that spot," she said with a smile and carefully got down.

"Uh, I just wanted to tell you that we have the go-ahead to hire, so you can tell personnel to post it in-house and out right away."

"Thanks," she said. "I'll do that."

"Are you okay?" Ben asked.

"Couldn't be better. And you?"

He moved his head in a circle. "Fine." He nodded. "Just keep up the good work."

She gave a quick salute. "I will," she said, but she was pretty sure Ben thought she'd eaten a few too many Froot Loops.

ON FRIDAY AFTERNOON, Walker left her a voice mail with instructions to dress "hot." Tight jeans and a hot shirt with some Bellagio heels.

Trina frowned at the message. All of her jeans that were tight were too tight to zip and she didn't know where her hot shirts were. She'd packed them away at six months of pregnancy and the suckers were still in boxes from when she'd moved into the condo.

On Friday night, BJ dropped off Danielle at Trina's while he went to pick up a pizza. "How are you feeling?" Trina asked the pregnant woman.

"Huge. Just when I think I can't get any bigger, I do," Danielle said, sinking onto the sofa and bending over to roll a musical ball toward Maddie.

"You know that the baby puts on most of its weight the last few weeks, don't you?" Trina asked, going through a box of shirts she hadn't worn in—forever.

"Yes. Does that mean my baby's going to weigh twenty pounds?"

Trina laughed. "Well, Walker told me that the Gordons historically have big babies."

"Does that mean it's too late to put in an order for an economy-sized model?" Danielle asked.

"Afraid so." Trina held up a flowy halter top with beads below the bust. "I wonder if I can still fit into this."

"That would be great for tonight. Just make sure you wear it with a pair of killer jeans and high heels," Danielle said.

Trina gave the pregnant woman a second look. "How do you know what I should wear?"

Danielle smiled coyly. "Because I know where Walker is taking you tonight."

"Where?"

Danielle shook her head. "Can't tell. Sworn to secrecy."

"You're no help," Trina fumed.

Danielle paused. "Just dress like a sexy groupie and you'll fit right in."

Trina shook her head. "I cannot imagine where he's taking me since it's not Halloween."

"Not by the calendar," Danielle said. "That's all I'm saying. BJ should be back soon. You need to get dressed. Go scoot. I'll stay here with Maddie girl."

Trina grabbed three shirts and two pair of jeans and went upstairs. With the help of underwear that felt like she'd been swallowed by a python, she was able to zip up one pair of the jeans. She tried on and discarded the first two shirts, tried on the third and returned to the first one, a green one that fit tight at the bust and fluttered over her abdomen and hips. After stepping into a pair of green leather Bellagio heels, she looked in the mirror and added some eye shadow, liner and mascara.

"Just this side of a 'ho,'" she muttered to herself, rubbing away some of the eye shadow. The doorbell rang and she heard Walker's voice. Her heart bumped in her chest, which was very stupid. They already knew each other. No need to get worked up, she told herself as she spritzed on some perfume.

The doorbell rang again and this time she heard BJ's voice. No heart-bumping that time, her evil inner twin told her. Trina bared her teeth at the mirror and put on a pair of dangly earrings.

With nothing else to help her stall, she turned off her light and headed downstairs.

She walked into the kitchen to find Maddie in her high chair, picking up Cheerios with great deliberation while Danielle and BJ ate pizza.

BJ glanced up at her and made a choking sound.

Walker, dressed in a leather jacket, worn jeans and a black T-shirt, stood next to Maddie's chair, holding a box of Cheerios. "In advertising, we have to stay on top of company goals and sometimes even provide our clients with new goals in order to—" Walker looked up at Trina and broke off midsentence. He looked her up and down and up again.

Trina couldn't deny a little rush of pleasure. Walker rarely stumbled over his words. "How about that?" Trina said, glancing at Maddie. "You're in the same room with her, but she's not crying."

Walker gave the box of Cheerios a shake. "Her lower lip started to poke out, so I bribed her again."

BJ chuckled. "Walker's not good with babies. It's like dogs. They smell his fear. Maybe he'll get better after our baby is born and he gets a chance to play uncle." He took another bite of pizza. "Gotta tell you, I never thought he would date a woman with a baby, but I can see why he would make an exception for you. One hot mama."

Danielle whacked him on the arm. "BJ, you're embarrassing her."

BJ looked contrite. "Sorry. I just meant it as a compliment."

"Thanks," Trina said and looked at Walker's ear, needing to focus on something neutral. Not his eyes. "Ready to go?"

"Ready," he said and they walked toward the foyer. He opened the door. "Hot mama," he said in a low voice.

She shot him a sideways glance. "Cute, very cute." He shut the door behind them. "I'm guessing that you still haven't told BJ about Maddie."

"Not yet. He's got a lot going on right now. I want to pick the time that will have the least impact on him."

"Do you really think such a time exists?" she asked, walking toward his car.

He shrugged. "I don't want to gum up his aspirations to try to be a good husband and father."

Trina digested his response. Despite Walker's belief that Gordon men were rotten fathers, he'd done everything he could to help BJ successfully step into that role.

She wondered why he thought BJ could do it and he couldn't. Or maybe Walker just didn't want to do it.

He stopped and turned toward her when they got to the car. He leaned toward her. "I don't know what you're thinking, but I'm pretty sure it's not good. I just want to give you something else to think about. You had nine months to get used to the idea of having a baby. You gave me less than five minutes."

## CHAPTER EIGHTEEN

*YOU HAD NINE MONTHS to get used to the idea of having a baby. You gave me less than five minutes.*

Walker's words reverberated in her head throughout the drive to wherever he was taking her. Which ended up being a barbecue restaurant, if one used the term restaurant loosely. It was more of a stand with picnic tables. The locals knew it was the best.

"Best barbecue in Georgia," she said, unwrapping her sandwich and taking a sip of limeade.

"Best barbecue, period," Walker corrected. "I've eaten a lot of barbecue between Texas and Georgia, so I should know."

"Except ribs," she said. "Best baby back ribs are at a place called Carolina Roadhouse in Myrtle Beach, South Carolina."

"Sit-down place?" he asked, chowing down on his sandwich.

She nodded, taking a bite.

He shook his head. "That's for sissies."

"Don't knock it until you've tried it," she said, smiling.

"Is that an invitation?"

He met and held her gaze and she felt a zapping sensation that she wished she could blame on the spicy barbecue sauce. "We'll see."

"How did you end up in Myrtle Beach? Can't see your mother approving of that trip," he said, stealing one of her potato chips.

"She didn't. That was the reason I wanted to go. I was nineteen and I went with a group of friends right after final exams my freshman year at college."

"Girls gone wild?" he asked.

She paused, taking another bite of her sandwich and thinking back to that time of complete insanity. "Looking back, I'd refer to it as girls gone stupid. One of my friends was arrested for dancing naked on the beach. She'd used a fake ID to get into a bar and drank way too many hurricanes."

"Bet that drew a crowd," he said dryly.

"My other girlfriend got arrested at a party where they were serving brownies with a kick."

"Okay, and what about Carter-Aubrey?" he asked, referring to the name her mother used.

Trina made a face. "Trina," she corrected. "Nothing illegal. Something incredibly stupid and rash, but not illegal."

"What'd you do?"

She shook her head. "I'm not telling."

"C'mon, you can trust me," he said. "I'll keep your secret safe."

Too embarrassing, she thought. "This is like stretch marks. I don't show them to just anyone." She balled up her paper and stood. "Thank you for the best barbecue sandwich I've ever eaten."

He looked up at her. "You're really gonna leave me hanging about what you did in Myrtle Beach."

"I told you the interesting stuff. My friends were much more adventurous."

He stood and leaned toward her, his mouth inches from hers. "You're lying, Carter-Aubrey Katherine, but that's okay. I'll find out your secret sometime."

His closeness made her heart race as if she was running a sprint. "Not from me," she promised, but the huskiness in her voice lacked the necessary punch.

He chuckled and his eyes gleamed with a dangerous expression. "Oh, sweetheart, you may as well have just said I dare you."

"No, I didn't," she said quickly. "I just said—"

He put his thumb over her bottom lip, stilling her words and her breath. "Don't worry. It won't hurt a bit," he teased then dropped his hand from her face and snagged her wrist. "Come on. Time for part B of our date."

"What's part B?"

"You'll see soon enough."

Walker drove to a bar on the other end of town. He escorted her inside where a man dressed as Alice Cooper checked ID and hard rock music vibrated off the black painted walls. The dim lighting was offset by sporadically placed black lights and lava lamps

"What is this?" she asked Walker, gawking at men dressed in spandex, with long hair.

"It's rock star impersonator night, featuring favorite rock bands, Kiss, Alice Cooper and Aerosmith. Hey, look, is that a Gene Simmons wannabe?"

Trina looked at a man with a painted face and black spiky hair who kept sticking out his tongue. "I think so." She looked at another with long dark blond hair wearing skinny pants. "David Lee Roth?"

He put his arm around her hip and lowered his mouth to her ear. "Yep, and don't look now, but here comes Madonna."

Trina gaped at a rather stout woman with platinum hair who had strapped herself into a bustier with cone-shaped cups.

"Hate to be around if the snaps bust on that one," Walker muttered.

Trina couldn't swallow a laugh. She punched Walker's shoulder. "You are so bad. Why in the world did you bring me here?"

"It's not dull, is it?" he asked, looking around. "Hey, here comes your dream guy."

A Steven Tyler look-alike, with his long brown hair, skinny body and puckered lips, winked at her as he walked past her. She felt a remnant of the silly thrill she would have when she'd been in high school.

"So is he your dream guy?"

"Fifteen years ago," she said. "This is like going to the circus, only better because I don't like the circus."

"Yeah, well, let's go take a look at the dance floor. If this is a circus, then that's gotta be the center ring."

They walked into a room with tables alongside a large dance floor where a myriad of costumed people gyrated and played air guitars.

Walker snagged a waiter. "Can you get me a beer and glass of white wine? Thanks, guy," he said and pulled two chairs together so they could sit.

Putting his arm across the back of her chair, he leaned toward her. "Okay, we're going to play name the rock star. Winner chooses our next date."

His thigh pressed against hers distracted her. "Next date?" she echoed.

"Yeah, unless you just want to go ahead and admit I'll beat you and I can go ahead and plan the next date."

An obvious ploy to get her involved and committed to another date. And she couldn't resist. She pointed to a woman with long, long dark hair. "Alanis

Morissette." A woman dancing beside her had long wavy blond hair and wore a gypsylike dress. "Stevie Nicks."

"Chick singers," he said with more than a little disdain. "There's a real rock star. Mick Jagger."

So it went for the next hour and a half. The music was so loud they both had to stay in each other's faces in order to hear and be heard.

Trina, bless her insane soul, didn't find it a bit of a hardship to sit so close to Walker and trade opinions on the costumes.

The disc jockey revved up the crowd with a string of hits by Aerosmith. "Wanna dance?" Walker asked.

Feeling a stab of self-consciousness, she shook her head. "Nah, that's okay."

"C'mon," he said, rising.

She shook her head. The Steven Tyler look-alike Trina had seen earlier strutted past and Walker grabbed his shoulder.

"Hey!" he said and pointed toward Trina.

Her stomach sank. "Oh, no." She shook her head as the guy approached.

"Come on," the look-alike said. "You'll blow my chances of winning the contest if you say no."

Somehow she ended up on the floor dancing to "Walk This Way," which segued into "Sweet Emotion." The DJ slowed things down with Aerosmith's recent ballad.

Walker tapped Mr. Not-Quite Steven Tyler on the shoulder. "My turn," he said and the rock star grinned and moved on.

Walker pulled her against him. "Does this mean I'm gonna have to get collagen in my lips to get your attention?"

She laughed at the image and sank against him. "It's not just the lips. It's the whole charming bad-boy persona who sings both hard rock and love ballads."

"Sappy love ballads," he said in disgust. "There's only one good reason to put up with a sappy love ballad."

"What's that?"

"It gives me a way to get close to Carter-Aubrey Katherine, also known as hot mama," he murmured then kissed her right there on the dance floor.

And she let him.

After they left the club, Trina leaned her head against the back of the passenger seat in Walker's car, and wondered what tonight would have been like if she and Walker hadn't spent that one night together that had changed everything. She couldn't possibly unwish Maddie, but she wondered, especially now, how things might have progressed for them under normal circumstances.

"Too quiet," Walker said, breaking the silence. "What's going through that beautiful brain of yours?"

"I was wondering how we would have felt about each other if we'd had a different beginning."

"What do you wonder?"

She shrugged. "I don't know. If you would ever have asked me out on a real date. If we would have gone out a second time."

"Yeah, we would have."

She gave him a second look. "How can you be so sure?"

"It's obvious we wanted each other on some level even if we didn't admit it," he said. "I wouldn't have been able to have sex with you all night long on the wedding night I was supposed to share with another woman if I hadn't wanted you."

"That was rebound sex for you. I could have been anyone. Plus, you were probably mentally having sex with Brooke."

"Trina, I don't remember everything about that night, but I do know that I wasn't pretending to have sex with Brooke. Sweetheart, I was in you, no mistaking that."

She felt a rush of heat at the visceral image of Walker sliding inside her. She adjusted the vent so that the air hit her face.

"And you may not want to admit it, but you had to be feeling more than pity for me to keep going."

"I never said I didn't find you attractive."

"That's good to know," he said in a dry tone that made his cockiness appealing. He pulled his car in front of her town house and cut the lights. "Speaking of our next date, since I'm the clear winner of the name-the-rock-star game tonight—"

"You are so not!" she retorted. "I won the game. I left you eating my dust. You couldn't name any of the women except the Madonnas and that's because they had pointy boobs."

He laughed. "Okay, then you plan the next date. When and where?"

She opened her mouth and paused, realizing she'd stepped into his trap. "You know I could say never and nowhere."

He leaned across the console. "But you wouldn't do that because you're not a bad sport, right, Carter-Aubrey Katherine?"

She shot him a dark look. "If you don't stop with the names—"

"Shut me up," he dared her. "You know how."

Another dare. So tempting. She hesitated.

"Carter-Aub—"

She kissed him. She pressed her lips against his and he immediately responded, opening his mouth and inviting her inside. She slid her tongue past his lips and the interior of his car heated up.

He tangled his hands in her hair and Trina felt herself tilt toward wildness. Something about the way he touched her lit all the darkened candles inside her. The way he kissed her made her want to give more, get more.

He pulled back slightly and shook his head. "Another night. Another hard-on. Let's do something tomorrow night."

She shook her head, remembering the date she'd made early this week. She'd deliberately made a date for the night after she went out with Walker to keep herself in check.

"Okay, Sunday. What about Sunday?" He kissed her again when she hesitated. "Say yes."

"Okay," she managed, her mind thick with the fog of arousal. "Sunday."

ON SATURDAY MORNING, Walker got up and went for a jog. He returned to find BJ carrying Harry's suitcase down the steps.

"Time for me to go," Harry said. "The doctor has released me. He said I can drive."

"Good for you," Walker said. "But there's no rush if you don't feel ready to leave."

Harry grinned. "I think a little privacy would do wonders for your stress level right now."

"You think?" Walker asked, returning his uncle's wily grin. "You know, I'm gonna miss fussing at your for stealing my beer."

"Took the rest of it," Harry said. "I found it in the desk drawer in your office. You might want to buy some more."

Walker chuckled and shook his head. "You want me to give you a ride home?"

"No, BJ here is going to cart me while Danielle catches a few extra winks. I think she's having a tough time sleeping. BJ told me that later today they're going to start cleaning the house they plan to rent."

Walker felt a tsunami wave of relief. As much as he loved his brother, this living situation just made him feel itchy.

Harry lowered his voice. "How are things going with Trina?"

"They're going," Walker hedged, not wanting to share his odd mix of thoughts and feelings about Trina with anyone.

Harry sighed. "Well, try not to screw it up too much."

"Thanks for the vote of confidence," Walker said.

"Hey, you know I think you and you brother and sister are the best things my lousy brother ever did, but I have seen the Gordon disasters in three generations. On the other hand, BJ seems determined as hell to do the right thing. If you and BJ could get on top of this fatherhood situation, it would be like giving your father the ultimate finger."

"Poetic way of putting it," Walker said and gave his uncle's shoulder a squeeze. "You know you've always got a place here if you want it."

"I do, but I also know it's time to go," Harry said.

Walker went with him to the foyer. "Don't be a stranger."

"Oh, I won't be far. Matter of fact, I'm coming back in town to take Aubrey out to dinner tonight," he said with another grin.

"You're kidding," Walker said, surprised at Harry's speed.

"No sir. She's a good-looking woman. Wound a little tight, but I might be able to help her with that," he said with a wink.

"I gotta warn you. Trina told me her mother and her father were arguing when her father was killed in an accident."

"I know. That's sad," Harry said soberly. "But just think if she could use up all that energy she uses for arguing in bed."

Walker covered his ears. "Harry, don't tell me any more. I don't want to be guilty by association."

Harry snorted. "Who's talking? You've done a helluva lot more than associate with Trina."

BJ returned. "You ready, Uncle Harry?"

"Sure am. Take care of yourself and what's important to you, Walker," Harry said and walked outside.

His uncle's words lingered with Walker throughout the day while he caught up on some work in his home office. He thought about Trina. And Maddie.

When he thought of Trina, he felt a mix of anticipation and the sense that he could count on her. Crazy because she hadn't made a commitment to him, but he knew well enough that she was a damn strong woman.

At least six times, he looked at the phone and thought about calling her and making up some reason that she should see him tonight instead of waiting until tomorrow.

But then he thought about Maddie and his stomach clenched. She was so cute, cute as hell, really. Unfortunately she scared the hell out of him, too. He knew it didn't make sense that a little baby should scare him, but she did. She didn't like him. Maybe she shouldn't, he thought, ugly memories of his father sneaking into his mind.

Late in the afternoon, he took a break and watched a ball game while BJ and Danielle left to clean the house they were renting.

Walker wondered what Trina was doing. He

thought about calling her again and procrastinated. She would like some uninterrupted time with Maddie.

His restlessness got to him, so he went to Charley's Sports Bar and grabbed a beer and a burger and watched another game there.

His cell phone rang just as he started his second beer. "Walker," he said, looking at the caller ID, and frowned. It was similar to BJs, but it wasn't his.

"Walker, this is Danielle. My water broke and I can't find BJ."

## CHAPTER NINETEEN

WALKER'S GUT FELL TO HIS FEET. "Your what broke?" he echoed.

"My water," Danielle said. "It's a sign of labor. I'm sorry to bother you, but I've called BJ several times and he's not answering. He said he would be right back and he would be bringing me a sur—"

She broke off and he heard her take an audible breath, then another. "This is starting to hurt."

Walker began to sweat. "Where are you? I'm coming right now," he said, and threw a twenty on the bar and left.

Danielle gave him the address as he got into his car. "I really want BJ. I think this is it."

"Hold tight, I'm coming. Do you have your doctor's number?"

"It's at the house," she said, her voice quivering. "What if something has happened to BJ? What if I have to do all of this alone?"

"You won't have to do this alone. BJ will be there. I'll be there." He pressed on the accelerator.

She made another sound of audible breathing. Walker checked his watch. Five minutes since the first time she did that.

"You know, I understand why Trina told me to get an epidural," Danielle said in a choked voice. "I felt crampy earlier, but I didn't want to say anything. I was embarrassed after the first time, but after my water broke." She took another breath. "This is really intense."

Walker decided to keep her on the phone with him for her sake and maybe his, too. "You're gonna have a baby soon. You and BJ never told me what you're going to have."

"We don't know," she said. "We wanted it to be a surprise. Where is BJ?"

"I don't know, but we'll find him. Do you want me to call him now?"

"Yes. No. I don't know. I just wish he was here with me."

"He will be. You're gonna be okay. The baby's gonna be okay. Everyone's gonna be okay."

She took more deep breaths. "How do you know? What if BJ was in an accident? What if I don't get to the hospital in time?"

Walker felt the sweat dripping down the back of

his neck. "There will be a good explanation for where BJ is. Later on, we'll laugh about it."

"I'm not laughing now. I'm hurting," she said in a voice that bordered on a wail.

"I'm going to get you to the hospital in no time. Just stay with me, Danielle. I'm almost there." He made three more turns and finally arrived at the address Danielle had given him.

Parking in the driveway, he rushed out of the car and left it running. Danielle appeared on the front step looking so scared and so young. He couldn't help thinking that Trina may have looked the same way when she went into labor with Maddie. The image tore at him.

"Here, Danielle. Let me help you to the car," he said and ushered her to the back seat of his car. "Just stretch out and try to relax. Can you tell me your doctor's name?"

"Scott. His name is Dr. Sean Scott."

"Okay, I'm on it," he said and dialed information. When he was connected with the doctor's emergency service, he gave the phone to Danielle. She answered questions about her condition, then returned the phone to him.

"They said to go to the hospital," she said with a laugh that bordered on hysterical. "I wasn't interested in an at-home delivery. I didn't even want a natural delivery. I just wanted a safe delivery with minimal pain with my husband. Ow!"

Walker swore under his breath. "I'll be at the hospital in just a few minutes."

"I hope they have someone who can give me an epidural," she said.

*Me, too.*

They arrived at the hospital and Walker took over the job of filling out the insurance papers so that Danielle could be admitted. He wondered who had done this same job for Trina.

While Danielle was examined, Walker made several calls to BJ's cell phone. No answer. He made another call to highway patrol on the terrible off chance that BJ had been in an accident, and was relieved to learn of no such reports.

The nurse told him that Danielle was asking for him, so he entered the labor and delivery area. In one room, he heard a woman screaming; in another, a woman was moaning clearly from pain. Again, he thought of Trina. He remembered that her labor had been long and hard and she'd been denied the epidural she'd requested.

He was led to Danielle's room. As he pushed open the door, he saw her sitting on the bed with her feet dangling over the side, her head bowed and her eyes closed with her arms over her belly. A moment passed and she looked up at him.

"I need to walk," she said. "Do you mind doing it with me? If BJ can't be here, I sure wish Trina could be."

She barely spoke the words before Walker dialed Trina's cell number.

"Hello?"

"It's Walker. Danielle's in labor. We can't find BJ. Can you come to the hospital?"

She paused less than a half beat. "I'll be there as soon as I can."

Walker paced up and down the hallway, alternately worrying about his brother and wanting to club him. The insidious thought that this was part of the Gordon curse slithered through his mind. Looking at poor Danielle, he sure hoped not.

Trina arrived, dressed in a black dress and heels. The rush of relief that swept through him knocked him sideways. He met her gaze and nodded.

"Hey," she said to him then turned to Danielle. "Hi, sweetie," she said, hugging Danielle. "How are you?"

"It hurts, but they said I should walk," Danielle said. "I'm only at three centimeters."

"So they're waiting on the epidural," Trina concluded sympathetically. "You're gonna get through this and you're going to have a beautiful baby. It really will be soon," Trina said with an encouraging smile.

"But BJ's not here," Danielle said, her voice catching.

Trina hugged her again. "You're going to be okay. It's all going to work out. You'll see."

Danielle sighed and looked at Trina. "You look pretty. What did I interrupt?"

"I'd just finished dinner, so you didn't interrupt anything. Do you want to walk some more or take a break?"

"I'll walk a little more," Danielle said.

"I've got you covered if you need to make some calls," Trina said to Walker. Behind Danielle's back, she mouthed, *Where's BJ?*

He shook his head. "I'll be back in a few minutes." Walker called BJ, then he called the highway department again.

Grabbing two cups of coffee, he returned to the labor and delivery area. Trina stood outside Danielle's room.

"The doctor's examining her, so I thought I would give her a little privacy." She accepted the cup of coffee and took a sip. "Thank you. Where in hell is your brother?"

"No idea. I've been torn between staying and going out to look for him, but I don't know where to look. Danielle said he'd left to bring her a surprise, but she didn't know what that was."

Trina shook her head. "I don't want her to feel abandoned."

He felt an ugly twist in his gut. "Like you did?"

She hesitated and closed her eyes for a few seconds. "It's just a horrible feeling to hurt that much and feel like you're all by yourself."

"I'm sorry," he said. "I'm really sorry."

"You can't be responsible for what you didn't know," she said.

"But I bet you still wanted to kill me when those contractions hit," he said.

She shot him a sideways look. "Oh, no, at that point, death would have been too easy."

The door to Danielle's room opened. "You can come inside," the doctor said.

"I'm at six centimeters," Danielle said. "I can have an epidural now."

"Oh, Danielle, that's wonderful. I'm so happy for you," Trina said.

"Where's BJ?" Danielle asked, looking at him with eyes full of hope.

"We're working on it. You just concentrate on you and the baby."

Danielle closed her eyes and sucked in a shallow breath. She panted. Trina took her hand.

"You're doing so good. A few more seconds," she coached.

"I want that epidural," Danielle said.

Trina glanced at the nurse. "Where's the anesthesiologist? If you can't get him here in three minutes, then I'll go after him."

Four minutes later, Walker and Trina stood outside Danielle's room again while the anesthesiologist administered the epidural.

"They stick her in the spine?" he asked, shuddering.

"Yep. By the time transition rolled around, I wanted to stick myself," she said.

"I don't see how women do it," he said.

"I guess there's a reason women give birth and men don't."

"Yeah," he said and looked her over. She looked classy and sexy. Not dressed for a trip to the labor and delivery room. "It was nice of you to come so fast. You never said what we interrupted."

"Yes, I did. Dinner, but I was mostly done anyway."

Walker had been running on sheer adrenaline, focused on Danielle and finding BJ. He looked at Trina's dress again and realization sank in. "You were on a date."

She shrugged. "Yes. First date."

Offended, jealous and pissed that he felt either emotion, he stared at her. "After we had that date on

Friday night with plans to get together on Sunday, you went out with another guy."

"You and I have not discussed exclusivity," she said. "Not so long ago, you were pushing me to go out with other men. You wanted me to get married."

"That was before you and I agreed to see what might happen between us," he told her, surprised that he felt hurt.

"I didn't totally agree," she said heatedly. "Besides I set up this date earlier in the week."

"That's supposed to make me feel better."

She moved closer to him. "Quit being a jerk," she said, her cheeks blooming with color. "I went out with David so I would keep my head straight about you."

He looked into her eyes for several seconds and saw fear, anger and passion. She was afraid of falling for him. The realization nearly knocked him on his ass.

"Did it work?"

She rolled her eyes. "We're not going to discuss this right now. Danielle is getting ready to have a baby. We have two centimeters before things get ugly."

"What do you mean two centimeters?" he asked.

"She's at six centimeters. Ten centimeters is baby time. Eight centimeters is transition."

"And?"

"She will hate every man who has walked the planet since Adam."

He felt a sliver of relief. "So I should stay away, right?"

She shook her head. "Not if you want you and your brother to live," she said.

The nurse opened the door. "You can come back in now."

Walker wasn't sure he wanted to, but he did. He watched Trina and Danielle interact over the next hour and his admiration for Trina grew. She reassured Danielle and praised her, gave her ice chips and put a washcloth on Danielle's forehead when the doctor halted the medication on the epidural.

As Trina had predicted, Danielle's mood turned ugly.

"Where the hell is your sorry brother?" she asked Walker, her eyes wide with pain. "He left me alone in that house, and now he's left me alone to have this baby."

She gasped as another contraction hit her. "He doesn't deserve this baby. He doesn't deserve me! He doesn't deserve to live."

Trina tossed him an I-told-you-so look.

Walker swore under his breath. This was all wrong. All wrong.

The door burst open and BJ rushed into the room with a panicked expression on his face. He immediately strode to her side. "Danielle, oh, honey, I'm so sorry. I went to get your surprise and the truck died on the way back."

"What happened to your cell phone?" she asked through gritted teeth.

BJ gave a sheepish look. "I threw it in the back seat when I was trying to fix the truck. When I started to call you, the battery died. I'm sorry, honey. I'm really sorry."

She made a strangled sound of pain as another contraction hit. BJ turned white with shock. "She's in pain. Somebody's gotta do something."

"Unfortunately it's part of the program at this point," Trina said.

Walker watched his brother weave on his feet while his eyes rolled back in his head. He jumped forward to catch BJ as he fell sideways.

Trina stared at BJ in amazement. "He fainted?"

The nurse called for help and the room turned into a cluster of confusion. Walker was so pissed at his brother he wanted to stuff the ammonia tablets straight up BJ's nostrils.

BJ shook his head as his eyes fluttered. "What happened?"

"You fainted," Walker said and lowered his voice just for his brother's ears. "Buck up and quit being a wuss. Your wife needs you."

BJ slowly rose to his feet and returned to Danielle's side. "Are you okay, honey? Tell me what I can do for you."

"If you ever get me pregnant again, I'll kill you," she said, spitting the words at him. "I want to push."

"Let me get the doctor," the nurse said.

Twenty minutes later, after encouragement from Trina, the nurse, the doctor, BJ and himself, Walker watched the doctor lift up a red, screaming infant.

"It's a boy," he said.

"Omigod, it's a boy," Danielle sobbed.

"You had a boy," Trina said, sniffing.

"We had a boy," BJ said, staring in disbelief, his face turning white.

Alarm rushed through Walker and he stepped forward to hold the ammonia tablets under his brother's nose. "Don't even think about it," he muttered.

BJ blinked then looked at Walker. "I have a son."

The doctor wrapped the baby in a blanket and placed him on Danielle's belly.

"He's beautiful," she said. "Oh, look at him. He's so sweet. Look at our baby, BJ."

BJ stared down at his freshly born son and began to weep.

With an awful sense of loss in his gut, Walker looked at Trina and began to realize how much he'd missed.

## CHAPTER TWENTY

WALKER GAVE TRINA A LIFT HOME. Since David had dropped her off at the hospital, she had no vehicle. He followed her into her house and while she paid the sitter, he went upstairs.

She knew what he was doing before she climbed up the stairs after him. He was in Maddie's room staring at her while she slept.

She stepped into the room and sure enough, he stood there in the dark, looking at Maddie. Although she knew he felt tortured, she wished she knew the thoughts running through his head.

He stood there next to her crib for several moments then turned to Trina. "What was she like when she was first born?" he whispered.

Trina's heart squeezed tight. She slid her hand over his and gently tugged. "Let's talk downstairs."

"The first three days, she was so sweet," Trina said as they walked into the den. "She didn't cry very much at all. Had a little pink rash on her cheeks and she didn't have much hair, but I, of course, knew she was the most beautiful baby ever born."

He cracked part of a smile and joined her on the sofa.

"She liked being bundled tightly in the beginning. I think it made her feel more secure. I thought I was going to have this sweet, quiet little baby."

"Not?" he asked.

"Colic," Trina said, wincing. "She had an arsenic hour every night. Maybe it was two hours when she cried and cried. I felt so sorry for her. And then when I couldn't get any sleep I cried, too."

"How did you get through it?"

"My mother helped some. Jenny Prillaman helped. It could have been worse."

"Or better," he said.

She shrugged. "She got better after about two months and when she started to sleep through the night at four months, I was sure I'd died and gone to heaven."

"When did you go back to work?"

"When she was three months, but I don't remember much of that first month. Ben cut me some slack, thank goodness."

"Did you ever think about calling me?"

"What could I say? Oops. Had a baby. Could you fly over and take a turn watching her tonight so I can get some sleep?"

"Yeah, you could have. If you had told me you

were going to have my baby, I would have come back sooner."

"But I knew you didn't want children," she reminded him.

"Sometimes it's not about what you want. It's about what's right."

Trina wasn't certain she liked the determined expression on his face. "I didn't want that for Maddie. I didn't want it for me. My parents fought all the time, but they stayed together out of obligation. I never want to be your obligation. I never want Maddie to feel like your obligation."

"That's why you blew a gasket when Alfredo told us we should get married," Walker said and paused. "So how do I convince you that the reason I want to be with you isn't because I feel obligated?"

"That's a tough one," she said.

"But not impossible," he said, pulling her closer.

Her heart thudded in her chest. "Brooke is a hard act to follow."

"You underestimate your appeal."

She looked into his eyes and could almost believe him. Almost.

"Until tonight, I was glad I hadn't been there when Maddie was born. The idea scared the life out of me."

"But now," she said, sensing he felt different.

"Now I feel cheated. I don't blame you for not

telling me you were pregnant. But I wish I could have been here."

"Why? If you think Danielle was testy, you have no idea what I was like."

"I wish I could have taken care of you," he said, lifting his hand to her hair.

"I still would have screamed at you and told you that you were the lowest form of life on the planet."

"I think I could have handled that," he said.

The strength in his gaze did something to her, got past her defenses, knocked the slats from beneath her.

He gently tugged her hair so that she moved her face closer to his. Then slowly, offering her plenty of time to push him away, he took her mouth with his.

Trina felt a bubble of emotion well up between them. It was new, strong and flavored with more than passion. The kiss went on and on and felt so good that she didn't want it to stop. She wished she didn't need to breathe and that he didn't, either.

He rubbed his mouth over her ear. "I want to make love to you."

Her chest squeezed tight. She struggled with conflicting feelings of want and need and fear. "I'm not sure that's a good idea."

"It's a great idea. We're both sober and we both want each other."

He slid his hands through her hair to the back of her neck and gently rubbed the taut muscles.

"I'm not on birth control," she said, because the way he touched her made her feel like a flower. "And I guess we both know that vasectomy of yours didn't take."

"You got that right. But, hey, I'm your condom-carrying guy," he said. "More than one in case we—"

She groaned to cover the rest of his suggestion and he leaned back on the sofa, pulling her on top of him. "If you won't let me make love to you, then let's just make out for a while."

Trina couldn't turn down that invitation because she loved the way Walker kissed. He French kissed her and squeezed her bottom, guiding her over his erection.

Her internal temperature heated up and she felt ripples of sensations in her breasts and between her legs. He didn't take off her clothes, but he managed to make her nipples stiffen even through the fabric of her dress and bra. He didn't slide his hands up her bare legs but his movements made her wet and swollen.

He stayed on the edge and she started to wish he would dive in and take her with him. She wanted to feel his naked skin against hers, his bare chest against her breasts. She wanted him to touch her with his hands, with his mouth.

She tried to swallow a moan as she wiggled over

his swollen erection. "Oh, Trina, you're driving me nuts," he whispered, but he still kept his hands on the outside of her clothes, driving her insane.

Hot and bothered, she pulled his shirt loose and slid her hands over the bare skin of his belly. He made a hissing sound of arousal at her touch. "How am I supposed to keep from ripping off your clothes if you're taking off mine?"

"Maybe you're supposed to rip off my clothes," she said and rubbed an openmouthed kiss over his naked chest.

"Okay, I'm taking that as permission," he said, and pulled down her zipper. A second passed and he was tugging her dress over her head. He unfastened her bra, and when she bent down to kiss him her breasts meshed with his chest.

They both said, "Ahhh."

He ran his hands over her from her waist to the sides of her breasts to her bottom as if he couldn't touch enough of her.

She pushed his shirt off him and he slid his hands inside her panties. Everywhere he touched her, she felt as if her skin sizzled.

His hair was mussed, his eyes dark, steeped with wanting. He squeezed her bottom then rose upward, pushing her on her knees.

"What are you doing?"

"I can't touch enough of you when I'm on my back," he said, pushing her panties down her thighs. "I want to get to all of you."

The rough edge in his voice revved up the heat inside her. With one hand, he cupped one of her breasts, toying with her nipple, while he slid his other hand between her legs where he found her wet and swollen.

"Oh, Trina, you feel so good." He flicked his thumb over her hot spot and she undulated against him. Between the sensual way he took her mouth and what he was doing to her body, she couldn't breathe.

It was so good, but it wasn't enough. She wanted more. Unable to stop a moan from her throat, she tugged at his belt. Arousal made her fingers clumsy, but she got it loose and then she unfastened his jeans and pushed the zipper down. It made a hissing sound of anticipation.

She plunged her hands inside his briefs and found him hard. She stroked him with both hands. He swore in a mixture of pleasure and pain.

"Damn, Trina," he muttered and slid a finger inside her.

She quivered. He rubbed and stroked her and she felt herself tighten with each stroke, each groan he made, each kiss.

"I want in," he told her and shucked his jeans and

underwear in one swift motion. He grabbed three plastic packets from his pocket and tossed two of them on the sofa table. He ripped open the third and pulled on the condom.

Caressing the insides of her thighs, he eased them open and slid between her legs. He snagged one of her hands with his and wove his fingers between hers.

That gesture, more caring than sexual, felt unbelievably intimate. He made the moment more intimate, when holding her gaze, he thrust inside her.

As if that connection didn't quite bring him close enough, he lowered himself and took her mouth.

Trina was overcome. She hadn't been touched or caressed or really even held like this in so long. Her heart filled up, crowding her chest so she couldn't breathe. A lump formed in her throat and she closed her eyes.

She hadn't realized how lonely she'd been. She'd become adept at dodging the depth and breadth of the feeling by filling her day with Maddie and her job.

The enormity of it contrasted with how she felt now in Walker's arms. Her throat felt so tight with emotion that she couldn't swallow. Her eyes burned and to her horror, she felt a tear stream down the side of her face.

Walker pulled back as if he felt her body tense. "Something wrong?" He studied her and surprise crossed his face. "You're crying."

Embarrassed, she swiped her eyes. "I'm sorry. I don't know why—" She broke off and shook her head.

"Does it hurt? Do you want me to stop?"

"No," she said quickly and took a deep breath. "It's just been such a long time. I must have a lot bottled up." She glanced away. "I'm sorry."

"No apologies," he said, covering her mouth with his finger. Then he grinned and pumped inside her. "If you've got a lot bottled up, that's okay. We can use all three condoms tonight."

After that, he seemed determined to take his time and her sanity. He slid down her body and attended to her breasts, then lower to her belly.

"Don't look at my stretch marks," she whispered.

He mocked her request by tracing them with his tongue. He went lower still and kissed her until the pleasure was too much and she arched off the sofa in a climax.

He worked his way up her body and slid inside her again. She shuddered and he swore. "You make me wish I'd brought more condoms," he said, thrusting inside her in a mind-blowing rhythm.

Still weak from her first climax, she clung to him. Every stroke sent her back up again, closer to the edge.

"Come on, baby, we're taking this ride together."

Just as she felt herself convulse around him, he thrust and she felt his pleasure vibrate inside every millimeter of her. He cuddled her head in his hand as if she were precious, as if he wanted to protect her.

It was difficult enough to tell herself to remain unaffected by his tenderness, by the way he held her hand and cradled her against him. She couldn't be swayed by his gentle kiss on her forehead and the way he stroked her hair.

After all, this was Walker, and what woman could really get to him? Trina wasn't sure that even Brooke had gotten to the core of him. How could she?

He made it hard to hold back her heart and keep it safe, and when he picked her up and carried her up to her bedroom, he made it nearly impossible.

MADDIE'S CALL AWAKENED Trina from a dead sleep the next morning. She threw the covers aside and was immediately reminded of her complete nakedness.

Grabbing a robe, she slipped her arms through the sleeves and tied the belt. Oh, what a night. She caught a quick flash of her head in the mirror on her dresser and made a face.

Her hair was a tangled mess, mascara smudged beneath her eyes and her lips were so swollen she looked like someone had hit her in the mouth. The true cause of the swelling was that Walker had kept her mouth busy in the most pleasurable way.

Yawning as she walked to the bathroom, she felt a few twinges of soreness. He'd kept her body pretty busy, too. Avoiding looking at the mirror, she washed her face, brushed her teeth and brushed her hair.

"Coming, carrot cake," she called as Maddie's voice grew impatient. Shuffling toward the nursery, Trina vaguely recalled that Walker had left around two in the morning.

"I can't lie next to you when you're naked when I'm out of condoms," he grumbled. "Now I understand why we couldn't stop the first time we got together."

"Because we were drunk?" she'd managed.

"No, ma'am," he said and kissed her. "But we'll talk about that more later. Get some sleep. I'll see you in the morning."

Trina pushed open the door to the nursery and Maddie let out a shriek and bounced on her mattress. Trina automatically smiled. How could she not?

"Good morning to you, too, little one," she said, scooping up her daughter and transferring her to the padded changing table to change her diaper. "Thank you for giving me a few extra winks this morning," she said. "Very nice of you."

Maddie lifted her lips in a gummy smile and chortled. Trina put her daughter on her hip and walked downstairs. With Maddie toying with her hair, Trina prepared a bottle of formula and oatmeal with apple juice. She put Maddie into her high chair and began to feed her.

A knock sounded at the door, surprising her. Scooping Maddie out of her chair, she went to the front door to find Walker armed with a bag of something from a bakery and two cups of coffee that smelled wonderful.

"Good morning," he said, his gaze taking in Trina and then Maddie. "Beautifuls."

Trina smiled at the plural. "Thank you. I'm surprised you're awake." She stepped to the side to let him in.

He brushed his mouth over hers. "I don't usually sleep late."

Her heart picked up. "With an infant, the word is never, but Maddie usually wakes up happy, so that makes early wake-up a little less painful. Right, sweetie?"

Maddie stared solemnly at Walker.

"She still doesn't like me," he said.

"She doesn't know you," Trina corrected and returned to the kitchen. She slid Maddie into her chair again and lifted the spoon to feed her. A thought occurred to her, making her pause.

Maddie kicked and banged on the chair.

Trina turned to Walker and gave him the spoon. "Why don't you feed her?"

He stared at her for a half second like a deer caught in headlights before he rallied. "Okay," he said. "I'll do it." Sounding as if he were talking himself into it, he took the spoon and sat in front of Maddie.

Trina watched them look at each other and the trepidation she saw mirrored in each of their gazes tugged at her.

He dipped the spoon into the oatmeal and lifted it to her mouth. Maddie glanced at the spoon, then at Trina, then at Walker. Daughter looked at father and father looked at daughter. It was almost as if a negotiation for world peace was taking place.

Maddie looked at the spoonful of food again, kicked her feet against the high chair and opened her mouth like a little bird.

Trina breathed a sigh of relief. One baby step forward. Walker finished feeding Maddie while Trina dug cholesterol-laden egg croissants out of the bag. She cleaned up Maddie, which resulted, as always, in protests, then put her on the floor on a blanket with her favorite toys.

She felt Walker watching her every movement. "Admiring my technique?" she asked, hoping he wasn't noticing how ragged she looked.

"Very efficient. How long do we have?"

"Five minutes. Eight tops," she said and took a bite of the croissant. "This is evil."

"There are two chocolate croissants in the bottom of the bag. Did you see them?"

Trina groaned and shook her head. "Your middle name is Satan, right? Do you know how many calories these things have?"

"How many did we burn last night," he said more than asked.

Trina stopped midbite and met his gaze. He smiled and she felt a girly flutter.

He took a sip of coffee and narrowed his eyes, probably because it was still hot. "We could burn some more during our date this afternoon."

"Which I've planned," she said, feeling a surge of heat rush through her.

His gaze darkened and it occurred to her that he was way too sexy for her good. "What did you have in mind?"

She swallowed over the arousal that swelled inside her. "A picnic in the park," she said. "With Maddie."

He stared at her for a half second, then gave a slow, sexy grin. "Okay, I can do that."

He could do a lot more, but she wasn't going to think about that. At least for the afternoon. Since Walker was available, she asked him to watch

Maddie while she took a shower and pulled herself together.

Slipping back downstairs, she rounded the corner and stopped abruptly at the sight of Walker and Maddie. He jiggled Maddie's musical ball and mashed a squeaky stuffed elephant

When Maddie made fussy noises, he reached toward her. His hand hovered over Maddie for a moment, then he pulled back and rubbed his hand over his face. He pulled an animal cookie from the little box and offered it to her. Maddie took the cookie and stuffed it in her mouth.

Trina sighed. He didn't want to touch Maddie; he didn't want to pick her up and hold her. Her heart tightened and she wished it could be easier.

"She doesn't usually bite," Trina said, trying to diffuse his tension and hers.

He glanced up at her, his gaze serious. He shrugged. "I know. You want to pick up some chicken for this picnic?"

"Sure," she said, wishing things could be different. Wishes were like pennies in the fountain, though, she thought. Many were tossed in the water. Most didn't come true.

Hours later, after a drive in her car with the top down and a couple of strolls around the park, she and Walker spread a quilt on the ground and nibbled on the Colonel's fried chicken. He sneaked a few teensy bites to Maddie, which her daughter loved.

"Do we really want to encourage her to like fried chicken?" Trina asked.

"It's gotta be better than that stuff you give her out of the jars." He made a face and gave Maddie another teensy bite of chicken.

"Just don't give her any French fries. The new research says French fries are terrible for you."

"What's the research on animal cookies?" he asked, giving her a sideways glance.

"I don't give her nearly as many as you do."

"That's because I'm still negotiating with her," he said. "She isn't sure she likes me yet."

"Or you're not sure you like her yet?" Trina bit her lip as soon as the words escaped her mouth. She should have swallowed that question, bit off her tongue if necessary.

He met her gaze. "I like her pretty much for someone I haven't known very long and considering the fact that she cries every time I get near her."

"She's not crying now," Trina pointed out.

"Because I'm giving her something to eat that tastes a helluva lot better than that nasty tasteless stuff she gets from a jar."

"Are you criticizing what I feed your daughter?"

"I wouldn't want to eat it, but I'm no baby expert."

Maddie began to fuss. She bobbed up and down on her well-padded bottom and looked expectantly at Walker.

He glanced at Trina. "I've created a monster."

She smiled and nodded. "There's a way out, though."

"What?"

"She likes to move almost as much as she likes to eat."

"Stroll," he said and stood.

"Swing," she corrected, pointing to a playground close by.

"She can't hold on by herself."

"They have swings for little kids with molded seats and straps and plastic things that keep them in the seat. Here. You take her while I clean up." She picked Maddie up and held her toward Walker.

He froze for a moment, looking at Maddie, as she was suspended. Her daughter wiggled, making a sound of protest. Walker paused another half beat, then took her in his arms and headed toward the playground.

Trina saw Maddie tilt her head around his arm to look at her, but her baby girl didn't cry. Trina let out the breath she was holding. She watched the two of them for a moment then tore her gaze away to clean up the remnants of their little picnic and return the stroller and blanket to her car.

Afterward, she made a wide circle and came up behind Walker as he pushed Maddie. She studied them for a moment and fighting the feeling of matchmaker, she tapped him on the shoulder.

"Hey," he said. "Where'd you come from?"

She shook her head and put her finger over her lips. "Go in front of her and push," she whispered.

"Why?"

"Just do it."

Shooting her a long-suffering gaze, he walked to the front of Maddie and began to push her. Maddie chortled, her wisp of red hair flying in the breeze. She batted her feet.

Walker cracked a slow smile and gave the swing another push. "You like this, don't you?"

Wheeeeeeee. Trina could practically feel Maddie's joy. She remembered the sensation of flying in the air with only a rubber seat and two chains for support. Pumping her legs, she went higher and higher with the wind pushing back her hair and that great euphoria racing through her.

She watched Maddie experience it. She watched Walker give it to her.

An internal camera snapped a photograph, then another and another. She sealed the images in her heart. She would have dreamed these moments during her pregnancy if she'd dared. But of course she hadn't dared. So why did her eyes burn and her throat tighten as if she was going to cry any minute?

The three of them returned to Trina's town house and Walker drove home with a promise to return later. Tired from the outing, Maddie fell asleep in her car seat. Trina allowed her to nap for an hour, but knew better than to let her sleep too long.

After approximately one hundred games of pat-a-cake and peekaboo, two strolls around the block, Maddie was falling asleep in her oatmeal. Trina put her to bed and lay down on the sofa.

A little while later, she awakened to Walker's lips brushing her cheek. He was sitting beside her on the couch. She wondered how long he'd been there.

"Are both girls all tuckered out?"

Trina nodded. "Pretty much. I had to work at it to keep Maddie awake. If she'd gone to sleep too early, she would wake up in the middle of the night ready to party. Did you get a chance to talk to BJ? How are Danielle and the baby doing?"

"I ran into him when he came back to the house for a shower. The good news is Danielle and the baby are doing great. They leave the hospital tomorrow."

"That all sounds good to me," she said, hearing resignation in his tone.

"It would be," he said. "If they were going home to their own house."

Realization hit her. "Oops." She winced. "I can let them borrow my bassinet. I've got a bunch of other baby things, too."

"I'll let BJ know. He was picking up a crib when his truck broke down, but I don't know what else they need."

"I think I'll give Danielle cleaning service for the next month as a gift."

He raised his eyebrows. "Pretty generous considering you don't know them very well."

"They both seem so young. Hopeful," she added. "But a little clueless. It makes me want to help them with the odds."

He nodded and rubbed his chin. "Yeah. Maybe I could pay for their move."

"Would that be a gift for yourself or them?" she asked.

He chuckled. "I can't lie. I want my own place back."

"Can't blame you."

"That's good to know," he said, sliding his hands under her shoulders and pulling her face toward his.

"Why is it good to know?" she asked, feeling a mixture of suspicion and pleasure.

"If you can't blame me for wanting my house back, then you can't blame me for wanting to stay with you until Danielle and BJ leave."

"That's a huge jump," she said, but tilted her head to one side to give him more room to nuzzle her throat.

"You have a big bed. Wasted space."

"I like to spread out sometimes."

"That's okay. You can spread out on me anytime you want." He gently pushed her down and slid on top of her.

He felt like a big, masculine sexy quilt on top of her. "I think you're confused. You just invited me to spread on top of you."

"You don't like this?" he asked, rubbing his open mouth over her throat.

"I didn't—"

He covered her mouth with his in a nibbling, inviting kiss that quickly turned hot. His hands wandered over the outside of her shirt over her breasts and down to cup her bottom. He rubbed against the inside of her thighs and she felt a steaming surge of want rip through her.

"I brought a box of condoms."

"A bit presumptuous," she forced herself to say, but oh, he felt so good.

"Determined," he corrected. "And prepared." He pushed up her shirt and lowered his head, then unfastened her bra and opened his mouth over her nipple. "I want to hear you moan some more."

Then he proceeded to make it impossible for her to keep quiet.

## CHAPTER TWENTY-ONE

MONDAY MORNING STARTED OUT crazy. Although Trina arrived at the office five minutes late, Amelia was nowhere in sight. Trina wondered if her wonder assistant was ill.

She needed something to clear her sex-clouded, sleep-deprived brain. She didn't know who was more determined to make up for lost time, her or Walker. Her legs felt like overstretched rubber bands, and her lips and chin were chapped from kissing. She couldn't recall a mojito hangover that had left her less coordinated since the night Maddie had been conceived. The thought scared the daylights out of her, but she reminded herself that they had used protection every single time.

Her cell phone rang before she could grab a cup of coffee. "Hello."

"Good morning, Carter-Aubrey," her mother said in a too-perky voice. "How are you?"

"Fine, thank you, and—"

"Good, I'm going to have a barbecue to celebrate the birth of Danielle and BJ's new son on Sunday night. I want you to be there."

"Isn't that a little early?"

"I've already spoken to Danielle. She loves the idea. I'd like for everyone to bring a little gift."

"Everyone?" Trina echoed, sinking into her chair. "Who are you inviting?"

"Just family. It's going to be casual. Harold has agreed to handle the grill."

"Harold?"

"Yes, Harold, the baby's great-uncle. Is there something wrong with your phone, darling? You're repeating everything I say."

"No, my phone is fine. I'm just surprised."

"Well, Harold has been so nice and generous in advising me about opening my home for special events. I think he would like to do something for BJ and Danielle, but he's a bachelor and a man, so he doesn't really know what to do." Her mother gave a coy laugh.

Trina felt a shot of alarm. "Mother, are you dating Harry?"

"Dating. I don't know that you would call it dating. We've been to dinner a few times. I prepared dinner for him yesterday and we took a nice drive."

"Mother, what are your intentions with Harry?" Trina asked. "We both know he's filthy rich."

"We haven't discussed his financial status," her mother said in a snippy tone. "Very much. Harold enjoys my company."

"He's a very nice man. I would like for you to be careful."

"Whatever do you mean?"

"I mean he's still recovering from heart surgery and you need to be careful with him."

"I don't know what you're insinuating, but I assure you I'm not a promiscuous woman. Harold has assured me that his doctor has given him a clean bill of health. He's ready to resume normal activities."

"I wasn't talking about sex, Mother. I don't want you to get him so upset he has another heart attack."

Her mother gasped. "That was uncalled for. Harold would tell you I've been nothing but kind. And as far as sex is concerned, I've firmly informed him that I won't go to bed with him until he's been tested and gives me the results."

Trina blinked. *Sex?* Her mother was considering having sex with Harry.

"Hello? Carter-Aubrey? Are you there?"

Trina cleared her throat. "Yes, I'm here."

"Back on task. Arrive at four o'clock and please pass along the invitation to Walker. Ta-ta."

The call disconnected and Trina stared at the

phone. Her mother and Harry. Sex? She shook her head. "Don't think about it," she whispered.

Hearing a rattling sound in the outer office, she rose from her chair and saw Amelia in a state of fluster. Her hair was disheveled, mascara smeared under one eye, and her buttoned cardigan sweater was off by two holes.

She glanced up with a lost expression on her face. "Sorry I'm late. I'll get your coffee right away."

Trina's office line rang. "I'll get the phone. No problem." She took the call from personnel and scheduled appointments for three interviews.

As soon as she hung up, Amelia appeared with a cup and placed it on Trina's desk. "There you go," she murmured, tugging at her lopsided sweater. "Sorry again that I was late. I, uh—" She gave a wan smile. "Monday morning mania."

Trina looked down at the cup. Of hot water. No coffee, just hot water.

"Damn, damn, damn. I can't believe I did that," Amelia said and reached for the cup.

Trina stared at the woman in surprise. She'd never heard Amelia swear. She'd always been so perfect. Something was very wrong. "I'd like you to close the door and sit down for a minute."

Amelia fluttered her hands in front of her. "I really— It's just—"

"Just for a minute," Trina said and waited for Amelia to close the door and sit down. "Is something wrong?"

Amelia sucked in a quick breath. "No. Nothing's wrong." She gave a quick smile that was more of a grimace. "Just a Monday."

Trina could see that the woman was wound tighter than a bad perm. "It's okay. You don't have to be perfect every minute. You just seem not yourself this morning. Is there something I can do to help?"

Amelia began to sniff and snort. Tears streamed down her cheeks. "It's William," she wailed.

"Is he hurt?"

She shook her head. "No, no."

"Sick?" She didn't want to say her next thought. Dead? Had he died? Amelia shouldn't have come to work if her fiancé had died.

Amelia shook her head again. "No. He wants us to take a break from each other." Her voice broke and she buried her face in her hands.

Trina's heart wrenched for her always-composed assistant. Grabbing several tissues, she rounded the desk and patted Amelia on the shoulder. "I'm so sorry. I can tell this has caught you off guard."

Amelia sobbed and shook her head. "He's moving away without me."

"Oh, I'm so sorry."

"I have to find an apartment or move back home," Amelia continued. "He moved out yesterday."

"That fast? He didn't give you any more notice than that? Prick," she muttered, feeling a stab of indignation. "I know this feels like the end of the world."

"It is," Amelia said, sobbing. "Without him my life is meaningless. I don't know how I can go on."

"I know it's awful to get your heart broken. It's happened to me more than once." She wondered if it would happen again.

"I've never had my heart broken. I can't remember not loving William." She sniffed. "We have to get back together. I have to believe we will. How else will I live?"

Trina bent over to hug Amelia. "In the meantime, you still have to put one foot in front of the other. I think I can find a place for you to stay temporarily. It's a nice place and you'll be very safe there," she said, wondering how much she would need to twist her mother's arm to let Amelia use a room in her house. "And since you need to take care of yourself, you can accept a job with Bellagio. You know how much we love you here."

"But what if William comes to his senses and realizes how wrong this is and that we really are meant to be together? I need to be ready to go."

"In that case, you can give two weeks' notice and

be on your way. But for now you need to take care of yourself."

"Because William isn't going to take care of me," Amelia wailed and began sobbing again.

"I think you should take off the rest of the day. Go back home."

"I can't go back there right now. I can't bear it. He's gone."

"Okay, go to my place. Take a nap. Take a Jacuzzi bath. And there's a chocolate croissant in the white bakery bag on the counter. It's all yours." She grabbed a notepad from her desk and jotted down her address and basic directions. "Turn right out of the parking lot, south on the interstate, second exit, second right, third left. And we'll have a few drinks tonight."

"I don't really drink very much," Amelia said.

"We may want to make an exception tonight. And your sweater," Trina said, pointing at Amelia. "You might want to recheck your buttons."

Amelia glanced down and shook her head. "I'm ruined. I'm totally ruined. I'll never be any good again."

"Wrong. You've just had a shock. You're a resilient woman. I knew that the first time I saw you." She opened the door to her office. "Now get a Jacuzzi and eat the chocolate croissant."

Trina watched Amelia leave the office wearing a

lost expression on her face. She felt a pang of sympathy. A broken heart was a terrible, terrible thing.

Fighting the sting of guilt, she dialed the extension for personnel. Amelia would recover, Trina told herself, and when she did, Trina wanted the young woman working for her.

"Mary Henderson, personnel."

"Amelia Parker is going to join Bellagio. I'm calling dibs."

For the sake of Amelia's privacy, Trina didn't elaborate. Within five minutes, however, she'd negotiated a room for Amelia at her mother's home and arranged for Jenny Prillaman Waterson to visit that evening to help commiserate with Amelia. Trina gave Jenny strict instructions that the new bride could not rave endlessly over her new husband, but Jenny was supposed to provide some "hope" factor. Between making follow-up business calls, she made a list of things to pick up at the grocery store on the way home.

AFTER PUTTING IN a long day at the office, Walker picked up take-out food on the way home for BJ, Danielle and himself. He also picked up two bouquets of flowers, one for Danielle and the other for Trina.

He complimented the new parents and ate some

Chinese food. Looking forward to a quiet evening with Trina tonight, he drove to her town house and was surprised to see extra vehicles in her driveway.

Curious about the occasion, he rang her doorbell and listened to loud music playing inside. He felt a stab of discomfort. Was she having a party?

Without him?

Trina opened the door and stared at him in surprise. Music boomed from inside the house. "What are you doing here?" She looked at the flowers and blinked. "Did we have plans?"

"I did. Here," he said, giving her the bouquet of daisies.

Her face softened. "Oh, Walker, they're beautiful and such a nice surprise. My favorite flowers. Thank you so much," she said and kissed him. "But you can't stay."

*Kiss me. Slap me.* "Why?"

She pulled the door closed behind her. "My assistant got dumped by her fiancé. The poor thing is devastated and doesn't really have many friends in town, so we're having MAP night."

He frowned in confusion. "Map night? Is she taking a trip? You can just use Mapquest—"

"No, no, it's not that. MAP is an acronym. It's a girl thing," she added.

"And the acronym stands for?" he prompted.

She hesitated a half beat. "Men are pigs. Nothing personal," she added.

Whoa. "Sounds hostile. So what are you girls doing?"

"We play girl-power music, eat junk food, drink martinis or margaritas, in this case both because Liz is here and she can drink everyone under the table. We also trash men and console the victim."

"Liz Colburn?" he asked, remembering the woman from Marc and Jenny's wedding.

"Right and Jenny. Anna couldn't make it because she swears she's ten months pregnant."

"Jenny Prillaman, Marc's wife is here? She's gonna trash men? She just got married."

"Yeah, I know. She's supposed to represent the light at the end of tunnel."

"And you and Liz?"

"Liz is the kind of woman you want on your side when you're in a dark tunnel. She knows how to knock a man on his ass both figuratively and physically. She used to be a bartender and now she's married to a very wealthy older man. But I've probably told you more than you want to know."

She'd told him enough to scare him. "Where's Maddie?"

"She inside enjoying the extra company."

"They're corrupting her to become a man hater,"

he muttered. "One more thing to keep my daughter hating me."

"She doesn't hate you. She's just not used to you."

"Who's going to take care of her if you get smashed?"

"I'm not getting smashed. I've only had one margarita and one martini." She paused. "Okay, so I already got a little buzz, but I'm not having any more. It's almost her bedtime."

"I'll watch her," he said, curious about Trina's Map party and feeling protective of Maddie.

Her eyes widened. "You can't really want to take care of her," she said. "And I don't want to have to explain you to them."

"You can bring her upstairs. I'll watch her there," he said. "Away from the evil influence of angry women."

"We're not evil," she said. "You must be desperate to get away from the new baby if you're willing to subject yourself to a chick party and watch Maddie."

Her assessment irritated him, but he couldn't blame her. After all, he hadn't given her a reason to think anything different about him. "I'll go upstairs. Bring Maddie when you're ready."

Trina hesitated, studying him for a long moment, then she opened the door and peeked inside. "Coast is clear." She gave him the flowers. "I really love them, but I don't want to have to make Amelia feel bad. Could you please put them in some water upstairs?"

"Yeah, just don't send anyone upstairs with sharp objects."

"You should be safe if you don't come downstairs. I'll try to sneak a margarita up to you later." She met his gaze for a moment that made him feel a kick in his gut. "I'm surprised you're volunteering. Let me know if you decide to bail."

Her last statement may have seemed innocent enough, but it clawed at him like barbed wire. He didn't want her to think he was the kind to bail. Feeling a shot of possessiveness, he slid his hand behind her neck and pulled her mouth to his for a quick kiss. "Don't forget," he said. "Men are good for a few things."

He climbed the stairs, put the flowers in water and prowled the second level. He hadn't had the leisure to notice much about Trina's bedroom. Before, he'd been single-minded about getting into her bed.

While "I Will Survive" blared from the speakers downstairs, he looked around. Pink, aqua and ruby-red bottles adorned her dresser. A stuffed long-eared rabbit and a photo of Trina holding a tiny baby sat propped on the opposite end.

He picked up the photo and studied it, realizing it had been taken in the hospital. Trina held Maddie in the protective cocoon of her arms. Her hair was a mess, her face weary, but her eyes were full of pride and amazement. He could almost hear what she would say—"Look at her. Isn't she beautiful?"

His gut clenched at the intimate joyous moment the photograph had caught. It must have been one of Maddie's first photos. Her little head looked pointed, her nose smashed and her face red. Her tiny palms curled in tight fists.

So fragile, so tiny, he thought, and felt a wave of protectiveness that surprised him. He hadn't been there. The weird sense of loss twisted at him again.

He returned the photo to the dresser and wandered to the top of her nightstand where a stack of books shared space with a lamp. He turned on the small lamp with swingy fringe tassel on the shade and checked out the titles. *What To Expect When You're Expecting, Baby's First Year, How To Be a Single Mom.*

He realized again what he'd already known. Although Trina may not have planned her pregnancy, she'd dived right into being a mother. For all her chic single attitude, she was solid.

Hearing steps behind him, he glanced up and spotted her in the hallway with Maddie propped on her hip and a margarita glass in one of her hands. He smiled at the image and walked behind them.

"Hey there," he said in a low voice.

Trina whirled, but saved the margarita. "Ready for carrot cake duty?" she asked.

He nodded and followed her into the nursery.

"Keep the light turned off and stay quiet," she said and put the margarita on Maddie's little white dresser. "She might not mind the switch as much if it's done in the dark. There's a secret to getting her to relax. I'm the only one who knows it."

"What is it?"

She hesitated as if she wasn't sure she wanted to tell him.

"It's not a state secret," he said.

"It may as well be," she whispered with a hint of testiness. "It took me over a month to figure it out. A month of not sleeping through the night."

He shrugged. No response would be adequate.

She looked down at Maddie and lifted her hand to her face. "You stroke her face. Very lightly, touch her eyelids and her eyebrows and talk to her. It doesn't really matter what you say. The tone is what's important."

She nodded toward the rocking chair. "Ready?"

"Yeah," he said and Trina passed Maddie to him as he sat in the rocker.

Maddie made a little sound of protest and Walker tensed.

"Soft strokes," Trina coached in a whisper.

He lifted his fingers to Maddie's baby-soft skin and touched her forehead. After a moment, her eyelids drooped and he stroked them, too. Two minutes later, her little body relaxed and she began to breathe evenly.

The baby beast had been tamed. She was asleep. Trina was the smartest woman in the world.

After he put Maddie in her crib and held his breath as he lifted the rail, he grabbed the margarita, left the nursery and closed the door. The music had been turned down and the sounds of the women's voices carried upstairs.

MAP party. This was an opportunity he couldn't pass up, so he ditched his shoes and went downstairs.

"All of us have been dumped," said one woman who sounded like Jenny Prillaman. "Even Liz."

Silence followed. "Once," another woman admitted. "But I did all the dumping after that. At least you're not in the same shape Trina was when she got dumped."

Another silence followed. "That was a mutual dumping."

"Yeah, but that guy had to be a total jerk not to at least help while you were pregnant."

"He didn't know," Trina said. "I didn't tell him."

"Why not? You could have gotten some serious money."

"I didn't want serious money. I don't want to be some man's obligation. Ever," Trina said. "If he doesn't want me for me, then I'll pass."

"I don't know who I am without him," another woman said in a shaky voice. "I don't know how I can go on."

"This is your opportunity to find out who you are. Trust me, girlfriend, this is your time to fly. Your time to do everything you wanted to do, but didn't have the freedom or the nerve before."

"Liz is right," Jenny said.

"But it hurts so much."

"You just take it one day at a time," Trina said. "And when one day is too much, you take it one hour at a time. When an hour is too much, you just get through one minute. After a few weeks, when you're still alive, you realize you're stronger than you thought you were. You can count on yourself even when you can't count on a man."

The women continued to talk, but Trina's last sentence hung in his mind. He wondered what it would take to get her to count on him. He knew she could want him, but could she need him? He wanted to be the man she knew would be there for her.

Serious stuff, he thought, and returned upstairs to her bedroom. He propped the pillows behind him and pulled a book from her nightstand. *Baby's First Year.*

An hour later, Trina opened the door and lifted her finger to her lips in a shushing sign. She closed the door behind her and walked to his side of the bed, whispering. "Please be quiet. Liz and Jenny have left, but Amelia is sleeping down the hall."

He nodded, watching her grab a nightshirt and head for the bathroom. There was the sound of water, and he heard her brushing her teeth, followed by a quick gargle that made him smile.

Seconds later, she appeared and crawled into bed. She wrapped her arms around him. "You may not take advantage of me because I had three drinks to-night." She inhaled deeply. "Oh, you smell good."

He liked the way she felt wrapped around him. "You're right. I can't take advantage of you," he said in a low voice. "You're so noisy your assistant would hear you."

Trina pulled back slightly. "She's all the way down the hall."

"She'd still hear you," he said, sifting his fingers through her hair.

Trina scowled. "I'm not that noisy."

"Wrong," he said. "I bet if I took advantage of you, that I could make you moan."

Her eyes darkened. "The question is could you make me feel like moaning, but help me not to moan and also remember to use a condom."

That was a challenge he couldn't resist, and he quickly learned that she was determined to make it difficult. While he kissed her and slid his hands over her breasts, she pulled off his shirt and pushed down his pants.

She surprised the hell out of him when she wasted no time, sliding her hands down to cup his crotch and stroke. He captured her little moans with kisses.

"Quiet," he reminded her. "Stay quiet."

"That would be easier if you weren't so delicious," she murmured and skimmed her mouth over his chest, lower and lower. When he felt her wet mouth close over him, his brain fried.

Sweet Trina, the really good girl, had a wonderfully wicked mouth. She pushed him to the edge, so close. Too close. He reached for a condom in her nightstand and pulled her back up his body.

"How can you be so good and so bad at the same time?" he asked and guided her over the part of him that she had made so hard he almost hurt.

She made an *mmm* sound and he lifted his finger to her lips at the same time he slid his hand between their lower bodies and found her hot spot already swollen. Her gaze fastened on his, she opened her mouth and sucked his finger inside her mouth.

And Walker couldn't contain his own moan.

"WHY ARE YOU SO EDGY?" Walker asked Trina on Sunday as she stepped out of her car onto her mother's driveway.

"I just am," she said, eyeing the front porch warily. Her mother could sense when something was going on with Trina, and when Aubrey sensed a secret, she dug and dug and dug until she uncovered it. "Have you already made an appearance? Because if you haven't, you need to go back in. I don't want my mother to know about us."

"You want me to remain your secret boy toy. I can handle that. Is that why you've got your panties in a twist?"

She didn't appreciate his sexy, joking tone. "You don't understand. I'm protecting both you and me. She will grill you until you're fried, then pick the meat from your bones. And if she ever finds out you're Maddie's father…" Trina shuddered.

"She's gonna find out sometime," he said.

Her stomach taking a big dip, Trina looked into his eyes. She shook her head. "Not now. Not today." Reaching into the back seat to grab the marinated vegetable salad she'd prepared that morning and the wrapped baby gift, she turned around and he took both from her, surprising her.

"You wanna get Maddie?" he asked. "You can calm down. Your mother seems focused on food, Harry, Danielle and the baby."

Trina shook her head as she collected Maddie from her car seat and climbed the steps with Walker. "I can't count on that. She can tell when something's going on with me. That's why I avoided her when I first found out I was pregnant. I swear I think that woman can smell when I've had sex."

"So what if she can? You're a grown woman. What can she do?"

"She knows how to make me feel bad. She'll make me feel like a slut, when the truth is I'm really only a slut with you." She lifted her hand to the doorknob.

"Wait a minute." Walker closed his hand over hers and pulled her away from the door. He lowered his mouth to hers. "That's the biggest compliment I've ever gotten, but you're not a slut. You're just a man's dream come true—lady out of bed, tiger in bed. Don't forget it."

Trina felt her knees wobble and her breath disappear at the look in his eyes. "Uh, thanks."

"Thank you." He kissed her once more and led the way to the front door.

They arrived to the sight of Trina's mother cooing over the baby while Harry talked with Amelia, who was temporarily housed in one of Aubrey's guest suites.

Aubrey glanced up from the baby and looked at Trina and Maddie. Her face lit up. "There's my gorgeous Madeline."

Maddie kicked her feet in response and Trina couldn't help smiling. Maddie loved her grandmother and Trina couldn't wait until her daughter called her mother something embarrassing like pookie or gammie.

Aubrey swept Maddie into her arms. "I've missed you. Your mother hasn't called me to babysit. Why haven't you?" her mother demanded of Trina.

"I got the impression you've been very busy," Trina said, throwing a meaningful glance at Harry and waving at him and Amelia.

"Never too busy for my Madeline," her mother said and looked at Trina for an extra moment. "You look different. Has something happened?"

"I probably just need a haircut," Trina said, refusing to even glance in Walker's direction. "Or maybe I ate too many double dippers this week and put on some weight."

Her mother shook her head and furrowed her brow. "It's not that. I can't quite put my finger on it."

"Can I have a beer?" Walker asked.

Ever the perfect hostess, Aubrey switched gears and looked at him. "Of course you can. I'll be right back. Harold, do you think we should start the grill?"

"Whatever you say, gorgeous," he said.

Her mother giggled.

Trina gawked. "Omigod," she whispered. "I really need to warn him that she could kill him."

"Already done," Walker said. "Harry says he's a master at causing ulcers."

Trina shuddered. "I just hope she won't—"

"He's not your father," Walker reminded her.

She took a quick breath and nodded. "You're right, and thanks for distracting my mother."

"No problem, just remember you can run, but you can't hide forever."

"There are just some things I'd like to delay," she said and headed toward Amelia and Danielle.

Amelia was slightly improved. She only looked lost every other minute instead of every minute. Trina invited her to help get the meal ready to keep her busy. She took turns holding Danielle and BJ's new baby boy, John Walker, a sweet infant.

She remembered holding Maddie in her arms at this age and how precious those moments had been. Feeling Walker's gaze, she looked at him and felt her heart twist at the connection she felt with him. It took her breath away.

During the meal, she put two blankets on the floor for Maddie to entertain herself.

"Why two?" her mother asked.

"She's scooting," Walker said and Trina shot him

a shocked glance. He wasn't supposed to know that about Maddie.

Her mother lifted her eyebrow.

"You told me that outside," he said to Trina. "When I helped you bring in the food and gift."

"That's right," Trina said, a little too cheerfully for her own ears. "We have a little scooter now. Life as we know it will be over soon. She's going to be crawling any minute."

"Wait until she's walking," her mother said and Trina let out her breath.

Everyone enjoyed the meal and sat on the porch afterward. Aubrey rotated between holding Maddie, John Walker and flirting with Harry. Trina figured she might escape scrutiny if she didn't stay too late.

The doorbell rang, interrupting the relaxed, friendly mood. Her mother excused herself to answer the door.

She returned with an ashen face. "Carter-Aubrey, there's someone at the door. He—he wants to see you. It's—"

A big man with dark eyes, a dark ponytail and tattoos on his biceps walked from behind her. "Hey, Kat, long time."

Trina froze.

"Hey," the man said, and waved his hand. "It's me. Stan."

Trina felt Walker's hand on her shoulder and she

took a shaky breath and stood. "Stan, let's talk in the foyer," she managed and was surprised when her feet moved. Why was he here? He was ancient history, a closed case. She had written him a note telling him to leave her alone.

"Okay, but don't you think you should introduce me first?" Stan asked and gave the bad-boy grin that had deceived her so well years ago. "I'm Stan Roch, Kat's husband."

Trina's blood pressure climbed through the roof of her mother's three-story house. "Ex-husband," she clarified. "Very ex."

Stan shook his head and made a clucking sound. "Not exactly," he said. "You should take a better look at those divorce papers. The judge never signed them."

Trina's blood ran cold. "But they have a seal on them."

"They might be sealed, but they're not signed. Now that I've had some time to think about our marriage, I've reconsidered the property division."

Trina's mother fainted.

## CHAPTER TWENTY-TWO

HORRIFIED, TRINA RUSHED to her mother's side and patted Aubrey's hands. "Wake up, Mother. Wake up." She glanced up at Stan. "We're not still married. You're wrong."

Harry joined Trina. "Aubrey, Aubrey, darlin'."

"Hey, sweetheart," Stan said. "I didn't make the law. I just had plenty of time to study it."

"Because you were in jail and couldn't rob any more convenience stores," Trina said as her mother blinked her eyes.

Walker stepped forward. "You should leave."

"Who are you? The new guy?" Stan grinned. "How does it feel to know you've been doing somebody else's wife? That could be a turn—"

Trina barely blinked before Walker threw Stan against the wall and wrapped one of his hands around Stan's throat. "Watch your mouth," Walker muttered.

"Careful, pretty boy," Stan said. "I've got owner-ship papers."

Trina panicked. Stan had always been mean. She didn't want Walker hurt. "Walker, don't—"

BJ came to Walker's side. "We're taking your sorry ass outside and you're gonna leave and not come back."

"Say what you want, boys. I've decided a differ-ent property settlement would be more equitable. That could take a while."

"Oh, my Lord," Trina's mother said.

Trina glanced at her mother. "It can't be true, Mother. It can't. We took care of this a long time ago."

"Funny thing," Stan said with a laugh. "That baby is legally mine, too. What's her name? Come to Papa."

Walker punched Stan flat in the face and blood spurted from his nose.

"Omigod," Trina said, feeling as if the evening had turned into a scene from a horror movie. This couldn't be happening. It couldn't be. "No," she said, scrambling to grab Maddie from the floor.

"She's not your daughter," Walker said to a bloody Stan. "She's mine."

"Oh, good Lord," Aubrey said and fainted again.

WALKER AND BJ TOOK STAN OUT of the house and put him on his motorcycle. Walker was so furious he wanted to throw the guy in a dump somewhere. By the time he and BJ took Stan outside, the ex-con didn't argue about leaving, but Walker knew he would be back. The guy was a parasite. He couldn't believe Trina could have gotten involved with him, let alone married him. His mind clicked at a hundred miles an hour as he and BJ climbed the steps to return to the house.

BJ stuck his hand in front of Walker as they reached for the door. "Are you really Maddie's father?"

He felt his brother searching his face and sighed. "Yeah. It's a long story."

"But you're not taking care of her. Hell, you're not even claiming her. What kind of father is that?"

"BJ, Trina didn't tell me she was pregnant. I didn't find out until I got back from France."

BJ stared at him and swore. He shook his head. "Why didn't she tell you?"

Walker shrugged. "It's hard to explain."

"I'm all ears," BJ said. "I can't believe you wouldn't look after your own baby."

"As soon as I found out, I set up financial support," Walker said, and raked his hand through his hair. "But I wasn't ready to be a father."

"I thought you had a vasectomy."

"I did. Apparently it didn't take."

BJ swore again. He was silent for a moment, then met Walker's gaze dead-on. "You got a baby. You're a father. Deal with it."

BJ opened the door and went inside, but Walker stood on the front porch, absorbing his brother's words. He thought about Stan and felt his blood heat to the boiling point. He would cheerfully have ripped the guy's vocal cords from his throat. He clenched and unclenched his fist and glanced down to see the skin on his knuckles cracked and bleeding.

Up until now, he'd been dipping his foot in the water, taking a few little steps toward fatherhood. In one second, everything became crystal clear.

Trina was his woman. Maddie was his baby. He walked into the house, ready to take on the chaos.

Aubrey was seated on the sofa with Harry's arm around her. She glanced up at Walker and narrowed her eyes. "You—you— How could you destroy my daughter's reputation and abandon your baby? You're not fit to walk the earth."

"He didn't know, Mother," Trina said as she cradled Maddie against her. "I didn't tell him."

Aubrey gasped. "How could you not tell him? He was the father. How could—" She made a choking sound and shook her head.

Trina bit her lip. "I think I should go now. It's late and Maddie's tired."

"Not until you explain how this could have happened," Aubrey said, rising to her feet.

Harry shot up beside her. "Careful, Aubrey, you've had a shock."

"Carter-Aubrey, how did this happen?"

"Usual way. Walker and I had sex and I got pregnant. I can't believe you want me to describe everything we did," Trina said, gathering Maddie's things. "We were both drunk. There, now you know."

"Oh, Carter-Aubrey, you know better than that."

"It was my fault," Walker said, moving toward Trina. "I got her drunk and took advantage of her."

Aubrey narrowed her eyes. "I should have known." She stalked across the room and stood in front of him for a half moment, then she slapped him. He saw it coming when she lifted her hand, but he let her do it.

Trina gasped. "Mother!"

Walker rubbed his jaw. "No, it's probably overdue. I apologize for compromising your daughter's reputation, Mrs. Roberts. I'm going to try to make it up to her."

Aubrey folded her arms over her chest. "You have a long way to go."

Walker heard Trina's muffled half sob and immediately turned toward her. Her eyes shiny with unshed tears, she bit her lip and made a weak attempt at a smile. The misery and shock on her face tore at him.

"I'm really sorry, Danielle and BJ, that this had to happen tonight. You, too, Amelia," Trina said, her voice unsteady.

"Oh, sweetie, don't you worry about us," Danielle said. "You go home and take care of yourself."

Amelia nodded. "Jacuzzi bath, chocolate, martini. Do you want me to call Liz or Jenny?"

Trina shook her head violently. "Oh, no. I just think I should go."

"Carter-Aubrey, there are things that need to be discussed."

"Not tonight," Walker said and turned his cheek. "Hit the other one if you want, but Trina needs to catch her breath."

Aubrey pursed her lips. "Good night then."

Walker nodded to BJ and his uncle Harry.

"I got your back," BJ said.

"Me, too," Harry echoed.

"Thanks," he said and escorted Trina out of the room.

Trina was silent as she walked to the car and fastened Maddie into her car seat. She closed the passenger door and moved to the other side of the car.

She whipped around to face him. "I met Stan in Myrtle Beach. The year I turned nineteen. He was a biker. I didn't dance naked on the beach or get busted at a pot party."

"You got married," he said.

"He was my one big rebellion," she said. "And the stupidest thing I ever did."

"Even stupider than me," Walker said.

She nodded. "I got Maddie. I wasn't with you to prove my independence."

"Why were you with me?"

She paused. "You were engaged to an unbelievably wealthy and beautiful woman. You couldn't have done better. I couldn't compete. I didn't want to want you." She closed her eyes and gave a sad smile. "But I did."

Her sadness hurt him so much it squeezed the breath out of his lungs. When had her pain become his pain? When had her laughter become his? At that moment, it hit him that he loved Carter-Aubrey Katherine Roberts.

He pulled her into his arms. "It's gonna be okay," he told her. "I'll help you with this."

She shook her head. "This is so not your battle, not your mess. It's mine. I won't let him get at Maddie. I don't care what I have to do. I won't let him get at Maddie."

Walker felt his jaw tighten, but he knew he needed to remain rational for Trina. "He doesn't want Maddie.

He's just trying to sniff around to see if he can get a payoff."

"I have a small trust. My mother set it up before my father went through most of his money for legal fees. I used most of it as a down payment for my condo, but maybe that would—"

"Don't even think about it," he told her, swallowing a bitter taste that another man could put her in such a vulnerable situation. "Don't talk to him. It would be like negotiating with a parasite. Let me see what I can find out for you."

She shook her head again. "Thanks, but this isn't your rock to carry. I need to get home. I want to put Maddie to bed and go through some files. I'll call my attorney first thing in the morning."

"I'll follow you home."

She paused and met his gaze. "I don't want you to come inside tonight."

"Why?"

She sighed. "It's crazy, but everything about my relationship with you has always been on the down-low and if I'm really still married, that just takes it too far for me."

"You feel like you need to be faithful to Stan?"

"No. I feel like I need to be faithful to me. So let me get this straightened out with Stan and if you're still interested—"

Her lack of belief in him pushed his exasperation to a new level, but he refused to take it out on her. "I'll just follow you home and then head to my place, but I want you to call me anytime day or night if you need me. And whatever you do, don't talk with Stan. If he comes to your house don't answer the door. Just call me."

She hesitated and gave a slow nod. "Thanks."

She turned around and got into her car and Walker would have given anything for her to feel like she could turn to him.

TRINA COULDN'T SLEEP at all that night. Digging out her long-buried divorce papers, she looked at them at least fifty times. Every time, she nearly lost her cookies.

It was horrifying, but true. Stan was right. The judge hadn't signed the papers.

Pacing from one end of her bedroom to the other, she wondered how this could have happened. How could it have slid past all these years? What if she'd gotten remarried? She would have been a bigamist.

Tempted to call the lawyer at home, she surfed the Internet instead, hoping for a quick fix. As long as both parties agreed, all she needed to do was send it back to court and get the judge's signature.

Stan, however, had already made it clear. Walker was right. Stan was a parasite.

Trina worried herself into a frenzy. At 5:00 a.m., she took a shower and got dressed. She ate yogurt followed by cocoa moochies, and got Maddie ready to go.

She backed out of her driveway, but was blocked by a motorcycle. Her stomach twisted. Stan.

He dismounted his bike, but left it in her path and strutted toward her. She glared at him through her closed window.

"I'm not leaving until you talk to me. You don't want to be late, do you?" he yelled.

She cracked her window one-tenth of an inch. "Hurry up. I need to get to work."

"Nice wheels," he said. "Bet you paid a nice chunk of change for this."

"You wouldn't be able to afford the insurance," she told him.

He shrugged. "Depends. Have you had a chance to look at your divorce papers?"

She lied, shaking her head. "I've been busy."

"You lie," he said, laughing. "If your eyes were lasers, you would have burned holes in them."

"If only I could do the same with you," she said.

"Kat, we can make this easy or we can make this hard." He waved at Maddie. "My baby girl is a doll. Maybe I could take her to visit my folks during my court-appointed visitation."

Wanting to smash his head into the concrete, she put her foot on the gas and screeched her brakes inches from Stan's motorcycle.

He ran after her swearing. "What the hell are you doing?"

"Oops," she said. "I couldn't see your bike in my rearview mirror. That's not your only mode of transportation, is it?"

He narrowed his eyes. "You bitch."

"I wouldn't bring my daughter into this discussion if you don't want anything of yours to get damaged."

"I want a million dollars," he said.

Trina's stomach twisted in panic. "I want to be four inches taller. Some wishes can't come true."

"If you want me to go away, I want a check from you with six zeroes. You're a trust-fund baby. That shouldn't be a problem."

"Go to hell. If your bike isn't moved in ten seconds, I'm running over it. Ten," she said and paused a quarter second. "Nine."

"You wouldn't want to mess up your car with my bike," he said.

Trina backed up. "Eight."

"You're crazy."

"Seven."

He swore and ran to his bike.

Trina was tempted to back over both him and his bike, but her hands were shaking. She'd never played a game of chicken where the stakes were so high.

Stan gunned his engine and waved at her as he rode away. His way of saying he would be back.

She took a deep breath then another and another. Fighting the urge to burst into tears, she focused on the task of driving.

She felt stupid and alone. It was the same way she'd felt when she'd found out she was pregnant with Maddie.

But she'd gotten through, she reminded herself. This was her mess. Her cleanup.

Four hours later after an emergency meeting with her attorney, she crunched numbers with her right hand and popped double-dipper chocolate-covered peanuts with her left hand.

A knock sounded on her door and she closed the desk drawer holding her stash of chocolate. She hoped it wasn't Walker, because she knew he wouldn't approve of her plan. He'd already left several messages on her cell and business phone this morning. "Come in."

Amelia walked in bearing a small bouquet of flowers in a vase. "I thought these might cheer you up."

"You're the best, the absolute best," she said.

Amelia shook her head. "You've been very good to me. And after seeing what you went through last night, I realize that my circumstances could be a lot worse than they are."

Trina smiled grimly. "Such as my circumstances."

Amelia winced. "I didn't mean to imply that your situation is the worst it could be."

"But it pretty much sucks the big one, doesn't it?"

Amelia looked at her sympathetically. "What are you going to do?"

"The attorney told me that Stan could drag this out for a long time. If it were just me, it would irritate me, but since I'm not planning to get married, I can deal with it."

"Doesn't Walker want to marry you?" Amelia asked.

Trina felt a knot form in her stomach. "I don't think so. Our relationship is very complicated and—"

"What about Maddie?"

Trina sighed. "He didn't want children and I don't want him to feel obligated to me or Maddie. I don't want to live that way."

"He didn't seem obligated," Amelia ventured.

"It would be impossible to tell," Trina said. "But what I need to focus on is how to get Stan to agree to the divorce. I have a little bit of a trust fund. Not much, because the money was used for my college education and then I used some for a down payment on my town house. I called the bank and I can get a second mortgage and a loan, but it's nowhere near what Stan is asking."

Amelia looked at her in shock. "You're going to pay that slimy sonovabitch?"

Amelia was so ladylike that it always got Trina's attention when her assistant swore. "I have to be pragmatic—"

"You're going to reward that scummy excuse for humanity by hocking yourself up to your eyeballs?"

Trina blinked. "When you put it that way."

Amelia shook her head. "There's got to be another way."

Trina sagged against her hands propped on her desk. "I don't know what else I can do."

"Why don't you ask Walker to help you? He's Maddie's father."

But he doesn't want to be. "This is my mess, not his. I need to take care of it."

Amelia looked unconvinced. "It seems to me that this is one of those situations when you need to rely on your friends. I think Jenny and Liz would agree."

"SHE WON'T TALK TO ME," Walker said to Harry as he pretended to watch a ball game at the sports bar. He took a long swallow of beer.

Harry took a long swallow of his beer, too. "Aubrey can't talk about anything but this. Trina won't talk to her either."

"I even went over to her house and she told me, with her nicest nearly debutante manners, to go home."

"Her mother says she's independent as hell. Do you know she threw her mother out of the labor room and didn't have anybody but the nurse and doctor with her?"

Harry's revelation made his stomach rumble, not from hunger. "She won't let me help her."

"Well, you know, there's always more than one way to skin a cat."

Walker stopped midgulp and studied Harry. He wore that quiet wily look Walker had seen his uncle wear a few times. It usually preceded something surprising for which his uncle refused to take credit.

"You've got something in mind," Walker said.

"Maybe," Harry said.

Walker sat quietly, knowing his uncle would appreciate his self-control.

"When's BJ moving out?"

"Maybe next week," Walker said, temporarily accepting the diversionary tactic. "I wanted to give Danielle a chance to rest."

"You've been a good guy through all of this."

"The least I could do," he said. "BJ's really stepped up. I gotta respect him for that."

"He doesn't know what he's getting into," Harry said.

"Do any of us?"

Harry glanced at him. "What are you going to do about Maddie?"

The question made him itch, but he figured he'd get over it. "She's my daughter. I'm gonna learn how to be a dad."

"Hmm," Harry said, his tone noncommittal.

"Thanks for your enthusiastic belief in me."

"I always believed in you. I wouldn't wish surprise fatherhood on you, but I think you could handle it." He paused a half beat. "If you want to."

"I didn't want to when I first found out," Walker said. "But something changed. I want to be there for Trina and Maddie."

"You could be a good father to Maddie without tying yourself down to Trina," Harry said. "Why bother with her?"

Anger spurted through Walker. "Because I want to be with Trina. I want to get rid of the bullshit so we can be together without hiding it."

"Sounds like more than a nice piece of—"

Walker grabbed his uncle in a fierce grip. "Don't ever talk that way about Trina."

Harry met his gaze directly. "You sound serious."

"I am."

"How serious?"

"I love her."

Harry cracked a smile and took another drink from his beer. "I think you just got out from under your daddy's shadow."

The light dawned. Walker realized his uncle had just goaded him into a confession of love. "You're a sonovabitch, Harry."

Harry nodded. "I might have a few friends who could help us out with the Stan situation. I could call in a few favors. It would help if we could get a judge to help us out."

"Who are these friends?"

Harry shrugged. "Just some good ol' boys. They like to call themselves the white trash mafia. Just friendly, persuasive guys."

"Harry, if Stan can claim that he signed the divorce papers under duress, it will be one big mess."

"He won't be singing to anyone. These guys are really good at what they do. I just need one flexible judge. You think you can find one?"

Walker thought of one family he could guilt into helping him. At another time, it would have been more than he could stomach to revisit his greatest humiliation. Now, he was thankful Brooke had walked out on him and if he could exploit the Tarantinos' guilt to help Trina, then so be it.

If you meet a man whose kisses make you feel as if
you're the most beautiful woman in the world
whether you're dressed in heels or tennis shoes,
he's a keeper.

## CHAPTER TWENTY-THREE

BY FRIDAY EVENING Trina was starting to panic. She hadn't seen or heard anything from evil Stan and she had no way to contact him to tell him that she would sell pretty much everything but her soul and her daughter in exchange for a divorce.

Stan hadn't given her a telephone number or address. How was she supposed to find him? Put a classified ad in the newspaper? *Looking for convicted felon's phone number. Please help.*

She'd eaten through another two bags of double dippers and she couldn't keep still. Trina paced while she watched Maddie scoot from one end of the den to the other like a caterpillar.

If the Stan situation weren't bad enough, then the Walker one was worse. She hadn't heard from him since Tuesday. So maybe she'd finally succeeded in making him give up on her.

The possibility made her heart hurt. She couldn't involve him in this, though. Even though she knew she'd chosen to handle this on her own, she couldn't remember feeling this lonely in her life.

The doorbell rang and she froze. Maybe that was finally Stan. Scooping up Maddie, she dashed to the door and looked out the peephole.

Her heart stuttered. Walker. A hundred emotions rushed through her. She tried to rein them all in, but it was impossible. Taking a deep breath, she opened the door. "Hi. It's really great to see you, but I'm still taking care—"

"I'm your personal deliveryman," he interrupted with a cryptic grin and pulled out a large envelope.

Confused, she took the envelope and opened it. "What—"

"You might want to let me hold Maddie," he suggested. "I wouldn't want you to drop her."

She allowed him to take Maddie as she pulled out the papers. "Why would I drop—oh, my God," she whispered, staring at the decree of divorce. "Oh, my God." She flipped through the pages and double-checked for signatures. They were all there. Her hands began to tremble and she looked at Walker. "How did you—how did this—" She broke off, words escaping her.

"Let's go inside," he said, and pulled the door open.

"Yes," Trina said, looking at the papers again, making sure she hadn't dreamed them into existence.

Walker led the way into the den. "They're real," he said. "They're not going to disappear."

"But how? Stan was determined to get money." A sickening thought hit her. "Did you pay him?"

Walker shook his head. "No, he changed his mind. I pulled some strings with a contact who could get a judge to move quickly. Your attorney had already gotten your signature on the papers Monday, so it was just a matter of getting Stan to agree."

It couldn't have been that easy. She studied his face. "Are you sure you didn't pay him?"

"I swear," he said.

She frowned. "How in the world did you get Stan to agree? He told me he wanted a million dollars on Monday."

Walker turned very still. "You talked to him?"

"He showed up as I was leaving for work on Monday. He blocked the entrance to my driveway," she added when she saw his jaw tighten. "I opened my window one-tenth of an inch."

Walker swore. "Well, it's a good thing he's gone now or I would rip him—"

Trina felt a shot of alarm. "Gone? You didn't kill him, did you? I mean, I thought about it, but—"

"No, I didn't kill him."

"There's something you're not telling me."

"I'm telling you the results. That's all you need to know."

Maddie began to flutter her hands over his jaw, poking at his mouth and nose.

"That's not going to cut it. If there's a body," she said, the ruthless expression on his face worrying her.

"There's no body. He's alive. He has even left the state of Georgia and I'm pretty sure he won't be back."

"Why?"

"He doesn't like the climate."

She narrowed her eyes. "Walker—"

"We have something more important to discuss."

Her throat tightened at his intent expression. She didn't know what he was going to discuss, but she'd never seen him this serious. "The divorce was pretty important," she said. "Thank you."

"No thanks for making it more difficult for me to help you."

She blinked. "Excuse me?"

"If we're gonna be together, then you've got to chill enough to let me help you."

Trina tried to compute the whole statement, but she got stuck on the words *we* and *together.*

"I realize I wasn't there for you when you got pregnant, but you need to know that I'm the kind of man who will be there when things get rough, when they're sticky."

She inhaled, but the air was thick with her nerves. "I always knew you could be a stand-up kind of man. I didn't want you to feel obligated toward me or Maddie. Because if you do things because you feel obligated, then eventually you might resent that person. I couldn't bear it if you resented Maddie or me. I couldn't—" Her voice broke and she bit her lip and closed her eyes. She couldn't look at him. She couldn't let him see what she knew was the naked emotion in her eyes.

"Oh, Trina," he murmured and pulled her against him. "Why are you so determined to think that I'm only interested in you because I feel obligated?"

She took a shaky breath. "You didn't exactly make a run at me before the wedding disaster."

"But we always clicked," he said. "Right from the beginning." He nuzzled her. "What can I do to make you see how much I want to be with you?"

She shook her head, feeling her eyes burn with tears. "I don't know. Just the fact that you ask that question is huge."

Maddie made a motorboat vibrating sound against Walker's neck.

Trina glanced up, smiling at her baby girl. Maddie made the sound again.

"Hard to hold on to a serious discussion with that, isn't it?"

Trina laughed through her tight throat. "Guess so."

Walker met her gaze. "I love you. I want to be with you."

Everything inside her came to a screeching halt. "Excuse me? Could you repeat the love part of that?"

"I. Love. You."

Hearing the words and seeing the meaning echoed in his eyes made Trina feel as if she were airborne. Walker's love was the secret wish she'd dared not make.

"I hope I'm not hearing things," she whispered. Her chest grew so tight she couldn't breathe. "What about Maddie?"

"I love Maddie, too," he said. "And I think I'm starting to grow on her a little because she's letting me hold her without screaming like a banshee." He paused and lifted his hand to her cheek. "What about Carter-Aubrey Katherine? What do you want?"

It was too much for her to absorb. The divorce problem solved. Walker loved her. Walker loved Maddie. Could it be true? Could it really all be true? A sob escaped her throat and she looked at him in horror. "Sorry, I can't seem to—" Her voice broke and her eyes swam with tears. "Oh, no. I'm crying."

"It's okay, sweetheart," he said, pulling her close again.

Maddie made an unhappy sound and grabbed Trina's hair.

"I don't want to cry," Trina said, unable to keep her voice from breaking. She couldn't stop her emotions. It was as if a dam inside her had burst.

Maddie's little face crumpled and she let out a long whine.

Trina laughed through her tears at her daughter's cry of empathy and wrapped one arm around Walker and the other around Maddie. "It's okay, carrot cake. Mommy is just so happy she doesn't know what to do."

She tried to collect herself. "I fell for you before you could see me. You are the dream I couldn't let myself dream, because it wouldn't come true."

He kissed her, and the kiss was full of love and promise. When he pulled back, he met her gaze. "I'm going to need some help with this father thing."

"I really believe you have what it takes." She couldn't push down a bubble of curiosity. "I have to ask if you think you'd be willing to do it again?" she asked.

"Do what?"

"Have another baby?"

"Do you want one?" he asked.

"Not right now, but maybe later."

He looked at her for a long moment and seemed to laugh to himself. "I never thought I would say this, but yeah, and next time I want to be with you for the whole thing. And I want to marry you first."

He kissed her before she could start crying again.

THREE WEEKS LATER, there was another wedding. This one took place in Trina's mother's backyard. The bride and groom looked deep into each other's eyes as they repeated their vows. Each had waited a lifetime to experience this kind of love, and their joy spilled over to the small group of guests.

After the minister pronounced Harry and Aubrey man and wife, Trina blew her mother a kiss. "I've never seen her this happy," Trina whispered to Walker.

"I still can't believe Harry is doing this. He's been running from marriage since before I was born," Walker said.

"Don't they look amazing," Trina said. "It's like they both had a makeover. Harry got rid of his bad comb-over."

"And your mother got rid of her attitude," Walker murmured. "At least, according to Uncle Harry, she has."

"Yeah, I know," Trina said, shaking her head. "When I asked her if she was marrying Harry for his money, she said no, he's a wonderful lover. That was more than I really wanted to know. But who knows? Maybe that's why she's been cranky all these years?"

Walker chuckled and slid his hand around the back of her waist. "Speaking of weddings, when are you going to make an honest man of me?"

At that moment her mother broke with tradition

and tossed her bouquet in Trina's direction. Trina instinctively lifted her hands and caught the flowers.

She met his gaze and felt her heart swell with the love in his eyes. "You know, Walker, I think it may finally be our turn."

# MILLS & BOON®

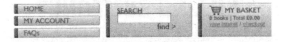

WEB/RS1 V2